THE PUNISHMENT
HAD TO FIT THE CRIME

Lord Dominic had no doubt that Sarah had come, in her daringly low-cut gown, from Captain Kendall's bed.

"My lord . . ." Sarah began to protest, her voice rendered high and thin by the cold fury in his eyes.

"Don't waste your breath with more lies," he said, looking at her hair and following the disarray down to where several strands lay on the swell of her breasts. Sarah felt her skin heat beneath his gaze, and her hand lifted to shield the bared flesh he studied.

But again he impaled her with his dark eyes, as he trailed his fingers just above the edge of her bodice. And how could she deny her guilt, when the trail of prickling fire she felt was so far from innocent . . . ?

EMMA LANGE is a graduate of the University of California at Berkeley, where she studied European history. She and her husband live in the Midwest and pursue, as they are able, interests, in traveling and sailing.

The Unmanageable Miss Marlowe

by
Emma Lange

A SIGNET BOOK

SIGNET
Published by the Penguin Group
Penguin Books USA Inc., 375 Hudson Street,
New York, New York, 10014, U.S.A.
Penguin Books Ltd, 27 Wrights Lane, London W8 5TZ, England
Penguin Books Australia Ltd, Ringwood, Victoria, Australia
Penguin Books Canada Ltd, 10 Alcorn Avenue, Toronto, Ontario, Canada M4V 3B2
Penguin Books (N.Z.) Ltd, 182-190 Wairau Road,
Auckland 10, New Zealand

Penguin Books Ltd, Registered Offices:
Harmondsworth, Middlesex, England

First published by Signet, an imprint of New American Library,
a division of Penguin Books USA Inc.

First Printing, September, 1991

10 9 8 7 6 5 4 3 2 1

PUBLISHER'S NOTE
This is a work of fiction. Names, characters, places, and incidents either are the product of the author's imagination or are used fictitiously, and any resemblance to actual persons, living or dead, events, or locales is entirely coincidental.

1

"Jane, you are expending energies you would do better to save." Dominic Moreland regared his elder sister with a fond, if faintly exasperated smile. "You are not to fret, by Dr. Dillingworth's specific order. He took great pains, not to mention an enormous fee, to tell you nothing will do for one suffering from inflammation of the lung but complete rest. And there is no need to say more. I shall willingly play Anne's escort."

"She is my eldest, Dominic. And I do want to be certain you are not put out."

"A poor brother I would be if I faulted you for illness, my dear." He took her pale hand in his. "I assure you I understand completely why it is you wish Anne to go on with her Season. It is absurd, but no fault of yours, a girl of twenty is close to being considered on the shelf."

"If only I had pushed her when she was eighteen," Mrs. Jane Pentworth opined. "But she was so shy, and then last year, it was she who fell ill. We cannot wait . . ."

" . . . another year. I do understand, Jane, and if I suspect that you are not displeased to have found a way to throw me upon the marriage mart as you and Ruth have been longing to do for years, know, too, I hold no grudge."

As her brother's smile had the power to transform his face, to soften and gentle its severe, if beautiful contours, Mrs. Pentworth not only smiled back at him but dared to observe, "You are thirty, after all, Dominic. You've restored the estates to what they were in our grandfather's time, and not a single debt hangs over you any longer. I should think time might weigh heavy on your hands."

Dominic laughed, a rare twinkle lighting his eyes of golden brown. "And you've the notion I might put that time to use filling the nursery at Ravensgate?"

Mrs. Pentworth was not without the spine to return with an owlish look, "Well, you do not seem averse to women, my dear."

He lazily conceded the point. "No."

"Dominic?" Aware of a new note in Mrs. Pentworth's tone, he cocked his dark brow at her and waited. "You've not avoided marriage because . . . well, because you've been harboring a *tendre* for Sophy all these years?"

"A secret, heart-wrenching *tendre* for Sophy?"

"Well, you needn't grin so odiously. I know you considered marriage to her."

"You were listening at keyholes, if so, Jane." He smiled at the thought. "As I recall, you and Ruth were accustomed to scolding me unmercifully for that particular sin."

"You were a proper little rogue who never heeded a word your wise sisters said." Mrs. Pentworth's gentle smile faded abruptly as coughing overtook her. The bout was long and difficult, and at the end her brother stroked her thin hand soothingly.

"I think you need your rest, my dear, not conversation."

"No, no! Talk to me a little more. I am bored in this bed, and I seldom have you all to myself."

Again he smiled. "The better to pump me. I know you."

The smile he elicited was a trifle wan, but real nonetheless. "I have always wondered why you did not ask for Sophy as Mama urged."

"Was I too far from the door for you to hear?" he teased, but then, seeing the dark half-moons beneath his sister's eyes, he left off. "I could not ask her, Jane. In the first place, I was only twenty and not particularly wild to settle, and in the second, I'd naught but Papa's debts to offer her. Can you imagine Sophy going without a new dress for years, or coming up to London for only a fortnight perhaps every second year? She'd have withered on the vine."

"Lord Matthew loved you like a second son, Dominic. He'd have settled a generous amount on Sophy, enough to pay off a great many of those debts." Dominic only shrugged, his expression unreadable. But his sister knew him. "You were too proud."

"Too foolish, more like," he said. "It has been a long ten years"

"Long, perhaps, but not wasted. You've been tested, Dominic, and found superior to the challenge. You are without equal, you know."

"Lord, Jane, I know you are a very prejudiced sister."

She giggled softly. "I think I have never before seen you discomfited, Dominic. There is even the faintest suspicion of pink on your cheeks, but I'll say whatever I wish. You're obliged to listen, as I am an invalid, and I wish to say I could not be prouder of you. You are not only the most compelling man I know, you are the most generous. Not everyone knows that side of you, but I do. Look what you did for my Arthur when he made those foolish investments on the 'Change, and that though you'd scarcely a penny to your name . . ."

Dominic placed a single lean finger over her mouth. "Enough," he warned.

She nodded, though her eyes were smiling. "I shall change the subject, if you demand it, and taking shameless advantage of my illness, inquire impertinently if you intend to pay court to Sophy now she is both free and out of mourning."

Her brother did not answer directly, but said, "I saw her last evening at a dinner. She is beautiful as ever. Few women can turn themselves out like Sophy. And she's accommodating. She has agreed to help Anne."

"Oh? Well, it will be very good for Anne to have a woman to look to until Ruth comes. Our sister ought to be here soon, but she is a wife before she's an aunt and cannot get away until Henry's gout is better. But are you thinking seriously of Sophy, then?"

"You don't approve?"

Keenly aware of her brother's perceptive regard, Mrs. Pentworth shrugged slightly. "Sophy is rather a cool person."

"That is a description that could apply to the majority of people in society. She's a pleasure to the eyes, though," he went on consideringly. "Exceedingly accomplished and well-bred, she'll conduct herself with the greatest elegance and discretion. Nor would I need to be concerned she was interested in me for my wealth." He gave a dry chuckle. "Her father has as much as or more than I, and she's married a title once. Neil was not an earl, but I cannot think there is such a difference between viscountess and countess.''

"You are not in love with her," Mrs. Pentworth exclaimed half-accusingly. "You cannot be and list her assets as if she were one of those investments of yours."

Dominic shifted his long legs into a more comfortable position. "Jane, I think we have already established, I do not harbor a secret *tendre* for Sophy. But that is beside the point, anyway. I don't believe in love as a basis for marriage. It is too fleeting an emotion. One might choose a mistress for love— she's easily discarded—but a wife ought to be selected for what she brings."

Mrs. Pentworth looked bewildered. "But you did not ask for Sophy when she could have brought you what you needed most."

Dominic's eyes darkened as he recalled that moment when his father's solicitor had told him he'd been left nothing, not one stick of furniture, not one horse, not even one book, that had not been put up as surety for some wager or other. "The imbalance between us was too great then."

"And now?" Mrs. Pentworth prodded softly, wishing to banish that shadow.

"Now Sophy would bring ease of entrée into the political and social circles she inhabits."

"As if you needed to be eased into those circles," his sister exclaimed at once. "You may have been an infrequent visitor to town over the years, but you're not unknown, Dominic. I have even been on hand on one or two occasions to witness how absurdly people fawn over you."

He regarded her with mock surprise. "But you said yourself, Jane, that I am positively compelling."

"Oh!" She swatted at him, and he laughed. "You'll see," she warned. "You'll be fawned over and toadied and toasted."

He grimaced. "Sounds dreadful. But as to Sophy, she is at home in those circles. You can't deny it. And at least she's not some young miss who has only her beauty to recommend her and would have me falling head over heels and feeling a fool. I've no intention of falling in love, Jane. You needn't waste your breath urging the course," he added as his sister opened her mouth to declaim, in fact, upon the wonders of love. "My life is my own, finally, and I like having full charge of it."

Mrs. Pentworth could not argue that her brother had not been at the mercy of others. There had been dozens of creditors to hold off while he worked his estates and invested what he could here and there.

She might have pointed out, however, that to win through as he had, Dominic had been obliged to take command of his fortunes in a way few gentlemen ever did, but Mrs. Pentworth did not think to say as much. Her illness drained her and made thinking clearly difficult.

Indeed, feeling her energies ebb, Mrs. Pentworth changed tack altogether. "One asset Sophy undoubtedly does possess is her connection through her father to political circles. With her at your side, Dominic, you would undoubtedly join Lord Matthew as a leading influence among the Tories. From what my Arthur says, they need your clear thinking and generous spirit."

In other circumstances, Dominic might have teased her by protesting he was no wild liberal reformer like "her Arthur," but seeing how pale she was, he forbore.

"We shall see what the future brings. I've made no decisions, only come to enjoy myself and take the measure of all the possibilities I've now the leisure to enjoy. And I shall enjoy playing the proud uncle while I escort Anne about."

"You are the dearest brother, Dominic." Tears welled in Mrs. Pentworth's eyes. "I shall remain forever grateful. Thank you."

"Anne and I shall get on famously, Jane. You've no need to thank me. And now, displaying some of the arrogance for which you and Ruth are forever chiding me, I shall decree it is time I departed and left you to the rest you need. Sleep well."

2

"Devil it, Kitty! Why is it horses are able to sense I've no experience with them?"

Sarah Marlowe flung the query at her cousin, an exasperated look in her eye as her mount, a gelding named Beau, sidled nervously. Kitty Ponsby only subdued a grin with an effort. Sarah could rarely be seen so completely at a loss as when seated upon a horse.

"Beau is only testing you, cuz," Kitty advised cheerfully. "Show him you are master, and we shall make the park in good order."

"You are quite certain it is not the fashionable time to be seen there?" Sarah requested the assurance after she managed to bring Beau around to face in the same direction that Kitty's seemingly more tractable mount faced. "I should greatly dislike making an utter fool of myself my first day in town."

Kitty's full-blown, quite pretty smile broke out. "I would not dream of putting you and Beau on display before all the *ton*, I swear it, Sarah. Particularly as I think you are a true champion to ride out with me, given your, ah, limitations."

Sarah giggled at Kitty's tactful hesitation, and was on the point of saying she was ready to get on with their expedition, limitations or no, when the door to the house Kitty's parents had leased for the Season flew open. A fashionably attired matron whose open face, plump figure, and soft brown hair and eyes proclaimed her Kitty's mother appeared.

"Girls!" The unexpected stir caused Beau to skitter again, and Mrs. Ponsby's broad brow creased at once. "You can manage Beau, Sarah?" she queried. "It would not do at all for you to take a tumble before everyone in the Park."

"Beau and I shall get on splendidly, Aunt Vinnie." She smiled at her aunt, and Mrs. Ponsby's frown faded a little before the force of the smile. "We are only just becoming acquainted, aren't we, old boy?'' Taking a calculated risk, Sarah leaned forward to pat the black's strong neck. Beau turned a large, dubious eye upon her, but otherwise displayed no sign of restiveness, and Mrs. Ponsby nodded, satisfied.

''Be certain you stay with Bert, girls.'' She gestured toward the young groom just behind them. ''There will not be many in the park this early, but one never knows who may be about. It would not do for you to be thought unattended. And remember, with no one but Bert by you, you may not stop to speak to any gentleman, unless, of course, he is accompanied by a lady known to you. Kitty, you are attending me?'' Mrs. Ponsby gave her daughter a sharp look. ''You must be on your best behavior. We shall never receive vouchers for Almack's, if you are not thought to conduct yourselves with the utmost propriety.'' Her strictures delivered, Mrs. Ponsby allowed herself a fond smile. ''I vow, though, should any one of the patronesses chance to see the two of you today, we would have the vouchers in no time. You both look quite, quite fetching for Sarah's first outing in London.''

It was Sarah who gave a gay wave and promised, ''We shall be the epitome of decorum, Aunt Vinnie,'' before urging Beau after Kitty, who had, perhaps purposely, departed her mother's presence without giving any assurance about her behavior.

When Sarah drew alongside her, Kitty wrinkled her nose. ''Mama has become the worst of sticklers.''

''Well, we are in town now, where our conduct will be a great deal more scrutinized than in the country,'' Sarah replied rather reasonably, but with a distinct lack of force. She was distracted by competing necessities: on the one hand she had to rein in Beau, but on the other she could not but gawk at the sights about her. London was new to her, as, since the death of Sarah's mother some ten years before, her father had shunned the extravagance and frivolity he associated with the capital.

Kitty, not so distracted, was able to summon more force to say, ''I would not mind so much, if I thought Mama were only concerned with our being received by this high stickler or that, but I know she's a great deal more in mind. Sarah, Mama is determined that I—that we, both—finish the Season with a title in our pockets. That is why she so relentlessly implored your

father to allow you to join me this Season. Oh, it is true, she
does believe your mother would have wanted you to have a
Season in town, but she particularly wished you to be on hand
for mine, because she is confident your beauty will attract
enough eligible titles that there will be one or two left over for
me.''

"Oh, come now, Kitty,'' Sarah protested, her attention
thoroughly caught, though Beau sidestepped nervously as a large
lorry passed. "You speak as though you are an antidote and
Aunt Vinnie as scheming as any general.''

"Mama is ambitious, make no mistake,'' Kitty exclaimed.
"She was proud as punch to get Delia a viscount when my sister
made her come-out two years ago, and now she wishes to do
even better for us. As for my looks''—Kitty shrugged her
plump, rounded shoulders lightly—"I know I am no antidote.
I am quite passable, but that is of little advantage, given my
small dowry and less-than-scintillating lineage. Mama thought
reinforcements called for, and though you've equally little
dowry and much the same modest antecedents, you've quite
remarkable beauty, though you are not, remarkably''—and here
Kitty grinned in the bright, infectious way Sarah had always
liked so very well—"the least puffed about it.''

Sarah looked surprised. "Well, I hope I'm not puffed about
something for which I've not the least responsibility. That
would be absurd. But tell me truthfully, Kitty, why are you so
bitter over your mama's hopes? Would it not be as possible to
be happy with a titled gentleman as an untitled one?''

Kitty's smile faded abruptly. "Perhaps, but I should prefer
a good man to a good title. I'm not like Mama or Delia. The
fashionable world is all to them, but I found too many of my
fellows at Miss Merriweather's the coldest, most supercilious
creatures. Do you know several shunned me after I, in a moment
of foolish candor, revealed we'd only ten servants at home.''

"Goodness! They'd have thought me a beggar,'' Sarah
declared with such wry fatalism her cousin laughed.

"And you'd not have minded at all, would you, Sarah? You'd
have told them buntly they were a pack of silly geese and found
all the company you needed in your watercolors. Then, of
course, they'd have come one by one to see what you were up

to and the whole affair would have ended with you subjecting them to drawing lessons.''

Sarah laughed. ''You have not forgotten those lessons, and yet it has been five years since I forced them on you.''

''I was so terrible!'' Kitty made a face. ''I could not even manage a straight line. But I am reminded of your other pupil. You do remember you cajoled Tom Woodward into sitting for lessons as well that summer? Do you know yet when he is to return from the Indies?''

''No,'' Sarah sighed, and seemed about to add something, but the passing of a barouche at a dangerous pace startled Beau.

As Sarah worked to control her mount, Kitty glanced to the vehicle and her expression changed. ''Why, it is Charlotte Manwairing,'' she cried, naming one of the good friends she had, in fact, made at Miss Merriweather's School for Young Ladies. ''And look! She is stopping at that milliner's ahead.''

Hoping to catch Miss Manwairing before she disappeared into the shop, Kitty spurred her mount forward and unwittingly strained Sarah's skill with Beau to the limit, for the gelding made to follow his stablemate at a pace beyond Sarah's abilities. Biting her lip, she fought to rein the horse in, and might have succeeded but for a whim of fate.

Some ten yards ahead, the driver of a wagon laden with kegs of ale, lulled into inattention by the rhythmic creaking of his conveyance, drove his rear wheel into a gaping hole in the cobblestones. When his frightened horses reared, the kegs slammed hard against the wagon's tailgate. It gave a great crack, and of a sudden some twenty kegs bounced crazily one after the other onto the street. Unsettled from the first by the novice rider on his back, Beau was completely undone by the sight of the large, heavy objects clanking noisily toward him.

Sarah uttered a scream as the gelding reared. She'd no time to think what to do, only a moment to cast about frantically in the hopes that someone, Kitty perhaps, would materialize before her to help her, but she saw no one near at hand, only heard Bert cry, ''Miss,'' behind her, as her eyes locked with those of a gentleman some distance away.

He was imposing. Even in that wild, frantic moment, when she knew she was losing control of Beau, Sarah remarked him.

Perhaps he stood out so because, while pandemonium erupted all around him, he sat his bay with such ease.

But then Beau bolted, surging forward with such power Sarah could not have controlled him had she possessed the strength of Hercules. All she could do was cling white-knuckled to her saddle and pray frantically she would not be thrown onto the hard cobblestones so far below her. The air rushed at her, tearing her hat from her head and sending her hair whipping wildly across her eyes. Terrified and half-blinded, she'd the sense that people were flinging themselves out of her path and that some were screaming, or perhaps it was she who screamed. There was no doubt Sarah did cry out when a carriage, quite unaware of her and her runaway horse, bowled out of a side street squarely into her path.

Beau reared and she screamed. And then, just as she lost her hold, just as terror surged through her, a strong arm encircled her waist, lifted her, and then plunked her down on a saddle hard against a male body.

Sarah flung up her head, took in an impression of dark hair and a strong face, before, accepting she truly had escaped death, she gave a sob of relief and flung her arms around the man holding her.

Dominic's mount, Ajax, shifted, uncertain of the new weight he carried, and Dominic reflexively drew the girl he held tighter to him. He was breathing hard still, for though the gallop had been brief, it had been swift.

He had noticed her approaching him before the incident with the wagon. She'd been wearing a hat at that point, but he'd caught the glint of the sun on her hair and idly looked more closely.

It was then the wagon had spilled its contents, causing her horse to rear. He'd seen clearly the terrified look on her face, and almost before the gelding had bolted, he'd set off after her.

The ride was not one Dominic cared to remember. Watching her ahead of him, bouncing like a rag doll, he'd grimly expected her to fly off and crack her golden head against the cobblestones before he could reach her. The silky weight of her hair spilled onto her shoulders and across his arm, its dishevelment a testament to the close brush she'd had with serious injury.

His breathing having slowed, he realized hers had as well. She was trembling still, though not crying, and Dominic leaned back to assess her condition.

He found himself studying a pair of absurdly wide eyes of a dark sapphire blue as she tightened her grip upon him, perhaps fearing he might yet allow her to tumble to her doom.

"I have you," he assured her in his authoritative way. "Are you hurt?"

It took Sarah a moment to reply, as if she had to think on it to be sure. Then, slowly, she shook her head. "No, I don't think so." Her voice was low, rough-edged with the fright she'd had, but having pronounced herself well, she rallied a little, straightening. "I must thank you, sir, you . . ."

She got no further, for a young urchin came running up with her hat. "I found this a ways back, miss."

From the look of pride on the lad's face, it might still have been the dashing little riding hat decorated with a jaunty pheasant's feather it had been when she set out. "Thank you very much. I am, ah, glad to have it."

Her rescuer said something grim under his breath, and Sarah cast him a rueful look after the urchin had taken himself off. "Not in the best of shape, is it?" She stroked the place where the proud feather had been. "At least I am whole, though, thanks to you."

"You could well have been as squashed as that pitiful thing," Dominic replied, anger overtaking him now his concern for her well-being was allayed. "You've no business at all riding a horse. Ah, here comes the villain now."

A bystander appeared around the corner, leading Beau, spent and winded, and Dominic called out to him, instructing him to bring the horse along and to examine him to be certain he'd done no damage to himself.

Sarah welcomed the diversion. Her fright having receded, she'd become far more aware of her position and of the man who had rescued her.

She had not sat in a man's lap since she was a child, and that man had been her father. Now, with a complete stranger, she sat with her breasts brushing his chest, her legs across his thighs, and his arm about her waist.

It came to her, as well, that the body holding her so securely was a fine one, well-muscled and lean. His chest was hard, strong muscles played in his thighs and arms, and the shoulder beneath her hand was broad. He smelled good too, but that seemed so intimate a thing to notice that she was more dismayed than pleased.

Sarah might have been a great deal less disconcerted by her position, however, had she not looked through her lashes to assess the man who'd rescued her.

He was striking. She deliberately did not call him handsome, for the word connoted to her pleasing, comfortable, boyish looks, and there was nothing boyish about her rescuer. All the soft edges had been chiseled from his features, leaving only decisive lines and high, arrogant angles. His was masculine beauty without apology. A hawk's perfect, imperious face, perhaps, beneath dark-brown hair that gleamed in the sun.

Only his eyes were not so frightening as a hawk's. They surprised, for though brown, they were a golden brown and surrounded by long, thick lashes.

And could light with a knowing gleam. She saw that gleam when he turned suddenly and caught her gaze upon him. It seemed as if he guessed she was admiring him, and then, dismay overtaking her, she realized such a guess would be child's play for him, accustomed as he must be to admiring looks from ladies.

"I . . . Oh! It is you," Sarah gaped, the intention to say she could stand alone and unaided routed. "I saw you before Beau bolted," she exclaimed, amazed she had not realized he was the same man before. "But you were on the far side of the kegs! How could you have reached me?"

What amusement there had been lighting Dominic's quite compelling eyes faded abruptly. "I reached you because I was prepared to go after you, and I was prepared because I could plainly see, as I said before, that you'd no business riding out in London's traffic."

The biting reply overlooked Sarah's question, which had been how could he have made his horse leap the distracting kegs, but certainly Sarah was not aware of the fact. She was listening, dismayed, as he added in the same curt tone, "Whoever is supposed to be looking after you ought to be whipped for ever allowing you on a horse in the first place.''

"Oh, no, sir," she cried, stung on her aunt's behalf. "The fault is mine entirely. Truly, I would not have you charge my aunt or my uncle where I am to blame. I did my best to appear at ease on Beau, and assured them I was.''

After a fraction of a second, during which Sarah thought she saw surprise register on the man's arresting face but could not be certain because the expression disappeared so quickly, he arched a single dark brow at her. "Very well, then, if you insist, I shall accept you are a consummate actress, but as a result, it is you shall have to bear the brunt of my scold. Not only did you nearly break your own neck, you know, but you endangered a good many other quite innocent necks as well.''

Sarah did not resent the scold, and that was not because his voice had softened slightly. She knew she deserved it, as she admitted in a voice strained with contrition. "I do realize the harm I might have done, sir. And the worst is, I never considered that I might endanger others. I am shamed to say I allowed my desire to view the Park to override all other considerations. The wheel on Uncle William's carriage is being repaired, you see, and it is my first day in London. But it makes no matter. I ought to have exercised patience, and rather than rattling on, I ought to be thanking you again for saving me. I might have died but for you.''

She was very beautiful, the girl he held, whose uncle had only one carriage, who made no effort to shift the blame for her foolish behavior to another, who was gazing at him, a little shy but very grateful.

Very beautiful. Her hair, alone, would have made her a prize. Thick and silky, it even smelled sweet.

But she possessed other assets. All other assets, Dominic amended dryly. Her wide-set blue eyes set off a lovely face. Her skin was smooth as porcelain. She'd a generous brow, a straight, slim nose, and a rounded but firm chin. Her mouth . . . was full, very full, yet finely drawn, which could be said, as well, of her body, of which Dominic could not but be very aware, they sat so close. It was full where it ought to be full, but finely boned and slender in all.

She was not mistress material, though she'd have made a magnificent one. Surely not more than eighteen, she was gently bred, judging from her clothes and speech, if not particularly well-to-do. The single carriage came to mind again, and with it the thought that she would be looking for a wealthy husband, titled preferably.

Sarah could not tell what he was thinking, only knew the way he studied her made her feel . . . odd. Breathless, really, as if she were waiting for something, and she could not tear her eyes from his.

"Let us see if you can stand now," he said, the unsettling moment passing as he suited his actions to his words and dropped her down to stand alone. Without the security of his arms about her, Sarah swayed unsteadily.

"You're certain you're not hurt?" he demanded, swinging down to take her arm and scan her closely for signs of undiscovered injury.

The touch of his hand was little after having had his arms encircle her, but Sarah experienced such a surge of feeling at the light contact, she was bewildered and moved away. "Yes, truly, sir, I am fine," she said, taking another step back that she might look into his eyes, for he was taller than she had realized. "I am only a little shaken. Oh, there is Bert!" She waved with undisguised relief at the boy. "He is our groom. If you will only help me to mount Beau, I shall leave you free to return to your business."

The stranger, if he heard her, took not the slightest heed of her request. Instead, he swung around to address Bert, who, though he was mounted, cut a negligible figure beside the broad-shouldered, imposing stranger. "Your mistress has not been injured, but that is only by God's grace, for she can scarce sit a horse, much less manage one in London's thoroughfares. There will be no difficulty getting her home, as the gelding's too winded to run away with her again, but if I ever see her mounted on anything again, I'll have her father or whoever is responsible for her taken before the magistrates. I expect I have made myself clear?"

Poor Bert gaped, then swallowed hard. "Yes, your lordship. She—"

Dominic waved a peremptory hand. "She would be difficult to resist, yes. But find the backbone to do it next time, man, or you'll be without a mistress. As for you . . ." He turned back upon Sarah before she could quite tame the grin that had begun to tease her mouth. "And what are you smiling at? I am in dead earnest."

She laughed then, and Dominic added her smile to her list of assets. It lit her lovely face.

"I don't doubt your earnestness at all, sir. It was your . . . your manner made me smile. I have never encountered anyone quite so . . ."

"Arrogant?" Dominic supplied dryly when she seemed to falter at such plain speaking. The twinkle sparkling in her eye gave him to know he had guessed correctly. "Well, let my arrogant manner be a warning to you. If I see you attempting to ride again, I'll snatch you off your mount, no matter if you are in the park with Prinny himself admiring you."

He would do it. Sarah knew he meant every word, but all she could do was laugh again, for the arrogant threat was entirely moderated by the fact that he'd begun to smile. Faintly, to be sure, but even a slight smile transformed his face, softening it, rendering him almost breathtakingly attractive.

"You would have the right, I think," she managed to return, if a moment late. "I realize you put yourself at risk of injury. And I thank you again . . ." Sarah hesitated, hoping he would give his name, but when he did not, she went on, "I wish I could repay you somehow."

"You can repay me easily, little one." The smile grew stronger and more powerful. "Only promise to stay off horses." Idly he flicked a gloved finger over the smooth skin of her cheek. "You've too much beauty to be so careless of it."

3

"Sarah!"

Sarah started, pulling her gaze from the uninteresting assortment of vehicles that had obscured the departing figure of the stranger quite some moments before.

"Kitty!" She turned to find her cousin looking very anxious. "You musn't be concerned. I am fine, really."

"You did not fall?" Kitty exclaimed, amazed.

"No, I did not, thanks entirely to a gentleman who caught me as I began to slip. Did you by chance see him?" Sarah asked, flicking another glance down the street.

"I never even saw Beau bolt with you," Kitty admitted. "I only knew something was amiss when a keg rolled by me. I turned to find Bert waving frantically, but I could not follow after him until the street was cleared. Luckily I came upon a small boy recounting the story of the runaway horse, and he directed me to you. But who was it rescued you? Did he give his name?"

"No, though he did admonish me against riding out in town again."

Kitty's brow lifted. "That was impudent of him! It was not your fault you lost control of Beau, cuz. Anyone might have, with those ale kegs clanking everywhere."

Sarah did not answer until, with Bert's help, she'd remounted Beau, now standing docile as a lamb. After arranging her riding skirts to her liking, she looked at Kitty with a smile frayed a bit at the edges by a delayed reaction to her brush with disaster. "Perhaps another might have lost control of him, Kitty, but I was certain to, I am so poor with horses. The gentleman was correct. I did not imperil only myself, but everyone I encountered. Only think what might have happened had a child run into the street!"

Kitty, moved by the sudden paling of Sarah's cheeks, leaned

over to clasp her cousin's slim hand. "Don't think on it, my love. Nothing awful did occur, and you were saved in the very brink of time by a dashing gentleman. At least I hope he was dashing?"

At Kitty's giggle, the dark look faded from Sarah's eyes. "Dashing?" she pretended to consider, tipping her head. "Actually, he was not dashing so much as arrogant."

"And handsome?" Kitty pried teasingly.

Sarah, enjoying the game, chuckled. "Nor handsome so much as compelling."

"Imperious, compelling, an excellent horseman too, in short, a nonpareil. I should say you did very well your first day in town, Sarah, falling into such a gentleman's arms."

Sarah was moved to laugh at that bit of nonsense. "Nor were they negligible arms," she confided, but then, blushing at the direction of her thoughts, she sought to turn the subject. "I do wish to say how sorry I am, Kitty. I've the distinct notion my very ephemeral good fortune has had the effect of causing you to miss someone in the park."

Kitty shot her a sharp look. "How did you guess?"

"You were very insistent about riding out at this particular hour, my dear. Is he someone of whom Aunt Vinnie does not approve?"

"Approve?" Kitty echoed rather bitterly. "Oh, she'd approve of him for someone else. She's known him all his life, you see, and knows he is all that is good and honorable and kind. Only he does not possess a title, and worse, he is a second son!"

"Johnny Carstairs?" Sarah guessed, for she had been to visit her aunt and uncle and cousins often enough in the summers that she had come to know their neighbors well.

Kitty's gaze softened. "Yes. It is Johnny. We are in love, Sarah. I am pledged to him and he to me, but it all seems so hopeless! Johnny cannot support a family upon the small income that is all his brother can afford to give him. Our only hope is that Johnny may find work as manager of a larger estate. He's done very well as Devon's manager, after all. We've hopes that while he is in town enjoying my Season, he can make himself known to gentlemen who may be in need of an agent.

"Mama wishes him well, of course, but she believes he is

far too young and untried to inspire such confidence, and is quite set against his interest in me. There is his lack of title, too, of course, and his lack of land to call his own. But I know he will succeed eventually, Sarah. He is so good! If I can contrive to meet him here or there, you'll not tell Mama, will you?''

"No, I'll not tell Aunt Vinnie, Kitty. I have always liked Johnny very much, as you know. But have patience with your mother, I beg you. She is only looking after your interests as best she can. Let Johnny prove himself, and I cannot but think she will come around.''

"I do pray you are right, Sarah," Kitty exclaimed fervently. "And I shall try to heed your advice. I know Johnny's situation must seem quite hopeless to her. But nothing is hopeless to me." She grinned. "And, though I have missed Johnny today, I am assured of seeing him tomorrow. He is invited to the Cranmers' ball, as are we! Oh! Would it not be the very grandest thing, if 'your' gentleman were to be there as well?''

Once Kitty had given voice to the notion that the stranger might attend the Cranmers' ball, Sarah could not get it out of her mind, and as a consequence, her eyes were sparkling with particular excitement as she sat before her pier glass the evening of the ball. Glancing into it, she saw her maid approaching. Maddie Cheers was a stout, older countrywoman with shrewd, if faded blue eyes, who had come into the Marlowe household when Mrs. Marlowe had first married.

"I'll not need that, Maddie," Sarah said, her glance dropping to the lace fichu the older woman held. "This strand of pearls will do nicely enough."

Maddie's eyes seemed to stab the bared flesh of Sarah's swelling bosom. "Are ye hopin' to snare that gentleman that rescued ye by flauntin' yerself, then?''

"I don't know what you mean, Maddie," Sarah protested with an airy sniff. "And I am not flaunting myself. Aunt Vinnie says I need not wear a fichu with this dress, that I shall be quite out of fashion if I do."

Sarah glanced up from her defiant examination of the dress's daring décolletage to find Maddie regarding her steadily, and a sudden grin lifted her mouth. "Oh, very well! I do hope the gentleman will be there and that I shall catch his attention. And I am, in truth, a little uncertain about this . . ." She waved her hand over the creamy swell that had never been placed upon public view before.

Maddie's grunt was ambiguous. " 'Tis an eyeful, right enough, but if yer aunt says ye've no need of more coverin', ye needn't worry. She'd not mistake the matter. As fer yer gentleman," she went on, a faint twinkle sparking her old eyes, "he'd be a blind man if he fails ta noteye, lamb."

"Or absent," Sarah added with a quirk of her brow. "He may not be present at all, for according to Kitty the Cranmers, like Uncle William and Aunt Vinnie, are not top of the trees. They are unexceptionable, of course, but not precisely the Prince Regent's confidants."

"And ye've the fancy yer gentleman is as lofty as a king's son?" Maddie asked as, conceding defeat on the fichu, she folded it carefully again.

Sarah watched idly, but her thoughts were on the gentleman who had rescued her. Random details she had not absorbed at the time came to her. The cut of his coat had been without flaw, its cloth the softest superfine against her cheek. His Hessians, for he had worn the high black boots with tassels swinging upon them, had gleamed with a mirrorlike finish, and his linen had been crisp and clean, his cravat elegantly knotted.

Yet, had he been dressed in the coarsest woolens, he'd still have been one to whom people deffered. Bert, attuned as servants often were to the merest nuances of demeanor, had addressed the man as a lord within a moment of encountering him.

"Aye, I do fear he may be well above the Cranmers, Maddie," Sarah said with a sighing, then smiled. "But . . . perhaps you'll say a spell for me!" She chuckled when Maddie looked taken aback. "I know you're a witch, Maddie. You read my thoughts too easily, and therefore it follows you can make him appear at the ball."

Maddie did not point out, as she might have, that if the man were so high and mighty, he could well be above considering a girl whose father's antecedents were of the scholarly class while her mother's father had been a down-at-the-heels baron.

Instead, Maddie pursued a topic of more interest to her than a gentleman her charge would likely never encounter again. "Mayhap I am a witch." She watched Sarah narrowly. "I did wish mightily ye'd lose yer interest in that Tom Woodward, and it seems ye have."

"Tom?" Sarah looked her surprise. "But I've not thought myself in love with Tom for an age. Since well before his father exiled him to the Indies. Though, of course, he remains one of my dearest friends."

Maddie shrugged dismissively. "Friend he can be. It was only as yer husband I dinna think him worthy. He's the sort who'll ever be a foolish boy. Look how he lost his family's jewels."

"I could not agree more, Maddie. It was unpardonably idiotic of Tom to wager the Woodward emeralds in a card game." Sighing, Sarah rose and crossed to the bed, where her shawl and reticule lay. "But I do think Sir Adrian was overly hard on him." She turned so suddenly her satin dress rustled. "Newly come to town, green as grass, Tom could not suspect the man seeming to act his friend was a villain. Captain Kendall!" Sarah spat the name with disgust. "He knew Tom had the emeralds. Tom admitted to me he displayed the necklace for the blackguard before he took it to have the clasp repaired. If only Sir Adrian had not been set on a Bond Street jeweler for his precious emeralds! He could have found a perfectly adequate man in Cumberland, but he would send the necklace off to London with Tom, and what should Tom do but flaunt it before a cardsharp who would scruple at nothing to get it. Tom told me Captain Kendall professed himself much taken with its history."

Sarah grimaced. "I don't doubt it! Very few necklaces lying about were once Queen Elizabeth's and none of them lie within the grasp of such a scoundrel. He tricked Tom. Oh, I know you think Tom to blame, and he was, in part, but how should he have guessed Captain Kendall was a cardsharp when the fellow lost to him night after night? Tom was too inexperienced to know the captain planned those losses to lure him on. And the final night they played, Tom said the captain ordered bottle after bottle of port. It is a wonder Tom was able to stand after he'd been plied with so much drink. Of course he'd no judgment left."

Sarah wrapped her Belgian lace shawl around her shoulders with a jerk. "Captain Kendall as good as stole the thing, yet he refused to sell it back when Sir Adrian approached him. Tom told me the rogue informed Sir Adrian he would have more than money for it, he would have a landed bride. Have you ever heard of such a thing, Maddie?"

Maddie had heard of many things and therefore was not as inclined as Sarah to dismiss the notion that there was a girl somewhere who could be enticed into marriage with a rogue if the man knew how to make himself friendly and happened to possess a magnificent, storied necklace. "There might be one or another—a wealthy lass, mayhap, who'd be wantin' a bauble her papa could not buy her. 'Tis a pretty thing, after all."

"It is the Woodward family pride and joy," Sarah exclaimed. "And I mean to see it is returned to Sir Adrian."

"What's this now?" Maddie turned sharply. "An' how would you be doin' that, missy?"

Sarah shrugged. "I don't know. But I shall find some means to see Captain Kendall returns it. Sir Adrian will forgive Tom then, I'm certain of it, and allow him to return from his exile in the Indies. It's the least I can do for Tom."

Maddie scowled dourly. "Ye said ye'd no interest in the lad."

"I've no interest in wedding him, Maddie," Sarah corrected carefully. "But I've every interest in him as a friend. And even had I not, you must agree I owe him the greatest debt. I know you have not forgotten that it was Tom came to my rescue when James attacked me that day."

Maddie did remember the incident with James Marlowe, Sarah's cousin. She'd been filled with murderous fury when a tearful Sarah had confessed the ne'er-do-well had lured her into the woods that separated the Woodward estate from the neat house and gardens owned by Sarah's father. The villain had thought to take advantage of her lamb, but Sarah had kicked and fought and held him off until Tom Woodward, hearing her screams, came to her defense before any real harm was done.

"Aye." She nodded slowly. " 'Tis true you owe the lad a debt, but methinks it'll not be easy pryin' that necklace from this captain's hands."

"I never said it would be easy, but I do intend to succeed.

I'll wager you a pound I do it before we leave London."

"Huh! I'd not wager on someat that'll likely see ye sent to the Indies alongside that foolish lad ye call friend."

"Papa could scarcely bear to see me come to London, Maddie!" Sarah's eyes twinkled. "I've little fear he'd exile me half a world away."

Maddie did not look reassured, though she agreed. "Spoiled ye, he always has," she affirmed direly. "Especially after yer mother. God rest her sainted soul, passed on. And 'tis headstrong ye are, missy, as a result. But ye'll do naught to bring shame on yer mother's memory. I'll not have it."

Sarah responded to the gruff warning by enveloping Maddie in an embrace that had little regard for the high-waisted evening dress she wore. " 'Tis you who've been mother to me most of my life, Maddie Cheers, and I'll not shame you—or at least," she amended, a saucy grin lighting her eyes, "I shall try not to."

"Och! Get on with you," Maddie scolded, a suspicious sheen in her eyes.

"Wish me luck?"

"With what, missy? Yer fine gentleman, the Woodward jewels, or only the ball ye'll attend tonight?"

"With everything, of course," Sarah said, laughing.

"Then luck to ye with the first two, lass. Ye'll not be needing it for the ball." Maddie's old eyes gleamed with pride as she took in the girl who stood at the door, sparkling and eager for her first ball. It seemed only a day or so ago Sarah had been a wee mite scampering about at her nanny's knees, and now, a child no longer, she was a lovely thing on the brink of womanhood. "Unless I'm daft, ye'll be the talk of the ball."

4

Maddie was not at all daft. Almost from the moment of her arrival at the Cranmers', Sarah was the object of considerable attention, and neither was Kitty ignored. Indeed, afterward, as they drove home through hushed streets, Mrs. Ponsby remarked upon the success of her girls with such excitement, Mr. Ponsby was moved to moderate her enthusiasm, saying with his gentle smile, "My dear, if you keep on in this way, you will give yourself a megrim."

Sarah rather hoped Mrs. Ponsby would heed her husband, for though Sarah had enjoyed herself, she was then experiencing some let-down. Maddie's powers had fallen short. There had been tall, dark men at the ball, but none tall enough, nor elegant enough, nor nearly so compelling as her stranger.

A half-dozen times she'd caught her breath, thinking, Let it be he, only to have the man turn and reveal a peacock's features, a flabby paunch, shoulders too narrow, or merely ordinary looks.

Nor had Captain Kendall's name been called. There had been several military men present, but none had been the holder of the Woodward necklace, and though Sarah accepted London was large, it did set her back just a little that she had failed on both fronts that evening.

Mrs. Ponsby, however, was blissfully unaware her niece had experienced anything but unqualified success, and in response to her husband's admonition, bent upon him a smile of such vigor an onlooker would never have guessed midnight had come and gone hours before. "You shan't hush me, William. I do not think I could be still. The evening was too, too successful! Oh, to be sure, none of the patronesses of Almack's were present, but I did not expect such fortune. Letty Cranmer does not fly in the very highest circles, after all. But she does fly high enough. I thought the Earl of Westphal displayed the most gratifying interest in you, Kitty. Two dances, he had."

"My feet are proof of that," Kitty muttered so low her mother was obliged to ask what she had said. "Only that I thought him a poor dancer and wish he will not single me out so again," she responded more loudly but no more amiably.

Mrs. Ponsby's eyes went very wide. "Kitty! Westphal is an earl. With an income of ten thousand pounds."

"Mother, the Earl of Westphal is forty years of age, if he's a day! He has bad teeth and three daughters, the eldest of whom is only five years younger than I."

Kitty sounded close to tears. She had been obliged by her mother to grant the earl the privilege of the supper dance, an honor she had hoped to accord Johnny Carstairs, and tired as she was, the disappointment seemed too great to bear. Sarah thought it wise to intervene before either mother or daughter said more than she intended.

"Aunt Vinnie only means that it is a feather in your cap you could draw an earl's attention, love, not that you must walk down the aisle with him tomorrow."

Sarah glanced at her aunt to see how Mrs. Ponsby took that, and was relieved to see her nod her head.

Kitty, too, saw, and recalling Sarah's advice not to flaunt her preference for Johnny, relented. "Forgive me, Mama. I fear I am fatigued past the point of civility."

Entirely mollified by the olive branch politely extended, Mrs. Ponsby patted her daughter's hand. "Of course you are weary, my dear. I daresay you danced nearly every dance. And Sarah has the right of it," she went on, reminded by the outburst how rarely direct tactics worked with her second daughter. Given time and patience, the child would surely come to see for herself where her best interests lay. "Only consent to be seen with Westphal and I shall be most pleased. It can do your credit no harm to have a man of his rank dangling after you."

In the interests of peace, Kitty overcame a desire to make a play on the word "rank," though the earl's breath, due to his teeth, no doubt, had been vastly unpleasant. Instead, she smiled at her cousin. "But I am not the only one who attracted attention from a nobleman. And yours, Sarah, was a marquess."

"I thought it quite wonderful," exclaimed not Sarah, but Mrs. Ponsby. "My two girls on the floor, one with an earl and the other a marquess. Lisle has never shown much interest in setting up a nursery, but as Letty, who is his distant cousin, pointed out, he is getting to those years where gentlemen must decide one way or another on the matter."

"Sarah was the only girl the marquess asked to dance," Kitty spoke up, as Sarah, her head tipped, considered the Marquess of Lisle in silence.

She was not surprised to learn he had danced with no other, though she had not noticed herself. He'd admitted to a dislike of the pastime. "Never cared much for capering about hoping I'll miss my partner's instep and, more fervently, that she'll avoid mine," he had drawled in measured tones as he led her onto the floor.

Sarah had not known precisely how to take the remark, but when she had looked closely at him, she thought she detected a hint of amusement lurking deep in the marquess's dark eyes. She'd not been certain of it, though. Nothing about the Marquess of Lisle suggested humor, for he had a heavy round face that was set in the blandest of expressions.

Still, that suspicion of a flicker in his eyes had prompted Sarah to chuckle and quip, "Then you are wise to partner me, my lord, for I am small enough I'll do you no permanent damage."

His bland gaze never leaving her, the marquess had replied slowly, if mysteriously, "I've the uncomfortable notion there may be some question on that point, Miss Marlowe."

Sarah had lifted her brow in question, but when Lisle had not chosen to clarify the remark, she'd not pressed him. The dance had begun, and much to her surprise, the marquess, though he was a heavy man, danced very well, as she informed him after the last note of the minuet died away.

Lisle's reply to her compliment had been immediate, if unhurried. "I take it, then, Miss Marlowe," he had said, putting his monocle to his eye, "that you enjoy the sight of a stout gentleman capering wildly?"

"Capering wildly?" she'd echoed, unable to restrain a smile. "I do not imagine you have ever capered wildly in your life, my lord. As to the connection between a gentleman's figure and the figure he cuts on the dance floor, there you are fair and far out. Figure has little to do with grace, as I am persuaded you are aware, for I saw you glance more than once in the direction of the wiry gentleman who cavorted like a monkey. Thin though the man admittedly was, he made a less-than-pleasing sight. I am certain his partner's insteps are bruised and battered, while mine are whole and hale.''

"Mine, too, tingle with good health, Miss Marlowe. Be assured you've my eternal gratitude for it. As to the rest . . . I think you are unusually observant.'' That same suspicion of humor flickered in his eyes before he exerted himself to bow over her hand, for they had come to Sarah's aunt. "Good evening, Miss Marlowe,'' he'd said before departing at the stately pace that she suspected was habitual to him.

"How old is the marquess, Aunt Vinnie?'' Sarah asked her aunt suddenly.

Mrs. Ponsby looked somewhat taken aback. "Well, I cannot say precisely. William, do you know?''

"Hey, what's that?'' Mr. Ponsby gave a little start as his wife's elbow disrupted the doze he'd been enjoying.

"Lisle. Do you know his age?''

Gathering his thoughts, Mr. Ponsby considered. "Probably's gotten to thirty or so. Why, does he interest you, Sarah?''

She smiled. "I suppose that is the way to put it. Because he was very different from all the other gentlemen, the marquess did intrigue me. I am surprised to learn he's only thirty, though,'' she mused. "He seemed rather older.''

"Perhaps because he is so ponderous and so pale,'' chimed in Kitty. "Lud! Does he ever venture out into the sun, do you think?''

"Now, Kitty,'' Mrs. Ponsby chided warningly. "You must not prejudice Sarah. Gentlemen are not weathered, after all. And the marquess's estates, so Letty says, bring in some twenty thousand a year.''

"Ah!'' Kitty's tone was as ironic as the glance she shot Sarah.

But Sarah's answering smile held only amusement. She did not fault her aunt for inquiring into the marquess's holdings. It was Mrs. Ponsby's duty to know who could offer what. Whether the marquess's earnings held any significance for Sarah was another matter entirely.

Twenty thousand pounds would never hurt, but it would not

be the deciding factor when she accepted a marriage proposal.
The man she would marry would be . . . Well, she did not know
what precisely. She had not got that far. She was still at the
point of deciding that though the marquess's looks were rather
droll, he had, in fact, amused her more than any of the other
gentlemen presented to her that evening. Time, she decided,
would have to tell what, if anything, would be between them.

And she did learn only a few evenings later that the marquess
could not remain in her thoughts when at last she encountered
one of the two men she'd been seeking at each entertainment.
Standing with the marquess, her aunt, and some others, when
she heard the footman at the doorway solemnly intone, "Captain
Charles Kendall," it was all Sarah could do to manage a casual
look to the door, the marquess quite forgotten.

There were two men, both turned out strikingly in scarlet
regimentals, their dress swords at their sides, and she could not
be certain which was the rogue who had fleeced her friend.

She could only guess Kendall was the raffish-looking dark-
haired one who glanced around the ballroom as if he were
scenting for prey. Studying her dance card, Sarah found to her
satisfaction that her next partner was Johnny Carstairs. He would
know which of the two men was the captain, and so he did.

"The dark-haired one," Johnny replied, but with a slight
frown. "I say, Sarah, you've not taken an interest in him from
across the room, I hope. He's a rum one, in my opinion, though
I confess I know only rumors against him, and they are more
likely to involve young men and cards than young ladies and
improper advances."

"No, no, I've not fallen into a sudden infatuation." Sarah
then made an excuse for her interest that was only close to the
truth. Sir Adrian's shame at his son's loss of the fabled
Woodward emeralds was such he'd forbidden the loss to be
spoken of by any in his family, and though she was not a
Woodward, Sarah felt bound by his wishes. "I heard his name
mentioned the other night and was only trying to guess who
he was from what I heard."

Johnny Carstairs was not the most prepossessing of men. To
Sarah he'd always resembled a good strong pony rather than a
high-spirited thoroughbred, but in that he fitted Kitty exactly,

for Sarah's cousin was rather sturdy herself. And Johnny did possess the friendliest, most humorous hazel eyes Sarah had ever seen. At that moment, they were twinkling. "Must have been a lady speaking. He's an enviable reputation with the muslin set, though most mamas are at least a little wary of him. He's not much to offer, as he's a third son. A bad lot, you know, we latter-born."

Johnny smiled, but it was a wry, self-deprecating smile, and Sarah was stung to protest softly, "Not all, sir. I have it on the best authority that second sons, particularly, are sterling characters."

Touched, Johnny inclined his head. "I rather fancy your source is suspect, Sarah, but I am grateful, nonetheless, for your support. I know it cannot be halfhearted." He grinned a little, recalling more than one time, during visits to Sussex, when she had acted downright incautiously in support of one cause or another. "Enough of me, however. Should you have some maggot in your head about Kendall, I shall continue to warn you off him. His pockets are nearly to let, though he does, through his sister, have good connections. His brother-in-law's the Viscount Whittingham. You met Whittingham's daughters by a previous marriage earlier tonight. Althea and Clarice Enderby. The two auburn-haired girls," he added when Sarah looked blank, "with Miss Manwairing."

"Oh, yes! The Misses Enderby." Sarah had needed the jog to her memory. Charlotte Manwairing, Kitty's friend, had quite overshadowed the two sisters. Sarah smiled slightly. More correctly, she had outdisplayed them. Kitty had confided that it was because she thought herself homely that Miss Manwairing rigged herself out in such an array of jewelry. Sarah could not know if it was for that reason or for want of taste. She could only stare in some awe at the diamonds and rubies that seemed to drip from the girl's hair, throat, ears, and all her fingers.

Given what she knew of Kendall, Sarah was not surprised to observe that he remarked Miss Manwairing's display. Before the next dance, he made his way to the heiress, who stood conveniently with his nieces, and led her out. He did not, however, confine his attentions to spectacularly turned-out heiresses that night. He did dance with other, more modestly got-up girls, but all of them also stood to inherit significant portions.

Sarah longed to take the man's measure for herself and pondered how she might meet him. She'd no baubles to catch his eye, however, nor did her father possess a purse the captain might hear of, or at least he'd not hear of it with any interest. Briefly she considered asking Johnny to present her, but feared the young man would either object or seriously question her interest in the captain. In the end, happily, Kendall solved her difficulties for her.

At the next interval, Sarah stood with her aunt, listening to Mrs. Ponsby sing the Marquess of Lisle's praises, when Captain Kendall approached in company with the Viscount Malthorpe, an unctuous gentleman well-known to her aunt and, indeed, to everyone.

"Mrs. Ponsby, I am honored." The captain bowed formally over Mrs. Ponsby's hand after the viscount performed the introductions. "I vow, there are not many ladies who would not pale to insignificance beside a beauty such as your niece is."

Mrs. Ponsby, no more immune to flattery than most, scolded him with her fan. "You flatter me, Captain, but I shall not, as a punishment, deny you my niece's acquaintance."

"I am charmed, Miss Marlowe." The captain bent his polished smile upon Sarah before dressing her hand to his lips.

Curtsying, she studied him from beneath her lashes and decided that even had she not known what a rogue he was, she'd not have been in danger of falling under Captain Kendall's spell. Despite the military garb he wore, he was too much the peacock to appeal to her. His chest seemed swelled with self-satisfaction, he swaggered more than walked, and he'd even allowed a lock of raven hair to fall with planned carelessness upon his forehead.

"I shall be disconsolate, Miss Marlowe, if you've no dance left for me." He cocked his head at her, a flirtatious smile curving his mouth. "I must lead out the most beautiful girl present."

"I think I could persuade my uncle to give you his dance, Captain. It is the minuet."

Though her tone was friendly enough, Sarah could not bring herself to flutter her lashes or smile coyly, the reaction the captain had inspired in the other young ladies he'd favored with his attentions. To Sarah's surprise, the restraint she could not quite overcome did nothing to put the captain off. Quite the contrary, his interest seemed to quicken.

His dark eyes gleamed as he bent on her so intense a look, it seemed to Sarah he meant to devour her on the spot. "You are delectable, Miss Marlowe," he purred. "I shall be forever in Mr. Ponsby's debt."

He continued his efforts to engage her when they danced, making much of having fought at Waterloo, only to assure her he believed all the perils he had endured in Belgium worthwhile, for they had kept beauty like hers safe from the rapacious French.

Sarah responded to the nonsense with a light laugh, testing the inspiration that Kendall was actually intrigued by an unaccustomed dose of disinterest. Given that he launched into a boasting discourse on his connections to the nobility—through his sister—she rather thought she was right.

But Sarah did learn one interesting thing before the captain returned her to her aunt. For reasons he glossed over, he had not taken rooms of his own but had accepted the hospitality of his sister and her husband. Sarah thought that a very good thing for her. Althea and Clarice Enderby's house she could enter, as she never could a bachelor's private rooms.

5

"Do come here, Kitty. That curl is not right." Mrs. Ponsby bustled over to pat the offending strand of shining hair into place, then considered her efforts. "Yes, that will do. Well, I believe we are ready, William. Sarah, you look lovely. Ah, wait! There is a wrinkle just here. Now, that is better. Girls, you will remember to keep your eyes lowered when you curtsy? You may smile when you are spoken to, of course, but do not be forward at all costs. Lady Ledbetter will expect the most exquisite manners.''

Sarah smiled as Kitty, trailing out to the carriage after her mother, rolled her eyes. Mrs. Ponsby had been chattering on in much the same way since they had received invitations to Lady Marietta Ledbetter's soiree. Charlotte Manwairing was responsible for the honor, for the marchioness was her great-aunt, and Mrs. Ponsby had duly blessed her. ''A dear, dear girl! Everyone knows of Lady Ledbetter, you see. Her soirees are quite famous. There can be no doubt that we shall encounter more than one of the patronesses of Almack's! You must be on your most exact behavior.''

To Sarah's relief, the first person they encountered at the soiree was neither an exacting patroness nor a haughty stranger, but the Marquess of Lisle.

He was at his ease among Lady Ledbetter's guests, and if Sarah did not need the reassurance of his company, Mrs. Ponsby did. Increasingly atwitter with excitement, she was chattering almost uncontrollably, exclaiming over the lineages of the guests, their exalted titles, their resplendent clothing, and so on, until Kitty seemed on the point of shushing her own mother.

By the sheer weight of his presence, however, Lisle managed to stem Mrs. Ponsby's flow, and he found them excellent seats from which to enjoy the diva Lady Ledbetter had invited to entertain them. But it was after the performance that he performed his greatest service, at least in Mrs. Ponsby's eyes, for he took it upon himself to present both Sarah and Kitty first to Lady Sally Jersey and then to Lady Emily Sefton, each of them a patroness of Almack's.

Mrs. Ponsby, when the marquess did eventually tear himself away, exclaimed delightedly over the reception Sarah and Kitty had received from the ladies Sefton and Jersey. The girls, in their turn, agreed with her that Lady Sefton had seemed to regard them with approval, but Kitty, in particular, protested that Lady Jersey had seemed scarcely to note them. ''She talked of nothing but herself, Mama.''

But Mrs. Ponsby would not be cast down. ''No matter, my dear, no matter!'' She waved her fan. ''It is well-known Sally Jersey finds herself to be her most interesting topic of conversation. The important thing is that she smiled upon you. Ah, here is Captain Kendall! We shall put the matter to him.''

Sarah glanced around in surprise. It did not amaze her she had not seen the captain earlier. The room was so crowded, she could not see people only five feet away. However, she had not realized Kendall would have the entrée to an affair such as this. Perhaps Charlotte Manwairing had procured him an invitation as well?

There was, of course, no indication on the captain's rakish face how he came to be among Lady Ledbetter's company. He held himself with his usual swagger and bent the full power of his gleaming smile upon Mrs. Ponsby.

''Now, what is the matter you wish to put to me, ma'am? I should be honored to be of service to three such entirely lovely ladies.''

''It is this, Captain.'' Mrs. Ponsby beamed. ''I believe Lady Sally Jersey was quite taken with my girls, but they are not so certain, for she did rattle on and on about her latest dinner, her next ball, the singer she means to have at her soiree, and so on.''

Sarah watched Kendall deliver a flattering reply. He was a smooth rogue, she granted him that, and she conceded him looks. It was only prejudice that caused her to see more self-absorption in his sleek, dark features than beauty.

''Sally Jersey could not but find both your girls the essence of loveliness. Certainly everyone else does,'' he finished, his black eyes coming to rest upon Sarah.

''You are too kind, sir,'' she murmured, though she knew him to be anything but.

''And you are too modest, Miss Marlowe,'' he chided with a wolfish smile.

The Earl of Westphal approached then to pay his respects to Kitty, and Kendall was able to separate Sarah slightly from her relatives. Instantly he took the opportunity to whisper in her ear, ''Tonight you are as enticing as a figurine of spun sugar from Gunther's!''

''Spun sugar is a most ephemeral thing, sir.'' Sarah glanced at him over her fan. ''I am not certain I care to be thought of as so insubstantial.''

Kendall laughed low. ''You are most maddening, my dear Miss Marlowe. You take me to task for a compliment with which I meant only to praise. I think you look more enticing than you know.''

"Do you suggest I am ignorant, sir?''

"Ah! At last you smile as you tease me mercilessly. I am entranced but not satisfied. No, I cannot be satisfied with a smile that is only a shadow of the vivid one you turn on Lisle so readily. Make amends. Come away where we can enjoy a modicum of privacy at least. The fresh air on the terrace will be a respite from the stuffy confines of these reception rooms. Come out with me.''

Sarah was reminded of the spider saying to the fly, "Only come closer, my tempting dear,'' but she wished to keep in his favor for the time being. Too, he'd a point when he said Lady Ledbetter's reception rooms were warm. "An irresistible invitation, sir, but we must ask my aunt's permission.''

The captain agreed readily, for he'd little worry Mrs. Ponsby would refuse him. Several of the French windows leading to the terrace had been thrown open, that Lady Ledbetter's guests might enjoy the night air as they chose.

"I confess I've serious doubts whether you will last the Season, Dominic.'' Lord Richard Beresford chuckled. Lady Ledbetter's terrace was lit by a succession of gay lanterns, and he could see his friend arch his brow in question. "It is all this attention you are receiving worries me. I've the greatest fear you will pronounce it tiresome and the social round frivolous, then hie back to the serenity of Kent.''

"Frivolous, Richard?'' Dominic inquired dryly. "Heaven forbid that I could see such dedication to the social round as I have witnessed since I came to town as requiring anything but the greatest discipline. My gravest concern is that I may be found to lack the necessary stamina.''

Lord Richard eyed his friend's powerful figure with a wry grin. "I don't imagine we shall find you laid low upon a sofa, smelling salts at the ready anytime soon, Dominic. It is not lack of stamina that affects you most, I suspect, but lack of patience with the hangers-on. You did not expect them, did you, from the endless line of eager mamas to the awed young men waiting avidly to see how it is you will tie your cravat on any given night?''

"Indeed," Dominic allowed with ironic emphasis, "I had not anticipated in any way how particularly fascinating my cravat would be. This night alone I have been beseeched at least half a dozen times to give out the secret of it. At first I replied with only a cool, and I hoped, off-putting look, but when that tactic seemed merely to whet interest in my toilette, I essayed the truth: that Deakins would not dream of allowing me to tie my own cravat. There are times I wonder whether I am his man or he mine, but no one will believe me. That one fellow, can't recall his name, the one with the paunch, Sir Somebody, accused me of modesty in the most wounded tones you can imagine."

Lord Richard chuckled. "Percy Kitely's the one you mean. He's deadly serious over his linen. Really," he insisted when Dominic laughed. "He's forever taking me to task for not living up to the standard of fashion Sophy invariably sets."

"She does set a high standard, but I cannot fault her on your behalf. She's been too great a godsend."

"Oh? And how is that?"

"It is her skirts shelter me from all those mamas you made mention of."

Understanding, Richard laughed. "Ah, yes, I can see Sophy would be entirely useful in that regard."

They fell silent a moment, the tips of their cheroots glowing red in the night. Absently Dominic registered a girl's laugh. Something in the sound teasing his memory, he glanced along the terrace but could see only a military man bending down to whisper in the ear of a lady the man's body hid from sight. From a gesture the man made, it seemed he was inviting his companion to walk in the shadowy gardens with him.

Lady Sophia still on his mind, Dominic put her in the place of the lady he assumed to be a dazzled girl. Would Sophy have allowed herself to be beguiled into a walk in dark gardens even when she first made her come-out? He smiled at the thought. Even then, Sophy had been too composed and cool to encourage forward suggestions. The man would not have approached her in the first place, or if he had, he'd have found himself escorting her back to her chaperon soon enough.

"But Sophy's rare, it would seem."

"Eh? What's that?" Dominic did not realize he had spoken aloud until Richard started. "Sophy's rare? As her brother, I can only agree, but as your closest friend, Dominic, I feel I must in honor add Sophy is as delightfully and entirely self-centered as any lady ever was.''

"Any beautiful lady," Dominic amended dryly. "A certain amount of self-absorption can be forgiven a woman of her looks and refinement, I should say.''

"I suppose," Lady Sophia's brother agreed, then after a moment added thoughtfully, "But what of Anne, Dominic? Forgive me if I am speaking out of turn, but though I believe you've enjoyed Sophy's company—she has kept the match-makers at bay, and she is accommodating company for you—I worry over your niece. The poor child seems shier now than she did when the Season began.''

The long breath Dominic expelled confirmed, he, too, harbored concern for Anne. "She does seem quiet as a mouse. I grant you that, Richard. But I cannot think what to do. Nor is Sophy to blame. She has done her best. She takes Anne on her calls, has introduced her to any number of young ladies, and presented her to at least a dozen young men.''

"Hmm. Sophy's very polished," Richard mused. "Yet I can imagine the very elegance and assurance we admire might actually unsettle a rather shy girl like Anne. Sophy's neither mothering nor girlish. She's more the sort Anne might aspire to being.''

From the corner of his eye Dominic caught a movement by the steps and, half-turning, watched the couple shift places slightly, so the man stood closer to the steps, one hand on the girl's waist, and she was turned with her back to Dominic.

It did not matter that he could not see her face. He knew her.

Her hair was not a silky tangle as it had been the last time he'd seen her. It was confined quite properly in a knot upon the top of her head. Several tendrils floated free, curling along the length of her graceful neck, but the artless look thus achieved she owed to a hairdresser, not a wild gallop through the streets.

He was certain she was the girl he'd rescued. He'd seen no other young lady in the past two weeks with hair so soft a gold. She was of the same medium height as well, fine-boned, and held herself well despite the foolish position into which she'd gotten herself.

"Dominic?''

"Yes?" He turned to find Richard looking at him expectantly. "Oh, Anne! Yes, I can see that she would find Sophy more awe-inspiring than not. I'll speak to her, assure her Sophy's like anyone, but I am not certain that will do the trick. She needs . . ." He paused, realizing he'd been about to say "a woman's hand," but caught himself. He meant, of course, "mothering hand." "We both need Ruth," he confessed aloud, referring to his sister. "Anne knows her well. Pray Henry does not remain gouty much longer. I've hopes for him now Ruth wrote to say he's been off his port a week."

"Which reminds me"—Lord Richard held up his glass—"my glass seems to have gone abysmally dry. Join me at the refreshment tables?"

"I'll follow you in a moment. The night air beckons me a bit longer."

Grinning, Richard clapped him on the back. "I knew it! You've already begun to find London's reception rooms unbearably stuffy. Soon you'll be making excuses to go back to Kent, muttering about the apple blossoms."

The remark did summon a vivid memory of springtime at Ravensgate with the faintest scent of the sea overlaying the sweet smell of apple blossoms, but Kent did not linger in Dominic's thoughts when his friend departed.

Glancing to his right again, Dominic realized he knew the man. Over the years, on one or another infrequent trip to town, he had encountered Captain Charles Kendall in the gaming houses Richard liked to drag him to. He'd never taken to the captain. Indeed, Kendall was the sort Dominic could find it easy to dislike. He displayed the worst of ingratiating airs toward those he considered his superiors, while reserving faintly contemptuous manners for those beneath him. There were, too, vague rumors about his predilection for play with exceedingly green young men.

The man's reputation with ladies was unknown to Dominic. Obviously, he conceded, moving toward the couple almost before he realized what he was about, Kendall had not committed any greatly scandalous act. He'd not have been received by Lady Ledbetter had he, but if a man could not be trusted at cards, he could not be trusted alone with a beauty like the one whose arm he now held and upon whom he was smiling as intently as if she were a juicy morsel he anticipated savoring.

What gave him the right to interfere in Kendall's effort at seduction, Dominic did not stop to consider—nor, for that matter, what gave him the desire to do so. It was enough that he did not like the man.

Neither Kendall nor the girl was aware of him until he stepped into the lantern light and his shadow fell on them. They both turned sharply.

" 'Evening, Kendall.'' He acknowledged the captain with a brief inclination of the head, but before the captain could get out a startled "Ravensby," Dominic looked to his companion.

The light was not such he could appreciate the deep blue of her eyes, but he could see they had flared very wide. She did not appear delighted to recognize him. Had she wanted to go into the gardens with Kendall?

Dominic smiled rather grimly down into her widened eyes. "Lady Ledbetter sent me to find you, my dear." He held out a well-kept hand. "And I shouldn't like to keep her waiting."

"Lady Ledbetter," Sarah repeated the only words that had registered at all to her, to give herself the time to stare.

He was her stranger! Tall, well-made, his dark hair gleaming in the candlelight, his features as severe and finely wrought as she remembered, he could be no other.

Yet he was uttering nonsense. Lady Ledbetter scarcely knew her. How could he have mistaken her for someone else, though, when he was staring directly at her?

"Ah, yes, of course," she heard herself say, and rather as if she were in a dream, she put her hand into his.

"Until later, Miss Marlowe."

It was as well Captain Kendall called Sarah's name. She might have floated off without doing him the courtesy of bidding him adieu. "Captain Kendall," she murmured.

He bowed formally at the waist, something he had never done before, and Sarah could only think it was because of the man who'd come for her.

"Kendall!"

Two fellow officers hailed the captain, and after bowing briefly to Sarah and the stranger, they swept Kendall off into the gardens with them.

Left alone on the terrace with the stranger, Sarah opened her mouth to ask . . . she knew not what, so many questions crowded her tongue, but he spoke first.

"Is there no one to look after you? Am I to make a habit of rescuing you?"

Sarah arched her neck the better to read his eyes and realized he was not merely staring at her, but glaring. "I wasn't aware I needed rescuing," she said, a trifle defensive before that look.

A single dark eyebrow arched sharply. "Weren't you? Did you wish to accompany Captain Kendall out into the concealing shadows of the gardens, then?"

"Oh!" She smiled in understanding. "You needn't worry over Kendall. I assure you I've every confidence I can manage him."

"You thought the same of the gelding, I imagine, and I can assure you, the captain is no gelding."

"Sir!" Sarah felt her cheeks go hot. "I appreciate your concern for me, but that was rather outside the bounds."

"Was it, now?" he shot back tersely. "I wonder how you can judge. Had you any notion of the bounds, you would never have been on this terrace alone with Charles Kendall, encouraging him to whisper forward suggestions in your ear."

If the man's imperiousness had amused Sarah before, it did not then. "I was not encouraging Kendall to anything," she protested with spirit. But when his brow arched sardonically, as if he were determined not to believe her, she felt her temper truly soar. "And even if I were, I cannot see it is the least of your affair. In future, you may count me lost to the captain's blandishments and pass on uninvolved."

Sarah did not bid him farewell, or wish him one, only whirled away before Dominic realized what she intended. He went after her on the instant and caught her by the French windows, literally taking her by the elbow and bringing her up short.

He had been harsh. He conceded it, but he had only spoken so for her own good. She could not afford even one misstep, for she was not, he knew, of the highest *ton*. Her uncle, as Dominic recalled it, possessed only the one carriage, and if that were not clue enough, he had the evidence of his own eyes. She was dressed with telling simplicity. Only one small strand of pearls encircled her neck and in her hair she wore nothing more elaborate than a ribbon. She did not need finery to enhance her beauty, but that was not the point. She'd have arrayed herself as all the ladies did, had she possessed the baubles.

"Let go of me!"

Sarah's command was robbed of some needed authority by the necessity she felt to whisper it. There were half a dozen people only a few feet from them, but Dominic was in no doubt about her mood. In the blazing light of the reception rooms, he could see quite clearly that her eyes, eyes that were bluer than he remembered, were also flashing.

"Be still," he ordered curtly when she tried to shake off his hold. "And calm yourself. This excess of emotion is no more within the bounds than gadding about with Kendall. I meant only to help you out of difficulty and point your way in future. You ought to thank me."

"Thank you?" she repeated, disbelieving her ears.

"Yes," he returned imperturbably. "Kendall can do your consequence only harm. And surely you can see that is something one in your position cannot afford."

Dominic had thought to add some cautionary note about the sort of young man she ought to seek out, someone honorable with unexceptionable manners, but she tried to free herself again, biting out with emphasis, "Someone in my position, sir, does not care to have her arm gripped. Leave off!"

He'd offended her and did not care a fig. She needed to hear a little plain speaking, it seemed, for she was too headstrong by half. "Someone in your position," he repeated the offending phrase with equal emphasis, "would seem to need the reminder that it is not acceptable in polite society to brawl in public. Nor, I can continue in this vein for hours, my dear, is it done for a young lady to return quite alone from a sojourn on the terrace. Inevitably speculation as to why she thought it necessary to charge off from her escort would arise."

Had Sarah been able to do him irreparable harm with her eyes, she'd have done it. He had been imperious at their first encounter, but never so odiously condescending! Worse, however, he was right. Unpleasant speculation would result if she returned unescorted. For herself, Sarah did not care, but she did care for her Aunt Vinnie, who would surely hear of it and fall into a paroxysm of worry over the precious vouchers to Almack's.

Not for anything in the world, though, could Sarah have conceded him the point in words. She could only turn, her back stiff and her chin high, and take her place beside him.

Dominic's mouth lifted just the least bit as he led her into the reception rooms. Whatever the girl's standing in society, she had the ability to carry herself like a duchess when she was furious.

"Dominic!"

Sarah's step faltered when her escort turned unexpectedly to greet a cool, elegant beauty who had separated from a group nearby. She was strikingly turned-out, with tall plumes waving in her hair and a fortune in opals around the neck. A thin eyebrow rising languidly, she glanced from Dominic to Sarah and back again.

"I could not find you." She pouted faintly.

"I was with Richard on the terrace." Sarah looked from the woman to her escort. And saw with a regrettable pang that his expression had softened. "Taking the air," he added.

"Blowing a cloud, more like," the woman returned.

He smiled. In contrast to his severity with Sarah, he was at ease bantering with the woman with the proprietary gleam in her pale-blue eyes. "More like."

Sarah might not have been present at all, they seemed so complete together, and thinking they would not notice if she slipped away, she made to disengage her arm from her escort's. He simply tightened his hold as he addressed the other woman.

"I find myself in the oddest circumstance, Sophy." He smiled slightly. "You see, I should like very much to present my companion to you, but though I have encountered this young lady before, on an occasion when I saved her a considerable bruising, I am in the embarrassing position of being obliged to admit I know her name only by the merest chance, while she does not know mine at all."

Even as Sarah was remarking to herself how little she cared for feeling like a stray animal brought in off the street to amuse her betters, the man turned to her. "I had thought to present myself when we joined your chaperon, you see, but as Sophy's come along to act in her stead, allow me to say, Miss Marlowe, I am the Earl of Ravensby and this is Lady Sophia Carrington.''

By sternly reminding herself no situation could be so awkward it could not, somehow, be carried off, Sarah dipped them both a curtsy she knew would have made her Aunt Vinnie proud. ''Charmed, I am sure. And may I thank you again for the rescue you performed last Tuesday, my lord?'' Sarah paused infinitesimally but long enough, she thought, for the earl to understand she distinguished that service from the one he had done her on the terrace. Still, just to be certain, she thought to add, ''You were very gallant then. And now I shall bid you adieu. My aunt will begin to worry over me if I do not return to her.''

So intent was Sarah on extricating herself from the earl and his . . . betrothed? that Dominic was obliged to catch her arm again.

''Lady Sophia and I will see you to her.''

''Oh, I couldn't put you to the bother. And there is no need. My aunt is just over there.'' Sarah inclined her head vaguely in the direction she had last seen her aunt. ''I shan't get lost.''

''It was not my fear you would,'' Dominic returned, his voice firming into the authoritative tone she knew rather too well.

He would have his way, she could see it in his eyes. No matter that she might not wish to expose her Aunt Vinnie to the condescension she was certain Lady Sophia, at least, would display no matter that Sarah herself did not wish to linger in the company of a woman to whom she had taken an instant dislike, Lord Ravensby would have his arrogant way.

''You are too kind, my lord.'' The deliberate irony had its effect, and Sarah was startled that her heart could leap so over no more than the sudden appearance of a gleam in the earl's golden-brown eyes. Smoothly, before an answering gleam could light hers, she turned to Lady Sophia Carrington. ''May I present my aunt, Mrs. Ponsby, to you, my lady? She will be most honored.''

6

"Come, do, Sarah! Go with us to Astley's. It will be ever so much fun."

Sarah looked up from the cup of hot chocolate she'd been stirring for the past several minutes into the eager face of Charles Ponsby. At seven he was her aunt's youngest. "I should like to, Charles. If you go again, I shall accompany you, but today I cannot. I've promised to accompany Kitty to Bond Street."

"Ugh!" Young Charles grimaced comically.

His slightly older sister, eleven-year-old Becky, aware of her grave responsibilities as the elder of the two youngest Ponsbys, scolded him at once. "You mustn't make faces, Charles. It is not polite." Then, just to be certain her errant brother minded, she added with authority, "And besides, if it thunders, your face will be frozen like that forever."

"It will not," Charles argued pithily, sticking out his tongue for good measure. "And I wish Sarah to come with us."

"I do too!" Becky shot back, stung that Charles had insinuated she was not as fervent in her desire to have Sarah with them as he.

Sarah smiled as the children scowled balefully at each other. "There is no need for this disagreement, you know. Although I cannot accompany you today, perhaps we can plan a pilgrimage to Gunther's tomorrow. I've enough pocket money to treat us all to ices."

"Oh, yes," both children cried simultaneously, and began to chatter about the sweets they particularly favored. Sarah listened, grateful for the distraction.

Until the children had joined her at breakfast, she'd been all alone, for she was the only early riser in the household, and her thoughts had been less than uplifting.

The meeting between her aunt on the one hand and the Earl of Ravensby and Lady Sophia Carrington on the other had been as awkward as she had expected. Mrs. Ponsby had been overcome, gushing her delight to meet them, singing the earl's praises for having "saved" Sarah, and so on. It was only natural. Ravensby and Lady Sophia were the very tip-top of the trees.

Sarah flushed with indignation to recall how Lady Sophia had met her Aunt Vinnie's enthusiasm. No smile had been in danger of warming her beautiful face. Arm entwined with the earl's, she had allowed her delicately thin eyebrows to drift upward as she listened to Mrs. Ponsby vow to excess how accurate were the reports lauding Lady Sophia's elegance and style. To Sarah those lifted eyebrows had seemed to convey astonishment—mild, of course, for surely a lady of her refinement never entertained a strong emotion over anything—that she had been asked to endure such a rustic as Mrs. Ponsby. It went without question she did so only because it was the earl who had asked the sacrifice of her.

Ravensby's reaction was not so obvious. He had not stood regarding Sarah's aunt as if Mrs. Ponsby were an inferior order of life. He had listened politely enough as she thanked him effusively and repeatedly, but when Mrs. Ponsby had paused for breath he had remarked, in a voice that if it was pleasant was also authoritative, "Young girls need looking after. As I am certain you know, Mrs. Ponsby, they can get into difficulties before they are even aware they have done so. Miss Marlowe, having only recently come to town, may need a closer eye than most."

The reprimand was too subtle for Mrs. Ponsby. She missed it entirely. "Oh, not Sarah, my lord," she had cried amiably. "She'll not mount a horse again, by her own declaration, and when she's on level ground, she is the most sensible of children. Now, my Kitty . . ."

Sarah had not heard the rest. The earl had flicked his gaze to her, and she had been, in a way that was most unusual for her, infuriated by the skepticism reflected in his eyes. Stiffening her spine, she had given him look for look, determined that he know she believed his questioning of her judgment entirely unfair. It was her Aunt Vinnie, not Ravensby, who knew her, and knew perfectly well whether Sarah would ever be in danger of allowing a man such as Kendall liberties.

His reply had been to arch his brow at her, and for half a second Sarah thought he intended to speak further to her aunt, to say specifically he had found her niece with a less-than-desirable *parti* upon the terrace, but Lady Sophia had intervened. In a bored drawl, she had remarked how thirsty she was and begged Ravensby to take her to the refreshment tables.

Sarah had hoped she might simply put the earl from her mind, forget she had ever encountered him or suffered his arrogance, but she was disappointed in her hopes. Mrs. Ponsby and Kitty had both been very full of her rescuer on the drive home. Both had agreed he was, in Mrs. Ponsby's words, "perhaps the most compelling gentleman in London," and in Kitty's, "so entirely masculine and elegant all at once."

Even Mr. Ponsby had spoken up. "A good man, Ravensby. Nothing overbred about him. Brought those estates of his back from the disaster his father had made of them. Most thought he'd fail, but he proved 'em wrong. And not by takin' the easy way. Didn't marry wealth, as it was believed he would."

"He is a proud man," Mrs. Ponsby declared as if she were on the very closest terms with the earl. "I was told tonight that he was on the point of asking for Lady Sophia and did not when his father's extravagances left him nearly destitute."

"Had I been Lady Sophia I'd have married him anyway," Kitty exclaimed dreamily. "If he were too proud to accept a large marriage settlement, then I'd have done without. There are not many gentlemen like him! Was her husband?"

It came as something of a surprise to Sarah that Lady Sophia was a widow, but not so great a one that she remarked aloud. At any rate, Mrs. Ponsby, frowning at Kitty's sentiments, was saying firmly, "No true gentleman would allow a lady of rank and sensibility to live as I have been told the earl did at Ravensgate. Why, the roof leaked, and he could not entertain for years. It would not have done at all for one such as Lady Sophia. No, no! And to answer your question, Kitty, Lord Carrington was quite attractive, yes."

"Carrington?" Mr. Ponsby queried as if his wife had lost her wits. "He was a mincing fop. Top o' the trees, I suppose, but nothing like Ravensby."

"Well," Mrs. Ponsby allowed reluctantly, "I suppose he was

not so . . . manly as the earl, but that is of no moment. Everyone says it is only a matter of time before Ravensby asks for Lady Sophia.''

''Are you certain, Mama?'' Kitty cast an excited smile at her cousin, sitting silently by her. ''I think it would be ever so romantic if Ravensby and Sarah formed a *tendre* for each other after the way in which they met.''

Sarah blessed the dark of the carriage for hiding the hot blush that rose in her cheeks. She, too, had harbored similar, quite pitifully impossible fantasies.

''I am absolutely certain, my dear,'' Mrs. Ponsby was saying. ''Now, Sarah, dear''—she leaned forward to pat her niece's hand—''I know you'll not get up your hopes in that area, for you are too wise. Perhaps next time you are rescued, you can manage an unattached gentleman, but you did not on this occasion.''

Having had the time to steady herself, Sarah was able to reply unaffectedly, ''I certainly hope there will be no other rescues, Aunt Vinnie, and I am only grateful the earl was on hand to save me, whatever his matrimonial plans.''

Her aunt applauded the sentiment, but Kitty hrrumphed in a most provoked way, ''Sarah Marlowe! I think you are entirely too prosaic.''

I hope to be, Sarah remarked grimly to herself, for to be anything but prosaic about the Earl of Ravensby would be the height of foolishness.

''Do look at this French walking hat, Sarah. Do you not think the ostrich feathers the height of elegance?''

Sarah eyed the silk creation skeptically. Perhaps she had taken an unfair aversion to plumes, but she could not like them. ''I prefer the cottage hat just there,'' she said, pointing to a hat farther back in the window.

When Kitty saw it, she rolled her eyes. ''Your father would prefer that one, cuz. It is entirely too simple. Ah, here is one you must like. Do you see the leghorn with only the one peach-colored rouleau?''

Sarah agreed she did like the leghorn better, and in harmony they strolled on to the next shop's windows to consider the

scarves and shawls on display there. They were not given much
time. No sooner had they reached it than they were greeted by
Johnny Carstairs' exceptionally amiable voice.

After the usual greetings, all very formal and surprised, for
Maddie's sake, for it was she accompanied the girls in place
of Mrs. Ponsby, the young man looked to Sarah. "You will
be particularly delighted by the goods in a shop just down the
street, Miss Marlowe."

"And why is that, sir?" she asked with a smile.

"Because there are reams and reams of watercolors on
display." He laughed when her eyes widened. "I knew you
would be interested. Ackners and Sons gallery has devoted its
premises to a display of the works of several different men.
Shall we go and see?"

The question was for the sake of politeness only. Johnny knew
very well Sarah had received training in the art of watercolors
from a Mr. Martin Aubermont, a friend of her father's who
was an artist in his own right. That she had been one of Mr.
Aubermont's favorite pupils, he did not know, but might have
guessed from the enthusiasm with which she exclaimed as they
entered the gallery.

"This is beyond anything marvelous," Sarah cried as she took
in the range of the exhibition. On the first floor, alone, there
were works by four different men. So absorbed was she in
studying their efforts that when Johnny and Kitty whispered they
had discovered a delightful courtyard in the back, she waved
them off without a word.

Maddie was not so distracted, however. "An' what's this,
missy?" she demanded. "Where's that minx an' the boy goin'?"

"Only the gardens, Maddie. Nowhere disreputable. Let us
forget Kitty a little and consider this amazing display."

In reply, Maddie muttered something dour about how amazing
it would be if Mrs. Ponsby were to appear at the exhibition and
find Kitty off without a chaperon, but Sarah did not listen, only
linked arms with her nurse and wound her way through the
gallery and up a set of circular stairs to the second floor, where
she discovered a new artist whose work was different from the
more traditional attitudes of the Sandby brothers, Thomas Girtin,
and Francis Towne on display below.

Entranced by the efforts of the artist with the unwieldy name of Joseph Mallord William Turner, particularly with those works in which he studied the effect of light upon water, Sarah quite forgot the time and Kitty and Johnny. She drifted from one room to the next, only to have her head come up sharply as she stood before an open window at the front of the building. Frozen, Sarah waited a moment; then her aunt's voice wafted through the window again.

"You are a witch, Maddie!" Sarah shot the old nurse an irritated look. "Whoever would have thought Aunt Vinnie would finish with her dressmaker so soon."

"Anyone could guess yer aunt'd not stay home, once the dressmaker was done."

Sarah did not acknowledge the entirely reasonable remark. She knew full well her aunt had even said she might try to find them on Bond Street, but Sarah had dismissed the possibility, as had Kitty, in the belief that Mrs. Ponsby would succumb to the desire to be fitted for not one new dress, but several. Just to be certain it really was her aunt outside, Sarah leaned her head out the window by her.

It was the worst thing she could have done. Her aunt caught sight of her, as did the Marquess of Lisle, the gentleman she had been greeting. Mrs. Ponsby waved her handkerchief. "There you are, my dears. Wait for us there, or we shall be hopelessly separated. Lord Lisle and I will join you as soon as we can make our way inside."

Glancing in the direction Mrs. Ponsby indicated, Sarah saw that at least they'd one thing in their favor. A throng of people crowded the doorway, preventing Mrs. Ponsby a quick entry. Indeed, the entire gallery seemed to have filled while she was not looking. Where there had been only one or two people in the room, now there was a crowd.

Quickly Sarah urged Maddie to fetch Kitty from the garden. The older woman argued against the plan, pointing out she would be leaving Sarah unprotected, but her charge effectively rebutted by observing that the consequences to all, should her Aunt Vinnie find they were in collusion against her, would not be happy. "I shall say you are in the necessary room, if she comes. Do hurry, Maddie. I shall be fine."

Hurry the old nurse did, but Sarah had been overly optimistic to think she could remain alone without difficulty. No sooner had she turned to gaze unseeing at a bright, mysterious picture of the Thames than a gentleman swinging a gold-headed walking stick appeared at her side.

At least Sarah took him for a gentleman until he leered at her. "Enjoying the exhibit, are you, missy?" he queried.

She lifted her nose in the air and took herself off to another picture. Unfortunately the man was persistent. "Hey, now, no need to stick yer nose up in the air. I've as much blunt in my pocket as any of the other gents yer likely to pick up here."

Sarah turned pink to her hairline. He thought her a . . . a lightskirt! "Go away," she hissed.

He perused the seductively rounded curves of her figure. "Can't think why I should do that."

"Because you will answer to me, if you do not," a low, decisive voice said from behind Sarah.

Even as a glad cry rose to her lips, Sarah could not but feel, too, the deepest chagrin. Of all the people who might have rescued her from such a predicament, she could have wished for anyone but Ravensby!

"Here, now! No harm done!" Sarah's accoster, taking in the dangerous light in the eyes of the man who stood a head taller than he, attempted his most placating smile. "Didn't know the lady was taken. That's all!"

As he slinked off, he darted a fearful glance back over his shoulder, but saw he need not worry. The girl's elegant protector had turned the full force of his amber gaze upon her.

"Great God," Dominic exclaimed, voice low and taut but nonetheless fearsome. "How could anyone know you are taken, innocent, or any way protected, Miss Marlowe, when you stand here in a public place entirely unattended? Are you determined to ruin yourself?"

Sarah shook her head, her thoughts quite scattered. Her father, while firm on his principles, had guided her with an indulgent, gentle hand. Never before had she encountered such a scathing look as she did then. "It is a confusion only," she stammered helplessly, unable to think of an explanation that did not involve Kitty.

"Confusion!" His brow arched contemptuously. "A girl of any breeding could not be confused on the matter. She would know that if she remained alone, she must leave herself open to the sort of ugly, demeaning approaches from lecherous strangers you have just suffered. I cannot imagine what your aunt is about to leave you like this. If she wishes to throw you at Lisle, why did she not take you with her? Can she possibly believe you would appear to better advantage alone?"

If Sarah had been at a loss for an answer when she had known herself at fault, now, when he insulted Mrs. Ponsby in such a contemptuous way, the words seemed to leap from her tongue.

"You are insufferable, sir! In your arrogance, you believe you know everything, when in fact you know naught!" Seeing a lady not far away turn at the sound of angry voices, Sarah lowered her voice, rasping out, "My being alone has nothing to do with my aunt. Nor, sir, has it anything to do with you."

Hands clenched, Sarah whirled away, angered all the more that she could not escape him altogether but had to remain in the room, aware of him, aware of his cutting gaze, aware despite everything that she wished he had not such a dreadful disdain for her.

Dominic had half a mind to wheel about in his turn and leave the chit to make do as best she could without his interference in her affairs. Already there were two dandies ogling her considerable charms.

Sarah gazed blindly at a misty rendering Turner had done of Lake Geneva. She did not appreciate it, did not even see it. She was seeing the contempt in Ravensby's eyes. It did not take a brilliant mind to guess who it was had observed to him Mrs. Ponsby was "throwing" her at the marquess. But he need not have accepted Lady Sophia's disparaging characterization of her aunt's hopes for her. That he had . . .

"You must take my arm, Miss Marlowe."

Startled, Sarah jerked her head up, her gaze colliding with Ravensby's. He cursed under his breath, and she wanted to die. He'd seen the tears clouding her eyes.

"Damn! I did not mean to make you cry."

"Well, what did you expect?" she flashed, taking refuge in anger lest she embarrass herself further and burst into tears in public, something no girl of "any breeding" would do. "You were hateful."

"I was concerned for you," he snapped, vexed by the exaggeration. Surely he had not been hateful, though he had, he conceded, been in a temper. It had infuriated him to stroll into the gallery and find her in the untenable position of being accosted by a toad.

"You were concerned for me?" Sarah demanded, her temper little better than his. "And that is why you insulted my aunt? 'Throwing' me at Lisle, indeed! She has done no such thing. And she knows nothing of my being here alone."

"If the fault for your position is yours alone, Miss Marlowe," Dominic replied levelly, "then I apologize to your aunt, but find myself all the angrier with you. Not that I wished to make you cry. I did not." His tone seemed sincere enough, but he did not look wildly remorseful. Indeed, Sarah thought his look more brooding than anything. "I did, however," he continued, his voice hardening, "wish to impress upon you the need to know and abide by the rules of society. They are for your protection."

And they were back to the beginning. "You may rest assured you succeeded in making your point, my lord," she said without humor. It rankled, particularly, that he would caution her to learn the rules of society, as if she were so ill-bred she did not know how to behave. But then she felt a ripple of frustration. She had, for just the one moment, acted as if she were ignorant of those rules.

And if she were not to appear completely lacking in either manners or common grace, then she owed him her thanks for rescuing her from the consequences of her actions.

"I do wish, however, to thank you for your intervention with that man, my lord. He was most unpleasant. Ah!" Her expression cleared and a smile of relief lit her eyes. "There is my party now. Excuse me, please."

She did not await any response Dominic might make. She sped from his company as quickly as she could with never a backward glance and joined forces with her cousin and an old woman who looked more nanny than maid. She had not, as she had said, been with her aunt. Dominic had jumped to the wrong conclusion when he'd caught a glimpse of Mrs. Ponsby and Lisle struggling with the crowd in the entryway as he climbed to the second floor.

"Dominic, here you are!" Lady Sophia Carrington, on her brother's arm, drifted in through the door behind Dominic. "We thought you were downstairs still. Is there anything of interest here?"

No sooner had she said it than Lady Sophia's eye fell upon Sarah Marlowe, who was just then greeting another pair of arrivals to the room. Lady Sophia smiled, albeit thinly. "I see there is, if you are interested in watching an ambitious child snare a title."

"Sophy!" It was her brother clucked protestingly. "You are being unreasonably hard on the girl. She's a remarkable beauty. It is no wonder at all Lisle is intrigued. As for her, it's as easy to marry a title as not."

The three looked on as the ponderous marquess bowed over Miss Marlowe's slender hand. Straightening, he said something to her, and despite his grave manner, she laughed. Really laughed, not merely responded with a polite titter.

Dominic swung about. "Actually, I was admiring this water-color of Lake Geneva, but as I am done, I've no objection to departing." Suiting his actions to his words, he propelled Lady Sophia and Lord Richard back through the door they'd only just entered.

7

Her third encounter with the Earl of Ravensby could not but prey upon Sarah's mind. Had she not had their first encounter to recall, his behavior might not have cut so deeply. He had been arrogant then, true, and even imperious, but he had not been rude or disparaging. His eyes had glinted with amusement, and he had touched her cheek and said she had beauty.

Why, then, the change? She had no answer, but that he found

her so wanting in all aspects of good breeding, he could not behave toward her with even ordinary courtesy, much less liking. It seemed to rankle him that he felt some sense of responsibility for her, having saved either her life or her limbs—whichever case best suited him at a given moment.

Sarah wished he had not saved her, that someone else had. Indeed, she wished she had never met him. Here was a man who seemed to have naught but distaste for her, and yet she could not simply walk disdainfully away from him. Never in her life had she imagined she would reply as heatedly as she had to the earl, and in a quite public place. And those tears! She could not think of the last time she had cried. It galled her to think she had lost her poise so, but she blamed Ravensby, in all. He had been unforgivably rude.

Ravensby's remarks on her breeding having left their mark, Sarah was as delighted as her aunt when they received invitations to a ball Lady Clarissa Edrington was to give. Mrs. Ponsby said the old dowager was of the very highest *ton*. Kitty whispered that her mother was a tactical genius.

"Just as Mother expected, your beauty has opened doors for us, my dear cuz," Kitty explained. "Lady Clarissa is a great-aunt to Lisle, and I am certain it is he procured us these invitations."

Sarah could not know the accuracy of Kitty's guess. The marquess did not even hint he had spoken to his great-aunt, but he was awaiting them close to the door, and he did present Sarah to Mrs. Drummond-Burrell, reputedly the most severe stickler of the several patronesses of Almack's.

To Sarah's surprise, the haughty woman thawed slightly when Lisle presented her. With the most measured of smiles, she allowed she had known Sarah's mother. "A very lovely girl she was, my dear."

"I am honored you should say so," Sarah replied, the sincerity in her tone such that she earned a rather more approving smile from Mrs. Drummond-Burrell, and when the marquess requested it, permission to dance the waltz.

He led her out proudly, as if partnering her lent him consequence. The notion was absurd, of course, but Sarah could not but be grateful for his manner. It was a balm to her bruised pride, and she did her best to be good company for him, even leading him on to describe the dancing classes he had endured with his sister.

"Harriet's a sack of potatoes, my dear. No point dressin' it up, and it was to avoid her weight I learned to be nimble." Sarah giggled at the thought of Lisle hopping about, even as a boy, just to avoid his sister's leaden feet. "You may laugh, Miss Marlowe," he went on in his droll way, "but Harriet was deadly, and I cannot tell you how grateful my feet are that you are too graceful to come near them."

Sarah had been paid more fulsome compliments, but she flushed a little beneath the unmistakable warmth of his look. As chance would have it, when she glanced away from the marquess, she found the Earl of Ravensby watching her.

He stood in the doorway, having just arrived. Lady Sophia on one side and a younger girl on the other. Sarah examined neither lady. Her chin went up as she held the earl's gaze. It was impossible to tell what he was thinking, his expression was unreadable, and therefore it was entirely possible to imagine the worst: that he was surprised to see her among such select guests; that he could not imagine she had been approved to dance the waltz; that she must have thrown herself at Lisle's feet to bring it off.

The moment ended as suddenly as it began. Eyes on her, Ravensby inclined his head, acknowledging her, if briefly, then turned away to do the polite with the flatteringly large group come to bid him, and his ladies, good evening.

Of course, they sought his acknowledgment, she thought rather bitterly. He was compelling as the very devil. Tall, broad-shouldered, dressed with elegant restraint in evening clothes of the same shade of dark chocolate as his hair, his severe, beautiful features schooled into a rather aloof expression, he exuded an air of self-possession and of mastery.

Sarah looked away when a beplumed dowager reached his side, and he smiled down upon the old woman. His cool expression softened then, and Sarah found herself biting her lip.

She was given ample reason to withhold her attention from the earl. Young man after young man came to pay her court, and some came who were not so young. Lisle returned, not to dance with her, but, as he said, to give her a moment's respite.

And Captain Kendall came, his scarlet regimentals seeming to set off his black eyes so they gleamed. "You are the success I knew you would be, Miss Marlowe," he said, lifting her hand to his lips. "You have even been approved to dance the waltz. I am so pleased! You were meant to dance that dance, you know." His voice dropped to a purr, that none of the young men crowding about might hear. "Lisle could not have shown you what a sensuous dance it is. I shall, Miss Marlowe. It would be my greatest pleasure."

She was just about to apologize, with a smile, of course, and say that her aunt had limited her to only one waltz an evening, but she happened by the merest chance to glance away from the captain's too-intense eyes and find, once more, Ravensby's piercing gaze upon her.

A thrill of defiance streaked through her, overtaking her good judgment. He had not accorded her the slightest attention but for the one cool stare when he arrived. He had danced several times, gone to the card room, come back, talked to several gentlemen, danced with Lady Sophia again, then led out an elderly dowager. Sarah knew all that, though it maddened her that she did, and knew, having followed his movements despite herself, that he had not only not asked her to dance, but that he had not even looked her way again. Not until now. And what would he do? Swoop down to separate her from the captain; decry her as an ill-bred upstart for dancing, and the waltz at that, with a rake like Kendall?

Sarah gave Kendall her hand and allowed him to lead her onto the floor. She regretted the rash act instantly. He tried to hold her far too close, though he did set her away after she pointed out coolly it was likely to be her last waltz, they would so scandalize the company. But he repelled her so, even his more proper hold made her skin crawl, and she suffered it for naught.

At least, she suffered for naught if her goal was to cause Ravensby to gnash his teeth, or, perhaps, to come and scold her. He quit the room, depriving her entirely of any notion how he was affected, for by the time she reached the floor and looked to see, all she saw was his back disappearing into Lady Clarissa's cardroom.

* * *

Lisle's interest, as well as the pretty manners Sarah and Kitty displayed, continued to bring invitations to the grander affairs of the social season. At all of them Sarah was surrounded by young men, many of them Johnny Carstairs' amiable friends, but never, though she saw him frequently, did Ravensby do more than incline his head in her general direction. Certainly he did not bring his niece, the young lady he escorted about, to meet her. Sarah met the girl by purest chance.

She was attending an affair at the home of Lord and Lady Dibble, when one of her more enthusiastic dance partners caught her dress with the toe of his shoe, tearing the lace flounce edging the hem. The rip was audible to them both, and, appalled, he apologized profusely.

She assured him it was nothing that could not be mended in a trice and went at once to attend it. Lady Dibble informed her a maid and a sewing kit could be found on the third floor in a room set aside for such crises. Though Sarah did not find the maid, she did find the sewing kit and set about doing the best she could with a tear that lay more to the side than the front of her hem.

She succeeded mostly at pricking herself several times, and, drawing blood at last, let out a pithy, frustrated, "Devil it!"

"Can I be of assistance?"

Sarah looked around in surprise to find the girl she knew from her aunt to be Ravensby's niece standing uncertainly in a doorway that gave onto a small balcony. "That depends if you can sew at all," Sarah replied with a smile. "And I am Sarah Marlowe, by the by."

"Yes, I know," the girl admitted softly. "You are much talked of." Sarah tensed a moment, but though the girl's eyes were downcast eyes, she seemed too shy and timid to have been hinting at anything unpleasant. Perhaps the earl and Lady Sophia had not discussed Sarah and the Ponsbys before her. "My name is Anne, Anne Pentworth."

A tall, slender girl with dark hair and great dark eyes, Miss Pentworth was not exactly pretty, Sarah decided, but she might have been attractive in an unusual way, if her expression had been even a little more animated and her hair dressed in a slightly more becoming way. She had too long a face to wear her hair swept severely back into a single heavy knot, no matter that she did wear a plume to dress it up.

"I can sew a little," she went on to say. "Enough to repair your lace, I think. Shall I try?"

"I would be eternally grateful." Sarah smiled ruefully. "Thus far I've managed more pricks to my finger than stitches."

Not seeming to detect the humor in Sarah's voice, Miss Pentworth replied seriously, "It is only because you cannot see clearly what you are doing."

As she seated herself on a little footstool and took the needle and thread in hand, Sarah observed Anne Pentworth thoughtfully. She seemed unnaturally solemn, but at the same time painfully uncertain.

"Shall I return the favor when you are done?" Sarah asked. "Or did you succeed at mending your dress?"

She was not at all surprised that Miss Pentworth looked at her blankly a moment before, coloring, she shook her head. "No." A pause ensued as the girl bent her head over her task, but then, taking Sarah by surprise, her needle in midair, she looked up again. "I did not tear it, you see. I only came up here . . ." Her voice trailed off, and she shrugged as if she could not say, or did not think Sarah would understand if she did.

But Sarah thought she did understand. "It must have been quiet and peaceful on the balcony. I don't wonder you sought it out. There have been times since the Season began I thought I would go mad if I did not have a moment of peace."

"You?" Miss Pentworth asked rather warily, as if she feared Sarah were making fun of her. "You seem very at home in society."

Sarah shrugged. "We've all different things at which we excel. I seem to excel at appearing gay. No, that's not fair." She chuckled at herself. "I do enjoy people. Still, I am from Cumberland and not at all accustomed to the sheer numbers of people I have encountered since coming to London. Nor," she went on after a moment's consideration, "do I think I wish to become entirely accustomed. That is, I do not wish to live permanently in town. I've a liking for solitude too."

"I was not only seeking quiet," Miss Pentworth admitted in a low, constrained voice. "I was hiding. Oh!" she cried tensely.

"I wish I could go home! I am weary to death of my Season."

A little taken aback by the girl's sudden intensity, Sarah prodded cautiously, "But you cannot? Return home, that is?"

Miss Pentworth shook her head. "My mother took ill. That is why she is not with me. To recover, she must have rest, and if I were to go home in the middle of the Season, she would fret and blame herself for my not faring better here."

"Well, I see only one solution then," Sarah announced after a moment, and when Miss Pentworth gave her a questioning look, she grinned coaxingly. "You will simply have to learn to enjoy your Season."

"That will be impossible!" Miss Pentworth sounded most forlorn. "I never know what to say to anyone. I am awkward, and I feel a quiz! My uncle is sympathetic, but he's no experience with girls. Both his sisters, you see, were older than he. Only his brothers were younger, and he has no notion how to help me go on. Lady Sophy, his . . ." Miss Pentworth hesitated, searching for the correct word, and could not know how Sarah held her breath, waiting to hear how the girl would characterize Lady Sophia. In the end Sarah was disappointed. Miss Pentworth simply skipped over her dilemma. "Lady Sophy has tried to be helpful. She has accompanied me to the modiste, taken me to Bond Street, and even offered to send her hairdresser to me, but I had encountered the man once and found him so dauntingly toplofty, I could not bear the thought of subjecting myself to him." Miss Pentworth shook her head mournfully. "If I cannot face a mere hairdresser, you can imagine how lost I am in society. And though Lady Sophia is generally on hand, she is so assured and elegant and accomplished, I feel the veriest dowd in comparison to her!" The girl paused to expel a deep breath, but before Sarah could think what to say to her, she smiled rather wanly. "I am sorry, Miss Marlowe! I did not intend to pour out all my difficulties, only, perhaps, to make friends. I don't know any girls my own age very well."

Sarah did know how to reply to that, and did so without hesitation. "I should be delighted to be friends! I do not know many girls in London well either." She shrugged when Miss Pentworth looked surprised. "It's true. While the young men have been friendly enough, the ladies have been distinctly more standoffish.'' Recalling the way Lady Sophia had regarded her aunt, she added, ''My lineage, though it is good enough for the country, seems somewhat suspect in town.''

Sarah was not the first girl with whom Anne Pentworth had made an effort to be friends. She had, in Lady Sophia's company, made duty calls at the homes of several young ladies, but had invariably been received with cool politeness. Why they had responded with no more than civility, she could not be certain, but she'd the unhappy suspicion the girls to whom Lady Sophia had introduced her felt too uncertain of their own consequence to care to be seen in company with an antidote, which was what she felt herself to be.

Her approach to Sarah had been quite unplanned, and undertaken only because Sarah happened to be at hand when Anne felt particularly dismal. To have her overture not only met with warmth but also a return of confidence won her to her new friend.

When Sarah said, then, that it was her antecedents the young ladies questioned, Anne snorted derisively. ''In my opinion the ladies' reticence toward you is likely to have a great deal more to do with the men's interest than with your lineage.''

''They are foolish, if so,'' Sarah replied. ''Most of the young men crowding around Kitty and me are friends of Johnny Carstairs' . . . a friend of the Ponsbys' from Hampshire. Oh, you may as well know!'' Sarah smiled ruefully. ''Poor Johnny hovers about us because he's a *tendre* for Kitty, but he must cloak his purpose, as his prospects are such my aunt does not approve his suit. Hence the reams of young men. Presenting them, you see, he's an excuse to linger.'' Anne laughed, pleased to have received the confidence, but she was not entirely convinced the young men thronged Sarah simply on account of her cousin and Mr. Carstairs. She opened her mouth to say as much, but Sarah had thoughts of her own to voice. ''We shall put Kitty and Johnny's woes to our use! Come down with me, and I shall introduce you to Johnny's friends. Are you a lover of horses, by any chance?''

Surprised by the question and certainly taken aback by Sarah's plan, Anne nodded slowly. ''Yes, of course.''

Sarah did not stop to point out there was no "of course" to liking horses. "Well, come along, then," she said instead, and standing, held out her hand.

Poor Anne felt she had been taken up by a whirlwind, when she'd only wanted a quiet coze. But neither, she found, could she disappoint Sarah, though she could warn unhappily as she slipped her hand into her new friend's, "I won't know what to say."

"Ah, but you will," Sarah returned with complete assurance. "All the young men, but particularly the one I've in mind to present to you, are mad about horses. Only tell Lieutenant Stevenson you understand he's come across a sound filly, and he'll be good for an hour."

Anne giggled nervously. That sounded too, too easy. They were descending the stairs, and the festive sounds emanating from the ballroom unnerved her. "I am such an antidote!" she protested.

Sarah ignored the sharp tug on her hand as she looked at Anne incredulously. "An antidote? Good heavens, Miss Pentworth! You really are off the mark. You might rearrange your hair, just to emphasize your eyes, for they are really quite lovely, but an antidote . . . ?"

There could be no doubting the sincerity of Sarah's amazement, and Anne felt her unflattering picture of herself fade just a little. "Well . . ." She fumbled. "That is, I have never been out in company much. But however I look"—her voice strengthened—"I do know I wish you to call me Anne. 'Miss Pentworth' sounds such an odiously worthy person, don't you think?"

Sarah giggled. "Odiously. And you will call me Sarah? I know!" she went on, after Anne nodded. "Why do you not come to call tomorrow, if your uncle does not object. My aunt's hairdresser is coming about one or so, and you will like her. Yes! She is a woman and a dear."

Head whirling, a new hair arrangement in her future, a friend at her side, and introductions imminent to what appeared to her frantic eye to be a battalion of young men, Anne Pentworth entered Lady Dibble's ballroom, her cheeks becoming flushed.

8

"Have you seen Anne since she excused herself, Sophy?"

Lady Sophia hesitated imperceptibly before inclining her head toward the far side of the room. "She and the Marlowe girl returned to the ballroom together. Later you must speak to her about who is and is not desirable as a friend, Dominic. The girl and her aunt will only use Anne, if you do not. Though they are now being invited to some of the better affairs, their hold on society is, shall I say, tenuous. They've not received vouchers to Almack's, for example, nor will they without a connection like Anne or, through her, you."

When Dominic did not reply, Lady Sophia glanced up to gauge the effect of her remarks. She could not have said precisely what his thoughts were as he studied the group composed of his niece, the Marlowe chit, her cousin, and an assortment of young men, but she was satisfied that he had heard her, for he was frowning perceptibly.

Dominic was considering one of Lady Sophia's remarks. In particular, that Miss Marlowe might befriend Anne to use her.

Anne would be susceptible to skillful blandishments and flattery from another girl. He knew she was lonely. Sophy had introduced her about, but it was not the same as being taken around by a mother, who would after the initial invitation invite the other girls to tea, call on them in the afternoons, arrange expeditions to Gunther's, and so on. Sophy had time only for the introductions. She'd her father's entertainments to arrange and preside over, her own friends to cultivate. Something had had to be left to the mamas of the girls to whom she presented Anne. And there had been, of course, tentative efforts. Anne had been invited on shopping expeditions, to card parties, and other amusements, but she'd not yet made a fast friend. When he'd inquired into the subject, Anne had shrugged and mumbled in her diffident way something about everyone being too busy to take a genuine interest in her.

What if Anne encountered a girl capable of seeming genuine in her interest? By her own account, Miss Marlowe could be an actress when it suited her, and she did have reason to try to play the good friend. As Sophy had said, she was in need of connections to families such as the Pentworths and the Morelands. But she'd other reasons as well. It was just possible she thought to retaliate for those remarks of his she had characterized as hateful. What a lark to cultivate Anne, then flaunt his niece's regard for her in his face.

The look in his eye darkening, Dominic watched Miss Marlowe split off one of the young men from her group and herd him along with Anne to her aunt. She was sending Anne off to dance without first consulting him. He'd no notion how suitable the young man was, only knew Mrs. Ponsby was a lax guardian.

Lady Sophia caught his sleeve as he moved forward. ''Dominic, I see what you intend, but I caution you not to fall in with their plans. They want you to go to them! They will establish a public connection with you in that way.''

''I intend to meet that young man, Sophy. And I've every confidence I am up to dealing with encroachers.''

With a grim smile, Dominic was off, Miss Sarah Marlowe his objective. He had not spoken to her in the week or so since their encounter at the gallery. The thought made him slow his step ever so slightly. He had not spoken to her by design. He did not accept he had been hateful that day, but it did nag at him that he had stung her to tears. Sarah Marlowe did not strike him as a young lady who cried easily. She had uttered a sob of relief when he'd plucked her from thin air, had trembled for a bit with reaction, but no more. Jane, even Ruth, would have sobbed for half a day. Sophy he rather thought might have swooned had she ever chanced to fall into such a hapless predicament in the first place.

And so he had held himself aloof from Miss Marlowe. He'd had no reason to speak with her. He was long past needing to puff up his consequence by being seen with the Season's newest beauty, and certainly he'd no interest in pursuing her into marriage.

A cooling period, he'd thought of it, or a time of disengagement. And no need to rescue her from some predicament or other had arisen to test his intention. True, she had danced as often as she pleased with Captain Kendall. Indeed, she'd flaunted at least one of those dances, tipping her chin at him as she slipped her hand into Kendall's and allowed the captain to lead her out for a waltz.

But she'd not again lingered on a shadowy terrace with the man. There had been no opportunity, perhaps, with more and more young men surrounding her each night.

It did not surprise Dominic in the least that Sarah Marlowe was a success with the gentlemen. He'd have been astonished were she not. She'd remarkable beauty, a radiant smile to animate that beauty, and seductive curves the feel of which he could remember beneath his hand.

She had not, however, as of yet, found quite the same degree of approval among the ladies, with the exception of the very old dowagers. When her bones permitted, he enjoyed leading out Lady Crowder, a great friend of his mother's, and once they had chanced to hear the girl laugh at something her young partner said. Likely it had only been an idle joke, but her laugh had been real and infectious. Hearing it, old Lady Crowder had smiled, and looking to Miss Marlowe, pronounced almost wistfully, "Lovely gel. Really a lovely gel."

Perhaps it was that very loveliness made the other, younger, ladies withhold their final approval. Perhaps it was a more legitimate objection to her lack of family, connections, or wealth.

Anne would make a providential connection. Shy she might be, but her family was the best. Would Miss Marlowe make a friend of her without caring a fig for her? Was she so cold? He could not know, and suspected his first inclination, which was to say, she was not.

He did see that, when she caught sight of him approaching her, Sarah Marlowe turned away deliberately and whispered with one of the young men in the group surrounding her.

It angered Sarah that when she realized Ravensby was approaching her, her heart should race but then should sink like a stone when she took in his expression. His face was as finely molded as a Greek statue's and as cool. He did not come to her on any pleasant mission.

At once she looked to Johnny Carstairs beside her. Kitty had asked if Sarah would distract her aunt a little, that she and Johnny might drift out to Lady Dribble's balcony unobserved. Ravensby would provide the perfect distraction. Already Sarah could see her aunt emerging from a circle of mothers intent upon him. "Ravensby is coming to inquire after Anne," she whispered to Johnny. "Go along with Kitty, if you still wish."

Johnny grinned at that and was gone, leaving her to face Ravensby. Sarah knew why he came. Taken very much with Anne, eager to bring the girl out of her shell if she could, Sarah had forgotten Anne's uncle. But reminded forcibly of him now, she recalled his remarks upon her breeding; his disdainful characterization of her aunt's hopes for her—that "throwing" her at Lisle still galled. He'd hold her and her family unworthy of his niece's company.

It hurt, that. She did not think herself so very unsuitable, and she had only thought to gladden Anne.

"Miss Marlowe, allow me, I beg you, to obtain you a glass of punch. It is my turn!" Arthur Farquahar, a wealthy young man turned out in the very latest fashion, elbowed his good friend, Mr. Ardrey, aside with a grin. "Don't listen to Ardrey, here. You gave him the honor only an hour ago!"

Mr. Ardrey was on the point of crying foul, for it had been Lord Edgemont Sarah had accepted her punch from, but both young men sobered suddenly as it seemed to Sarah a shadow fell on their group.

The two young men greeted Ravensby with something like awe, stammering their good-evenings. He returned the courtesies, but in such a way the gentlemen did not think to linger by Sarah. She watched them float away with a feeling of detachment, far less aware of their desertion than Ravensby's gaze upon her.

She looked up, her face set. Dominic had not realized he expected even an insincere version of a smile until he marked its complete absence. "My lord." She dropped a formal curtsy.

"Miss Marlowe."

His tone was no warmer than his expression. Sarah braced herself for some scathing remark.

"My lord!"

Mrs. Ponsby's cry startled them both. They had, variously,

forgotten her or never seen her in the first place. Perforce the earl had to greet Sarah's aunt, giving Sarah the opportunity to study him. She had almost forgotten how formidable he could be at close range. His powerful figure seemed the more daunting, as did, somehow, the impeccable elegance of his evening clothes.

And he was so very arresting with his dark hair and strong, chiseled features.

"I hope you do not mind I approved Lieutenant Stevenson to dance with your delightful niece!" Mrs. Ponsby exclaimed. "When the set was forming, I could not see you, and he is a nice boy."

"I should like to meet him, of course, Mrs. Ponsby." Dominic caught the flash of emotion in Sarah's eyes, for he had flicked his gaze to her, and knew she had taken exception to his reply, quite unlike her aunt, who was beaming as she ran on about Lieutenant Stevenson.

"You will like him exceedingly, my lord! His family is from Edinburgh, I believe. Is that not correct, Sarah?"

"Yes, Aunt Vinnie," Sarah addressed her aunt. "Lieutenant Stevenson's father is a viscount."

She shifted her gaze to Dominic. He did not mistake the challenge in it, though with her aunt standing at her elbow she could not outright glare daggers at him.

"Most unexceptionable," he agreed in return. "I wonder I have not encountered him before."

"He was only given his leave a short while ago!" Mrs. Ponsby replied, drawing the earl's regard to her again. "It was in response to an invitation from his aunt, Mrs. Derwent, that he came to have a taste of town."

"Mrs. Derwent?" Dominic frowned slightly. "She is a friend to Lady Crowder, is she not?"

"Yes, yes! I was just speaking with them both. Mrs. Derwent is in hopes her nephew will be able to remain in town for the remainder of the Season. He . . ."

While Mrs. Ponsby chatted on about the boy's leave and his regiment, Dominic wondered why her niece would send such a paragon as the boy seemed to be off with another girl. He'd not get the answer from her. She stood half-turned so that she seemed more absent from their trio than of it. He followed her gaze and saw her watching Anne and the lieutenant.

Anne was not smiling, he saw, but she was listening attentively as her partner talked. The lieutenant must have asked her something, for then, blushing a little, she made a reply that caused the boy to nod vigorously before he began holding forth again.

Curious, Dominic looked down and sustained a surprise. Sarah Marlowe was smiling, faintly but nonetheless distinctly.

"Now, then! They make a nice couple, I think." Mrs. Ponsby sounded rather proud as she looked out to the dance floor, as if she had thought of the pairing.

But she had not, as Dominic knew. "What made you think to pair Anne with the lieutenant, in particular, Miss Marlowe?"

For a moment Dominic thought she meant to ignore him, but then slowly she lifted her blue eyes to his. "Lieutenant Stevenson is exceedingly fond of horses, my lord, a subject upon which, as you may imagine, I've only the most limited conversation."

"Sarah!" Mrs. Ponsby looked uncertain, as if she had heard a note in her niece's voice she could not quite credit. But then she waved her hand, as if in dismissal of her suspicion. "That is, I only thought to say you have seemed to enjoy the lieutenant's company these past weeks."

"I have, Aunt Vinnie." Sarah managed a smile, regretting how close she had come to giving herself away. "Perhaps I ought to have said I hoped Anne would find it easier to talk with the lieutenant, as they share a common interest. She had confided earlier that she felt rather shy in company."

Sarah was unable to keep from looking at Ravensby half-defensively again. He surprised her, however. "She seems to be doing very well in that regard. You were most thoughtful, Miss Marlowe."

Sarah thought with despair she must be mad that so little could lighten her spirits. Particularly when Ravensby accompanied his praise with a searching look, as if he wished to fathom her mind and discover to what end she had exerted herself to be thoughtful.

"Sarah, dear, do you know where Kitty's got to?" Mrs. Ponsby's voice intruded between them.

At her aunt's question, Sarah flushed. Even if Ravensby had no notion she lied, it was difficult to tell a whisker with him looking on.

"Kitty excused herself for a moment," Sarah said, keenly aware of the heat rising in her cheeks. "She will return shortly, I'm sure."

Mercifully Mrs. Ponsby was not given time to ask where it was Kitty had excused herself to or with whom she had gone. The music ended, and Sarah was able to turn to greet the dancers.

"I see the country set suited you both." She smiled, looking from Anne's flushed countenance to Geoffrey Stevenson's smiling one. The poor man's smile faded, however, as he took in the earl beside her.

Immediately Sarah intervened, swinging about to give Ravensby an imploring look. Taller than the lieutenant, with broader shoulders, he did present a daunting figure. "My lord, allow me to introduce Lieutenant Geoffrey Stevenson. He is a great admirer of yours."

Ravensby flicked her the briefest look before he did what he had intended to do before Sarah had attempted to prejudice him in the young man's favor and extended his hand to the lieutenant. "An admirer of mine?" he asked.

Flushing nervously, Geoffrey Stevenson nodded. "I've always admired your horses, sir. The bay you are riding now looks a prime goer."

"I told Lieutenant Stevenson Ajax had outrun Lord D'Arcy's chestnut," Anne interjected. "It is true, isn't it?"

"It is," Dominic affirmed, smiling a little to hear what was an old feat, really, trumpeted about again. "By two lengths, but that was some two years ago. Ajax is older now, and not so swift, I fear."

"But to have beaten D'Arcy's mount by two lengths!" Lieutenant Stevenson exclaimed. "Perhaps, if you are at Tattersall's tomorrow, you will do me the honor of giving me your opinion on a filly I've my eye on?" Ravensby inclined his head in acknowledgment of the boy's request, and Lieutenant

Stevenson looked to Sarah. "I say, Miss Marlowe, as Miss Pentworth enjoys riding, why do we not get up a riding party for tomorrow afternoon? I should be delighted to put one of my mounts at your disposal."

"You are generous, Lieutenant, but I, ah, would fear the consequences, were I to ride out in town. I have been advised in quite strong terms that I may not, you see."

She looked to Ravensby then—how could she not?—and felt her heart lurch unsteadily in her breast. It was nothing, really, that amused look he returned her. He might have looked at Geoffrey Stevenson the same way. But Sarah had not thought to see that gleam in his golden-brown eyes again.

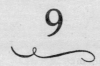

9

"Please, do allow us to organize an outing to Richmond, Mama!" Kitty begged just as Sarah, Charles, and Becky, all returned from an expedition to the ancient Tower of London, piled through the doorway of Mrs. Ponsby's sitting room with distinctly varying degrees of grace.

Charles, keen of ear when it suited him, had heard his elder sister's request and proceeded to jump up and down even more excitedly than he had been. "Richmond!" he cried. "The maze is there. I shall find my way out before you, Becky!"

"You never know your directions, Charles," his sister returned with a lofty sniff before, without pausing for breath, she rounded upon her mother to implore in a distinctly higher, more childlike voice, "May we go, Mama? Please, may we?"

Kitty's vision of an outing to Richmond had not included her younger siblings, but she was practical. Their entreaties added weight to hers. "You see! The children would be so amused. And Sarah longs to go too. Don't you, cuz?"

Sarah had been forewarned of Kitty's plan to get up a party

of young people, which must, out of politeness to a neighbor, include Johnny Carstairs. Once at Richmond, under the guise of exploring the famous maze, Kitty hoped she and Johnny might steal away for a little time together. Sarah sympathized, but in fact she said no more than the truth when she told her aunt, "Truly, I should like a change from the city, Aunt Vinnie."

Taking in the four pairs of eager eyes, Mrs. Ponsby relented. "Very well! It will be amusing, I don't doubt that. But I must approve your guest list, Kitty, and do set the date for sometime after this Thursday. We shall be too busy in the next few days to make any preparations for a picnic. I did say, did I not, that we've received vouchers to Almack's?"

Mrs. Ponsby's effort at offhandedness brought all the response she wished. "Almack's!" Kitty breathed, amazed. "But you are the greatest tease, Mama!"

Mrs. Ponsby beamed in delight as her daughter enveloped her in an enthusiastic embrace. "I thought it only fair to wait until Sarah returned to make the announcement, my dear. But I am so pleased!" Her brown eyes sparkled as brightly as either of the girls'. "We shall have new dresses! Mr. Ponsby has quite approved them, Sarah," she added, seeing her niece was on the point of raising an objection to more clothing. "He could not deny we shall feel the more confident to know we look well. As you must agree, child! Now, then, run along and make up your guest list for Richmond. We've an hour or so before our appointment at the modiste's."

The girls did spend a few moments in excited conversation about the famous Assembly Rooms they would at last see for themselves, then settled to the matter of the guest list for their expedition. As Kitty interpreted her mother's caution that she would approve the guest list to mean she would insist on the Earl of Westphal's presence, Kitty penned his name in without remark. Lady Anne Pentworth came to mind at once, as did Charlotte Manwairing, and Sarah suggested the Viscount Whittingham's daughters, Althea and Clarice Enderby. Kitty made no objection. She had known Althea at Miss Merriweather's, and though the girl was a trifle toplofty, Kitty liked her well enough.

Sarah also admitted she would prefer not to invite Captain

Kendall. Kitty, giving her a shrewd look, asked if the captain had been impertinent, to which Sarah replied, "No, not yet, but I think the maze might present him too great a temptation to miss."

Kitty laughed and penned in the Marquess of Lisle's name instead, then Lieutenant Stevenson's, observing that he and Anne Pentworth had seemed to get on rather well.

Sarah agreed, but vaguely, for a new concern had arisen to preoccupy her. She could not be certain, now she thought on it, that Ravensby would allow his niece to make up one of the party.

He thought Sarah's family quite beneath his in social standing. He had made that clear enough. Nor did he trust her aunt's judgment. Sarah only had to think how he had hastened to evaluate Lieutenant Stevenson for himself, though Mrs. Ponsby had approved Geoffrey to dance with Anne, to know that.

It was true as well he had not approved Anne's visit to Albemarle Street and Mrs. Ponsby's hairdresser. Anne had come, but said, when Sarah had made some reference to the earl, "Uncle Dominic will be most surprised by my new coiffure. He had left the house this morning before I remembered to tell him of your suggestion that I come. I wonder what he will say."

Sarah suspected she could guess. Never mind that his eyes had warmed for that one instant at Lady Dibble's. Teasing her about her ineptitude with horses was not allowing Anne to take her up as a friend.

Almost, Sarah asked Kitty to remove Anne's name from the list, but a certain stubbornness did not allow her to take that craven course. In the first place, she did not wish to miss Anne's company. And in the second, she thought it grossly unfair Ravensby's unfounded prejudices would keep his niece from an entertainment that would be fun for her, and relatively easy, too, for she would have both Sarah and Kitty by her.

Sarah's decision, after only a little thought, was to apply to the earl herself. She would, thereby, spare Anne both an unpleasant interview with her uncle and the subsequent embarrassment of having to tell Sarah and Kitty they were undesirable as friends. Her eyes kindled. By heaven, it would be satisfying, to make him admit that was a most unfair judgment!''

Sarah was, however, frustrated in her desire to get on to the interview. In a note thanking everyone at Albemarle Street for being so very amiable to her, Anne also added that she and Lady Sophia had both come down with the sniffles and would not get out before Thursday at the earliest.

Sarah accepted the delay as well as she could and tried hard on Thursday not to allow the prospect of a confrontation with Ravensby to overshadow her excitement at seeing Almack's at last. She'd her new dress to think on, as well as the problem of a hair ornament.

She'd no tiara, nor even the seed pearls Kitty would wear sprinkled through her hair, and she continued to refuse plumes. Mrs. Ponsby, in her element deciding such things, suggested at last Sarah adorn her hair with camellias.

''They will be the precise color of your dress, my dear! And so fresh and lovely, exactly like you!''

Sarah grinned at her aunt's effort to put the best light possible on the situation, and readily allowed Maddie to pin the sweet-smelling flowers in place.

Only once, as she was evaluating their effect, did Sarah's resolve waver. In her mind's eye she could see the elaborate headpieces the other ladies would wear. Lady Sophia's hair would sparkle with diamonds very likely. But then she thrust the comparison aside. Someone in her position had no choice but to make do with camellias.

The other ladies at Almack's that night did indeed sport most elaborate coiffures. And, if the rooms were nothing out of the ordinary, the company within them was awesomely select. A royal duke stood across the room, and it was rumored the Duke of Wellington was to come later.

As Mrs. Ponsby whispered a string of august names, Sarah felt a spurt of gratitude to Mrs. Drummond-Burrell. The haughty patroness had greeted them with dignified reserve, but there had been the faintest flicker of approval in her eyes as she had taken in Sarah's dress, a demure concoction of satin. Then, noting the camellias, she had inclined her head. ''Very nice, my dear. The camellias are a fetching touch.''

Buoyed by the approval of a woman renowned for her

discrimination, Sarah searched for Anne with a relatively martial gleam in her eye. And found her friend standing with her uncle and the elderly lady he occasionally led out to dance. Lady Sophia was not with them. Sarah was just digesting that piece of luck, when Anne, catching sight of her, waved.

Ravensby glanced up to see who had excited his niece's interest, and something very like surprise briefly animated his features, but no softer expression followed to warm his eyes as they met Sarah's. It was possible the old dowager claimed his attention before he had time to do more than register astonishment Sarah had been allowed through Almack's hallowed portals, but it made no matter.

Sarah's determination to approach him on Anne's behalf faltered. Face-to-face with him, she realized she had deluded herself. There was little likelihood he would give his consent, but rather much more that he would inform her in biting tones she was too ill-bred and had too great a taste for rakish company to be seen with Anne. After a hesitation, Sarah turned not toward her friend but toward Kitty and her aunt.

Her indecision cost her, however. Before she could attain the comfort of her allies, she was caught all alone, for Anne came hurrying to Sarah's side and brought her uncle, whose arm she held, along with her.

Sarah dipped the earl a curtsy and murmured good evening, without seeing any reason to lift her gaze above the intricate knot of his cravat. A large, square sapphire winked back at her, and all the confidence she had had in her simple camellias evaporated.

Sarah turned from Ravensby to Anne. And found her friend far too excited to note Sarah's constraint.

"What do you think, Sarah?" Anne queried, beaming. "Sykes did just as Mrs. Grigsby instructed her!"

Sarah felt a very poor friend, indeed, at that moment, for she had been so preoccupied with her own concerns, she'd not even noted Anne's new coiffure. It was, as Mrs. Grigsby had decreed, softer and more feminine, from the abundant curls adorning the top of her head to the curls tumbling gracefully down the back. Sarah's approval was reflected in her eyes. "You look lovely," she confirmed.

Anne glowed. "Uncle Dominic approves too! Don't you?" She smiled up at Ravensby.

An odd feeling tugged at Sarah as she watched a warm, teasing smile soften the earl's face. "You are fishing for compliments, minx—and never deserved them more. I do like this new arrangement very much. I believe"—he flicked his glance to Sarah before she was quite prepared—"we owe Miss Marlowe our thanks for putting her hairdresser at your service."

Ravensby inclined his head rather formally, his eyes veiled now. Sarah told herself that look was no more than she had expected. "It was my pleasure, of course, my lord," she replied with the same rather studied courtesy.

At once, she looked back to Anne, and the tight knot in her chest relaxed a little. "I am glad you are pleased, Anne. I admit I had some doubts how this would turn out. So many of us were giving suggestions, I feared poor Sykes would be hopelessly confused, and you would have curls sprouting from your ears."

Anne giggled, but whatever she meant to say about her maid's clarity of mind was lost, for Lieutenant Stevenson came. "Good evening, sir," he said to Ravensby. "I wish to thank you for your advice at Tattersall's. The gelding's gait is smooth as glass."

"I am glad I could be of service, Lieutenant," Ravensby returned.

"Miss Pentworth, you look . . ." Lieutenant Stevenson paused uncertainly, the ordinary politeness he'd intended seeming to wither on his tongue. "That is," he tried again, "you, ah, look quite different. Smashing!" he added gallantly, though he continued to look slightly puzzled.

Anne blushed, but it was obvious she was pleased. "Thank you, sir."

Sarah stifled a smile when the lieutenant continued to gaze rather bemusedly at Anne. At last, when it seemed enlightenment might never dawn, she took pity on him. "I think you really do approve Anne's new coiffure, Lieutenant. You cannot seem to take your eyes from it."

"Oh!" The young man grinned engagingly. "Deuce take it, but I could not for the life of me determine what it was had so changed! Very nice, very nice, indeed."

Anne looked exquisitely embarrassed, if delighted, and Sarah gave her a teasing grin. "I think we ought to cease mortifying Anne with our compliments and simply allow her to show off her new curls."

No slow top, Lieutenant Stevenson took Sarah's hint readily. "A dance before the Assembly would be the very thing, I quite agree. What do you say, Miss Pentworth? That is . . . ?" He looked at Sarah as he recalled he'd joined the group in the first place because he had reserved the dance on her dance card.

Sarah smiled. "It will be my pleasure to watch, sir."

She turned, having already rehearsed in her mind both the curtsy she would make the earl and the smooth departure that would follow. She did not get beyond the turn. Ravensby took her hand before she could begin to curtsy.

Dominic felt her tense, and it occurred to him to wonder whether Lisle's or Kendall's touch could put her off so obviously. His voice, as a result, was perhaps a little cooler than it might have been. "I cannot leave you to languish on the sidelines, Miss Marlowe, watching your dance partner with Anne. That would scarcely be fitting recompense, I think, for the favor you have done my niece."

"You've no need to do the polite, my lord," Sarah replied stiffly. "I've little fear I shall languish. Excuse me, if you please."

"I do not please."

Her eyes flew up to his. Then her heart began to beat decidedly faster in her chest. His amber eyes gleamed. "That bit about you languishing was the merest politeness, as you must know. Not suffering from blindness, I am well aware there are a host of gentlemen waiting to surge to your side the moment I relinquish you. Allow me to rephrase the question. Will you dance with me, Miss Marlowe? In all these weeks this is the first opportunity I have had to ask you. Those young men swarm so about you, no one else has any hope of getting through."

It was all nonsense. She had seen him cut through two of the young men like a knife parting butter. He only asked to lead her out because he felt a debt on Anne's account. If she said no, she would leave him in no doubt what she thought of his arrogant manner.

"You are absurd, my lord," Sarah said, her voice so low she had to clear it. "The honor would be mine."

It was a waltz. Sarah had forgotten it would be, and when she heard the music, a panic seized her. She had not expected to remain close to him. His hand was on her waist, warm and strong, his other held her hand. Suddenly painfully shy, she studied the superb sapphire again.

They danced in silence, adjusting to each other. Ravensby moved well. Sarah noted his grace, even as she registered the strength of his shoulder beneath her hand, and then the warmth of his breath ruffling her hair.

"I have seen you converse while you dance, Miss Marlowe." Ravensby's voice came amused but soft in her ear. "You understand I admire your hair. Who would not admire the essence of sunlight? And the camellias are a lovely touch. They appear, I think, almost as soft and smooth as your skin, but I enjoy your conversation too. Will you talk to me, Miss Marlowe, if I promise not to chastise you for encouraging Captain Kendall?"

She did look up then, and felt a spurt of resentment that he could make her so uncertain. She wanted to know if he meant what he'd said about her hair and her skin and the camellias. But he had mentioned Kendall.

"I do not encourage him," Sarah protested, her voice sounding unnaturally low.

She could not read Ravensby's expression. His golden-brown eyes probed but did not give much away. "A woman either encourages or discourages, Miss Marlowe. Riding out in the park is not discouraging."

Frustrated that she was no closer to Tom's necklace than she had been when she arrived in London, Sarah had agreed to ride out with Kendall the day before in the hopes he might drop some stray scrap of useful information. The outing had been a failure, however. She had learned nothing, nor had she seen Ravensby.

The thought that he had watched her when she was unaware made her stiffen so she threw them off in their dance. Their feet collided, but Dominic recovered easily, whirling her around in a circle so that she'd no time to think of anything but following his lead, if she did not wish to disgrace herself by falling in a tangled heap upon the polished floors of Almack's Assembly Rooms.

When he slowed their pace again, Dominic studied the top of her golden head a long moment. "I apologize, Miss Marlowe." He waited until she met his gaze, her eyes wary. "It was wrong of me to break a promise, and in the next breath at that. I did not ask you to dance that I might hold you captive for a lecture on Kendall, however much I believe you are in need of it. Will you accept a change of subject?"

He thought a scarcely perceptible nod was to be her only answer, until Sarah added, "And I accept the apology as well, my lord."

It was like her, that. He could not but smile. "How gracious of you, Miss Marlowe. And now we have established I am forgiven, allow me to say I really am grateful for the change you've wrought in Anne. In the space of only a few days she seems a much happier girl."

"Anne only needed friends her own age, my lord. She has sisters at home she misses."

Dominic appeared to consider a moment. "I don't doubt you are right. My point, however, is that I am grateful to you for taking up where they left off. And even going beyond that," he continued. "I know Anne's sisters well enough to say though they had a court of males surrounding them, still they'd have begrudged relinquishing even one of the young men, whether she would be pleased thereby or not. Now, how will you turn that off, Miss Marlowe?"

She did not think to resist the smile warming his eyes. She smiled back, but there was nothing coy about her when she shrugged her shoulders lightly. "Truly, you are too generous, my lord. I've no court. The young men are friends of Johnny Carstairs', who . . . ah, knows Kitty from Sussex."

"Ah, yes. The somewhat questionable courtship of Mr. Carstairs."

Sarah looked alarmed. "How . . . ?"

"I saw Miss Ponsby slip out to Lady Dibble's balcony with Mr. Carstairs, and I asked Anne directly if she knew why you would be deliberately vague with your aunt as to her whereabouts."

Sarah flushed deeply. "Johnny is the best of young men, truly. He is entirely devoted to Kitty, but my aunt would have her daughter wed a gentleman with better prospects."

Ravensby's remarks on Mrs. Ponsby's ambitions between them, she lifted her chin, but he only asked casually, "Does Mr. Carstairs have any prospects?"

It was a fair question, and Sarah answered without rancor, "Not yet, but he is applying all around to be the manager of an estate. He would make a good one, too, for he has long run his brother's estate successfully. Unfortunately Radley is not so large it can support two brothers with families."

"Your cousin would be happy married to an estate manager?"

Sarah looked a long moment into Ravensby's eyes before she was satisfied condescension had not prompted the question. "Yes. She's no aspirations to lead society, only to have dozens of children and a good, kind husband."

"And you, Miss Marlowe? Is that what you want?"

Sarah nearly stumbled again. The personal question had come unexpectedly. "I, ah, cannot say, my lord. I have not thought much of marriage."

"Not even to Lisle?"

He had not meant to ask that, and even as her cheeks heated, Dominic shook his head ruefully. "What is it about you, Miss Marlowe, that makes me behave as though I've known you all my life? I suppose it was the way we met. Forgive the impertinence?"

Sarah could manage no more than a mute nod, she'd felt so sharp a burst of pleasure to learn he felt some affinity for her. It would not do. He had meant nothing but that she seemed young and hapless to him. If he had said those lovely things about her hair and skin, it was only because he was glad for her that she looked so well.

And next time he saw her committing some folly, he would take her to task as scathingly as ever. The thought reminded her of Richmond, and just in time, for the final strains of the waltz were being played.

"My lord?" When Ravensby cocked his head in question, Sarah steeled herself and hurried on. "I've something to ask. My cousin and I are getting up a party to go to Richmond for a picnic, and we would like to invite Anne. Lieutenant Stevenson is to come, along with a few other young people. Will you give your permission?"

Immediately Dominic thought of Sophy. She had been less than delighted to learn Anne had taken up with Miss Marlowe to the extent of visiting her in Albemarle Street, no matter that the effects upon Anne had been for the better. "Of course they have exerted themselves on Anne's behalf," she had scoffed disdainfully. "They must, if they are to form an association with her. Mark my words; when Anne puts it about the Marlowe girl has befriended her, she will receive vouchers to Almack's."

And here was Miss Marlowe at Almack's, just as Sophy had predicted. Had she used Anne? Did it matter so much? Dominic asked before he could answer the first question, for he had caught sight of Anne approaching, a bright smile on her face for her new friend.

"When is the outing to be?" He glanced back at Sarah and found a guarded expression had robbed her eyes of their sparkle. She was, he realized, braced for a refusal that would, in so many polite words, imply she was not fit company for Anne.

"Sunday next."

Lord Matthew Beresford had invited a small circle of friends to gather that afternoon. Dominic was to go, while Anne remained home by herself. "Yes, I think a picnic to Richmond will do very well that day, as I am to be occupied elsewhere."

Convinced by the length of time it had taken him to decide that she would receive a negative, Sarah stood blank-faced for a long moment. And then a vivid, vivid smile lit her face. "Oh, I am glad, my lord! She will enjoy herself, I promise you. May I tell her now?"

He was thirty and had known dozens of women. But she very nearly succeeded in taking his breath away then, and when he smiled back at her, Dominic knew very well he smiled because he was powerless not to do so.

"I cannot see why not," he said.

Anne, when told, was in alt she would be included in what promised to be a gay group. Laughing up at her uncle later, she commended him for being the greatest gun. "I know Sophy is not very keen on Sarah, but I like her exceedingly. She's great spirit, and somehow or other when I am with her, I find it easier to be in company with young men. And I would only be better pleased by this entire affair, if you decided against the stuffy confines of Lord Matthew's tomblike palace in favor of the sylvan vistas at Richmond.''

"Minx," Dominic reproved. "You mustn't deride Lord Matthew's marvel of Palladian architecture. To do so only shows ignorance, and besides, I think you are beyond needing me at your side.''

"Never!" his niece returned, but with a smile.

10

"Really, Dominic!" Lady Sophia sounded, as Dominic had expected, as if she could not credit what she heard when he told her of the proposed expedition to Richmond. "I cannot conceive why you agreed. Their motives are so appallingly obvious.''

"Whatever their ulterior motives, Sophy, both Miss Ponsby and Miss Marlowe seem to genuinely like Anne, but more to the point, their friendship has lifted her spirits enormously. She is in alt over this new coiffure.''

"I did suggest Anne could make use of my hairdresser," Lady Sophia said, obviously piqued that Dominic's niece would prefer the ministrations of a nobody to those of her acclaimed man.

Dominic shrugged. "Anne is young, Sophy, and no doubt in awe of you. Miss Marlowe is her own age.''

"The girl is younger than Anne," she remarked rather pettishly.

Dominic, however, did not take the reminder of Miss Marlowe's youth quite as Lady Sophia had expected, for he shook his head. "She seems the elder, really.''

"Do you know who will chaperon the outing?" she asked rather quickly. "Surely not the Ponsby woman alone. You yourself have faulted her judgment. And who is to go? Will that Captain Kendall be included?''

Dominic kicked at the fire the rooms of Lord Matthew Beresford's house needed even in summer. He had not given thought to the possibility of Kendall's inclusion. Miss Marlowe had said "young people" were invited. It was a vague description at best, and he could not, now the question was raised, say with any certainty whether she considered the captain one of the "young people."

He could say with certainty Mrs. Ponsby did not consider the captain an unfit companion for a young lady. He had, after all, seen Miss Marlowe with him in the park. Still, Richmond, with its intricate maze and far-flung gardens, was a different matter, surely. "No, I am certain the Ponsbys are not so foolish. And as to chaperons, Mrs. Manwairing is to go along."

Mrs. Emily Manwairing was entirely unexceptionable, as Lady Sophia knew. Much as she did not care for any scheme that might somehow deepen the rather odd, intangible air of familiarity between the Marlowe girl and Dominic, she knew any further objections would sound very like nagging.

"I see." She gave in with a shrug. "Well, as long as you do not expect me to go, then I shall say no more. That is, you are still coming to Papa's gathering that afternoon?''

Dominic's smile reassured her. "I am looking forward to it.''

For many years Lord Matthew Beresford had been in the habit of gathering together, on those Sunday afternoons when the mood struck him, the more politically minded of his gentlemen friends. An elaborate buffet was laid out, and the gentlemen helped themselves between bouts of discussion and rounds of Lord Matthew's excellent port.

Dominic was one of the last to arrive that Sunday, and when he entered the library where some fifteen or so gentlemen were gathered, a strong and unexpected feeling of nostalgia tugged at him. He had attended several gatherings since, but it was his first, when he had visited Beresford House on holiday with Richard, that he recalled. He had been dazzled to find William Pitt among the guests, and listened in awe as the great statesman held forth on the short-lived Treaty of Amiens.

There was no one so august present that Sunday, Dominic

saw as Lady Sophia guided him to a seat by Richard. Though there was one minister in Castlereagh's government, the remainder of the men seemed, like Lord Beresford, beyond the age of holding positions of power.

Lady Sophia did not stay. Her role, after greeting her father's guests, was to oversee the setting-out of the buffet, for though her father's friends all appreciated her cool, elegant appearance, theirs was exclusively a gentlemen's gathering.

Dominic nodded to Lord Matthew as he slipped into his seat and acknowledged several of the men who raised their glasses in greeting. Lord Edgby, a paunchy old curmudgeon who sported a great drooping walrus mustache, was holding forth on the subject of the controversial Corn Laws. "Got to have 'em," he maintained gruffly. "Crop failures have been devastating. We'll all go under if something's not done. It's what the rabble wants, really. They've caught the French disease and would level society. Well, you see what a mess they've got in France as a result, by Jove!"

"Hear, hear, Edgby! You've the right of it," several gentlemen agreed at once.

Dominic's gaze strayed to the window. The day was one of those breathtakingly clear, shining days that are a reward after a prolonged period of drizzle, but Lord Matthew's library had not been designed with sunlight in mind. The furniture was dark and heavy, the thick curtains half-drawn. For all the light that found its way inside, it might have been a gray winter's day outside. When the man beside him lit a cigar, Dominic recalled how fresh the air had felt on his face as he rode through the streets. "It will be good to see the countryside again, particularly if the day is nice," Miss Marlowe had said to Anne when she had told her of the picnic.

"Eh, now! We've not heard from you, Dominic." Dominic pulled his gaze from the single narrow shaft of sunlight pooling on the Axminster carpet to look to his host. "You've lands, lad. You must support the Corn Laws."

The elder man's bristling brows were narrowed, as if he suspected already the answer he would receive, and Dominic smiled. "I think you have guessed, sir, that I do not."

"But that's lunacy!" exclaimed Castlereagh's minister.

Lord Edgby spoke up as well. "Do you wish to beggar yourself, boy?"

"I've not experienced the crop failures to which you referred," Dominic replied easily. "And therefore I've no need of additional grain tariffs. But even had I suffered losses, I should be against the tariffs. We've most of us the wealth to weather some adversity, but the poor have not. The higher prices on bread that have resulted strike hard at them and at the hundreds of discharged soliders who, though they struggled valiantly for us through long years of war, have come home to no reward, least of all decent labor."

For the space of a moment there was not a sound in the room. Lord Matthew's gathering had not, it seemed, entertained a dissenting view in a very long time. The response, when it came, came all at once. Dominic heard the word "reformer" murmured darkly, but it was Lord Edgby he answered, for the old man had the most piercing bellow and as well the most pertinent question.

"How'd you escape crop failures, boy, when the rest of us have suffered them year after year?"

"I implemented agricultural reforms on my estates, and they made a great deal of difference."

"You mean all that nonsense Arthur Young spouts?" the old gentleman would know.

Dominic nodded, for the former head of the Board of Agriculture had indeed influenced him. "I found that 'nonsense' kept my head above water when others around me went under."

Lord Edgby grumbled something about newfangled notions, but another gentleman returned to Dominic's criticism of the Corn Laws, saying, "It's no use concerning ourselves over the poor. They'll always be with us, and they always manage somehow."

There were wise nods as the comfortable notion was accepted as truth; then Lord Matthew turned the conversation to the glories England had earned in the recent wars with France.

Dominic listened, entertained by one or two keen remarks, but when Lady Sophia came to announce the buffet was served, he heard her with a relief that surprised him.

"Not greatly attuned to the harsh realities of life, are they?"

It was Richard whispered in Dominic's ear when they stood. "They're at the age of wanting to comfort themselves with past glories, I'm afraid."

"Perhaps they deserve that luxury," Dominic conceded. "They led England through a difficult time."

Lord Richard shrugged. "I suppose. Did Anne get off in good time?"

"Yes, and I am pleased to say she was looking forward to the day."

"As who wouldn't with the Marlowe chit about to feast one's eyes upon?" Richard chuckled. "Did I tell you I danced with her the other night? At the Bellinghams'. You were home with Anne when she was not feeling quite the thing. The girl's light as a feather, and amusing too. What a marvelous laugh! I'm afraid she encouraged me to give my impression of Prinny."

"Oh? I thought you reserved that trick only for young men you wished to impress. Ought Arabella to be concerned?"

Lord Richard shrugged at the reference to his mistress of many years. "Bella has a distinct advantage over any young girl," he replied as he selected a pickled eel from the delicacies before him. "With her, there's no question of getting leg-shackled."

Dominic chuckled, but as he filled his plate, he found Miss Sarah Marlowe lingered in his thoughts. The question of Kendall's inclusion in the picnic group had plagued him since Sophy had raised it. Alternately he would think it out of the question that Kendall had been invited, then he would revise his opinion completely. Miss Marlowe had not fallen head over heels for Lisle, but perhaps she had for Kendall. She certainly did not wish to be warned off him.

Damned little fool, he tried to dismiss the girl, but found he could not. Kendall would bend his best efforts upon her. She'd rare appeal, witness the way even Richard had sounded half-besotted.

Dominic's gaze fell upon Lady Sophia as she moved among the gentlemen, seeing they'd all they needed. Ever the perfect hostess, she flattered the men in her cool, elegant way, but not one would have thought to overstep the bounds with her. She was simply too composed.

Quite unlike Miss Marlowe, who was not remote at all, nor was she cool. Again witness Richard's response to her. Dominic flicked a speck of dust from his sleeve, displeased to have the girl dominate his thoughts so. His proper concern was Anne. She, too, would be susceptible to Kendall's blandishments, if, say, they were to find themselves alone in the maze.

Dominic was never to remember much of the buffet. Between idle bouts of conversation with the other gentlemen at his end of the table, he would find himself worrying over . . . Anne. It was his niece worried him.

After he'd eaten, Dominic gave up the struggle to keep his mind on a discussion of Wellington's strategy in Spain, and gave Lord Matthew the same excuse he gave Sophy: that he was anxious over Anne. "It is her first time to be out without a member of her family nearby. She is so shy, I wish to assure myself she is getting on well."

Lord Matthew thought his concern overdone. "Got to get her feet wet sometime, Dominic! Won't do any good clinging to you."

However, Dominic replied that Anne was young for her age with such finality, Lord Matthew waved him off with only a "hmpf." Sophy was no more pleased than her father, saying very coolly, when she realized she would not persuade Dominic from his decision, "Very well, then, go and see to her, but perhaps in future you'll pay my advice more heed."

"Perhaps," Dominic returned, but mildly, for, as he had been one of those invited to stay on for dinner later, he could understand Sophy's sharpness. "You must know your part in this afternoon was as successfully pulled off as ever, by the by. You are a superb hostess, Sophy."

Mollified slightly, she allowed him to kiss her hand, but could not be much pleased that Dominic then took his leave briskly, descending to the entryway below them without a backward glance.

He found Richard awaiting him, and his friend grinned. "Wasn't going to remain entombed if you were escaping, old boy."

The words reminded Dominic how Anne had all but called Lord Matthew's house a mausoleum, and though he could not agree quite, for he still thought of the house as the epitome of order and taste he had long admired, he did recognize that on that day at least, he experienced a sense of escape into a brighter world when Lord Matthew's door closed behind him. "You're riding to Richmond with me, then?"

"Well, of course, Dominic! I'm as fond of admiring beauty disposed upon the greensward as anyone."

Dominic chuckled, not bothering to deny he, too, expected a pretty sight.

And it certainly was that. Mrs. Ponsby had had a thick covering laid out upon the grass, and lounging upon it, soft pillows to cushion them, were some half-dozen young ladies, their pastel dresses in pretty contrast to the tans and greens sported by the young men disposed about them.

The two chaperons sat a little apart in comfortable chairs, and beside them sat a little girl drawing a picture as she sang a nursery ditty.

"There she is."

Dominic looked in the direction Richard indicated and saw Anne sitting by Kitty Ponsby. Just behind Miss Ponsby was the only older gentleman present. The Earl of Westphal, clad in sober black, looked so out of place Dominic could not blame her for preferring young John Carstairs.

Mr. Carstairs and Lieutenant Stevenson were nearby playing at a modified game of lawn bowling while the young people cheered them on.

Anne was the first to see her uncle, and her astonished "Uncle Dominic!" caused Mrs. Ponsby to turn so sharply she nearly toppled over in her chair.

Luckily Dominic was swift enough to catch her. "I hope I have not overset you, Mrs. Ponsby," he said, smiling faintly as he righted her.

Half to his surprise, the plump little woman caught his joke and laughed. "You very nearly did, sir!" she admonished, shaking her fan at him. "But I forgive you, as it is such a pleasure to have you join us. Would you care for refreshment?"

"Something for thirst only, thank you."

Lord Richard was welcomed as hospitably, and Westphal came to join them, weary, perhaps, of arranging his older bones upon the hard ground. Chairs materialized as if by magic, and when they were all comfortably seated, Anne asked what had brought him. "I thought you were to be at Lord Matthew's this evening as well."

"Richard and I decided it was too rare a day to remain indoors for the whole of it."

Everyone exclaimed in agreement, saying it was the perfect spring day, with even a softening in the air that hinted at summer. Dominic welcomed the wine when it was brought, and shooed Anne back to her seat with the younger people. That she was not the least reluctant to leave his side, he marked with pleasure.

It was Lieutenant Stevenson's turn at lawn bowling. Dominic sipped his wine and watched the young man knock down three pins. Idly, as everyone cheered, he ran his eye over the others in the group. Captain Kendall was not present, but neither was Sarah Marlowe. He had known it from the first, but had not confirmed his impression before.

He was just turning to inquire casually of Mrs. Ponsby if any of the group were attempting the maze, when he chanced to see Lisle trudging across the grass. That the marquess was not accustomed to outdoor entertainments was obvious. His pale moon face was unnaturally flushed, and beads of sweat stood out on his brow.

"Ravensby." Lisle nodded, but did not speak until he'd had a long drink of lemonade a servant rushed to serve him. "Surprised to see you here. Didn't know you were coming, but I suppose you fancy rustic entertainments, living in the country as you do." The marquess sat down heavily in a chair Mrs. Ponsby had signaled for. "Can't say I'm that fond of 'em, myself. The maze was hot as the devil! No breeze at all. I gave up trying to find Miss Marlowe and Charles. Thought I'd faint if I didn't."

Dominic had found it difficult to keep from smiling up to the part about Miss Marlowe and Charles. Then he stared in disbelief. Lisle had abandoned the girl to Kendall in the maze.

Dominic looked to Mrs. Ponsby. As unconcerned as the marquess, she laughed jovially. "Those two will find their way out, never fear. Sarah's not one to be lost for very long."

Not unless someone led her astray. Dominic tossed off the remainder of his wine. "I'll go and look for them. I've need of a challenge," he announced, and strode off before anyone could beg to join him.

The maze at Richmond was intricate and the hedges high. Inside it, sounds were distorted, and Dominic could not merely call out to fetch the pair to him. Nor, of course, had he any notion where to look. Kendall might have taken Miss Marlowe down any of a dozen paths. The thought that she would find it difficult to get away from the man if he had her in an isolated cul-de-sac led Dominic to redouble his pace.

Lisle had not overstated the warmth of the place. There was no breeze, and Dominic grew warmer as he continued on, his own footsteps on the gravel the only sound he could hear. Frustration took a toll. He cursed amiable Mrs. Ponsby fluently for her scandalously lax guardianship, before he turned his curses on Miss Marlowe herself.

Sometime later, stopping to get his bearings for perhaps the fifth time, he heard a familiar infectious laugh.

"No, no, sir! You won't pull me down that one. I'm certain that's not the way."

Dominic's jaw tightened dangerously. "Sa . . . Miss Marlowe!" he barked loudly enough to be heard in London. And again, "Miss Marlowe!"

A moment of silence followed; then, "Lord Ravensby?"

Though Sarah's voice was muffled somewhat by the hedges between them, Dominic recognized astonishment in her tone, but he did not think he detected relief. Had she desired privacy with Kendall?

"Where are you?" he demanded curtly.

The amused laugh that floated over the hedges did little to improve his temper. "I am here. Where are you?"

Again she laughed, for, of course, it was impossible to say where one was in a maze, and again Dominic's mood deteriorated. "I am near the center. Wait there and I shall find you."

"That may prove impossible, my lord. We are lost, I fear, but we shall try to retrace our steps to the center and meet you . . . no, not that way, sir, here. . . ."

Her voice faded away. Vexing chit! Dominic thought he would enjoy strangling her when he saw her, until it occurred to him that she might be wise to keep the captain moving.

Further along he heard the crunch of light footsteps, likely a child's, on the gravel somewhere ahead of him. Reassured that there were other people in the maze and that Kendall could not be assured of complete privacy, Dominic strode on, only to be obliged to move swiftly sideways as a young boy cannoned around a corner.

"You found us!" Dominic looked over the boy's head and into Sarah Marlowe's eyes. They seemed particularly blue. Perhaps it was the unclouded sky he saw reflected in them, or perhaps the blue ribbons woven through the brim of the chip bonnet she wore. They matched the robin's-egg blue of her dress.

It was a pretty dress, of thin light muslin, and clung to her figure in a way the satins and silks of her evening dresses did not. Her willowy waist, rounded hips, and full high breasts were all very apparent, though she was fully and properly clothed.

"I never thought we would come across you so soon," Sarah said, flushing a little when Ravensby remained silent, staring at her. "We have been walking for what seems like hours, haven't we, Charles?"

She was addressing the boy. The boy gazing up at him was Charles. Dominic thought he might laugh, though whether from foolishness or relief, he could not have said.

Sarah noted that Charles's eyes, wide as saucers, seemed glued to the earl. It was no difficulty for her to understand his reaction. She felt as if she'd been stricken by the same disease.

Ravensby appeared very much in his element there in the open, wearing his riding clothes naturally, unlike poor Lisle, who had looked as if he'd gotten up for a costume party in his buckskins. The earl's buckskins, by contrast fitting him like gloves, revealed altogether well-formed long legs. His coat, too, fitted well, no crease showing across his broad shoulders. Of a tan somewhat darker than his buckskins, it seemed to bring out the gold in his eyes.

"Lord Ravensby, may I present my cousin, Master Charles Ponsby?" Sarah collected her wits sufficiently to remember to present her awestruck young cousin. "I recommend him for maze work, my lord. Even if you are lost, he remains entirely brave and cheerful.''

"I am honored to meet a man of such determined spirits, sir." Dominic bowed formally, and Charles leapt to do the same, which made Sarah smile, for her young cousin rarely remembered his manners when his mother and father were urging him.

"Have you seen the Marquess of Lisle, sir?" she asked then.

"Yes." Dominic smiled, thinking of the marquess. "He became quite overheated and was forced to return to the shade."

"I knew he would!" young Charles exclaimed with a child's disdain. "I told you he would not last, Sarah!"

"Charles, you must not criticize the marquess," Sarah exclaimed, half-embarrassed for Lisle before the earl, whose smile she had not missed. "He is . . . that is, I am certain Lord Lisle did his best."

To her chagrin, Ravensby smiled outright at her stumbling attempt at a defense. And Charles did not look in the least impressed either. Poor Lisle, to be held up to the standards of a child, who possessed more than the ordinary child's stamina, and to Ravensby.

She glared just a little at the earl for his bad example, and though his lips twitched, he did, at least, wave a flag of truce. "Perhaps we ought to leave off considering Lisle and turn our thoughts to finding our own way out?" He held out his hand to Sarah, as he had once before, only this time he was not glaring at her at all. "I do believe this is the way out."

Sarah giggled, made almost light-headed by the friendliness in his eyes. "That is what I said every time we went down a wrong turn."

"I shall go ahead and see if it is a cul-de-sac!" Charles raced off as he had been doing all afternoon. "It doesn't end yet!" he called back at the corner before racing ahead again.

His cry left a silence in its wake, and Sarah felt suddenly constrained, all alone with the earl. She darted a look at him through her lashes only to find him looking down at her. Caught out, she blushed and said the first thing that came to mind. "Did you come out to Richmond on Anne's account, sir?"

The look he gave her then was unreadable, though not, she

thought, distant. When he did finally speak, it was to say only, "She seemed remarkably at ease."

Sarah nodded, smiling. Had someone told her her eyes were sparkling with particular brilliance, she would not have been surprised. She could feel happiness bubbling up inside of her, and though she knew her elation had little to do with Anne's ease at the picnic, she did not try to reprove herself. Useless to demand composure or caution on a beautiful bright afternoon when Ravensby had appeared out of nowhere, a smile in his eyes, to take her arm. She'd even an impulse to tell him how glad she was to see him, but some tiny kernel of good sense helped her to hold back words that would only embarrass him.

She compromised, saying, "Anne has enjoyed herself, but though she was not greatly in need of your support, I am glad you were available to rescue me again. I've become exceedingly weary of the famous maze."

He chuckled at her tone, then said, the smile fading, "And I am glad it was only from the maze you needed delivery, Miss Marlowe."

She tipped her head the better to see him from beneath the brim of her bonnet. "I think I have assured you I would not ride a horse again, sir."

"Yes, Miss Marlowe, I am aware that is all you have assured me."

He sounded almost wry, but Sarah could fathom neither why, nor precisely what he'd meant. She did not think she could ask, however, for he had dismissed the subject.

"I do believe I hear our advance guard returning." Light footsteps could be heard approaching rapidly. "Does the boy ever walk, I wonder?"

Sarah laughed. "I have never known him to, my lord. But I wonder what he shall have to report."

She knew when Charles burst into view, for he'd a wide smile upon his face. "We've done it, Sarah! Lord Ravensby's brought us out at last! Hooray!"

11

"Well, then, why do you think the earl came to Richmond, if not to see you?"

Kitty regarded Sarah with some exasperation. Her cousin, curled up in a chintz-covered chair, a letter from her father in her lap, had not received Kitty's delightful imspiration—that the Earl of Ravensby had sped to Richmond on Sarah's account—with the interest Kitty had expected.

Sarah, who, in fact, had only been holding her father's letter while she thought about the Earl of Ravensby and his unexpected appearance at the picnic, explained with authority, "He came on Anne's account, to see she was not uneasy without anyone of her family about."

"Did he say so?" Kitty demanded.

Ravensby had not said so precisely. Sarah could not think exactly what reason he had given. But she did know Kitty to be an incurable romantic who would, if given half a chance, spin impossible dreams that would only haunt Sarah.

"Yes, he said something to that effect, I cannot recall exactly what."

"And that is why he scarcely said two words to her before he tore off to the maze?" Kitty produced her trump card with a certain triumph.

But Sarah was unmoved. "From your own account, Kitty, he did not precisely 'tear off.' He assured himself Anne was doing well, and only came after me because he thought I would get into some difficulty, heaven knows what, with only Charles to protect me. You said yourself," she pointed out as Kitty tried to speak, "he did not depart for the maze until Lord Lisle returned to the picnic and announced he had left Charles and me to our own devices."

"Drat!" Kitty scowled unhappily. "That means nothing of much good came of our picnic, and it took such a lot of planning!

Not to mention the cost. Papa is appalled at the amount required to hire the extra servants.''

"You did not have your time with Johnny, then?"

Kitty shook her head. "I could not escape Westphal. He stuck to me like a burr. Even so, Mama read me a scold last night for my lack of courtesy to him! Can you imagine? And after I suffered him to sit so close to me on that wretched blanket that I could feel his horrid breath on my cheek!''

Kitty looked very close to tears, and Sarah went at once to take her hands. "You did the wisest thing, my love, however difficult it may have been. The two of you looked so incongruous in comparison to the other, younger, better-matched couples, Aunt Vinnie could not but have noticed, and I would not be surprised if that were what sharpened her tongue. Give her time, Kitty. You are right that she's her heart set on a good marriage for you, but she'll accept in time that it is with Johnny you'll make it.''

Kitty squeezed her cousin's hands in reply. "I do hope you don't overestimate Mama. I dearly do!''

"Well, now we've that settled"—Sarah smiled—"why do you not take yor mind off Johnny and Westphal by accompanying the children and me to Hookham's?''

"I cannot." Kitty giggled suddenly. "I am to be fitted for another new dress this afternoon. Poor Papa! I cannot imagine how Mama succeeded in persuading him I must have a quite new one for the ball Althea and Clarice invited us to attend. But I shan't quarrel, for Johnny will be there to see me look fetching!''

Sarah grinned as Kitty twirled about in an excess of foolish pleasure. Then, blowing her cousin a kiss, she went to join the children and their young nurse for the trip to the lending library. And if a smile lingered at the corners of Sarah's mouth, it was because she, alone, knew how very much she had hoped for an invitation to the Whittingham house. If she could find them, she had decided to steal the Woodward emeralds from Captain Kendall.

Her letter from her father had decided her. In it he had enclosed a note from Tom Woodward addressed to her. Poor fellow! He was suffering dreadfully in the heat of the Indies.

Accustomed to the cool climate of England, he said he drooped
even before ten o'clock, the heat came so early. By midday it
was difficult even to gasp for breath, and then, just when evening
promised relief, swarms of mosquitoes arose to make the nights
worse than the days. The thought that while Tom suffered so,
Captain Kendall sat cool and smart in his regimentals at one
pleasant ball after another goaded Sarah to the decision to take
action she knew very well would be viewed as criminal if she
were caught.

"Miss Marlowe!"

Sarah slowed her pace with the utmost reluctance. The
children and their nurse had disappeared through the door into
Hookham's, and she was not pleased to be caught alone by
Captain Kendall.

As she was on a busy street, however, and as he had already
leapt from his phaeton, she waited for him. Soon she would
be able to turn her shoulder to him, she assured herself. Soon
she would have the emeralds he did not deserve.

Her mouth curved into a particularly bright smile. "Captain
Kendall, I'd not have thought you frequented Hookham's."

"You do me an injustice, Miss Marlowe," he chided, dark
eyes raking her. "I come by frequently—and even enter on
occasion, depending upon who is inside. Have you made your
selections?"

Sarah did not want him hanging on her as she browsed. "No,
I have not. I am with my young cousins. Charles is seven, and
Becky is eleven. Perhaps you would care to assist us?" She
smiled innocently.

Kendall almost said yes. Drawn by the curve of Sarah's
generous mouth, he was tempted. But children? And what would
it gain him? He would not have her to himself, if she'd children
in her charge.

"I cannot! Alas, I've an appointment. I only stopped to greet
you and to assure myself you really will be attending my step-
nieces' ball."

"I would not miss it, Captain. I am certain it will be a most
successful night! But I must go along. The children will have
demolished the library by now."

When Kendall winced, Sarah fought a grin. What luck he'd not come along in time to see the children had a nurse in attendance.

He caught her hand before she could depart, however, and lifted it, soft, palm-side-up, to his lips. Through the mesh of her light morning gloves she could feel his breath hot on the more sensitive skin there. It was impossible not to pull her hand from his grasp.

He was not pleased. Sarah saw annoyance, perhaps more, flash in his eyes, and she made an effort to smooth the incident over. Shaking her finger in seeming play, she protested, "You must behave yourself, Captain Kendall. We are in broad daylight before a public place on a busy thoroughfare."

Turned up sweet, he grinned wickedly. "I am justly rebuked. But some other time, under cover of darkness, in the privacy of a garden . . ." As his voice drifted off, his eyes seemed to smolder. "Then we shall see my delectable Miss Marlowe."

Sarah opened the door to the lending library and stepped into the quiet, comfortable atmosphere, breathing a sigh of relief. Pausing by the door while her eyes adjusted to the dimmer light within the establishment, she'd a strange, prickling sense of being observed. Turning abruptly, she saw a man standing before Hookham's front window. Even had he not spoken, the outline of his tall, imposing figure against the light would have been enough to identify him.

"How amiable you are when you greet a friend by chance, Miss Marlowe. I wonder you did not forget your delightful young cousins entirely and go off with the captain. Surely that hot kiss upon your palm was some inducement."

Ravensby's tone was, on the surface, light, even amiable. But Sarah was not fooled, and though she could not make out his shadowed expression, his displeasure registered as a sudden coiling in the pit of her stomach. "Lord Ravensby," she said, making an effort to be calm. "Good morning to you."

He did not respond in kind. "In fact it is afternoon, Miss Marlowe. The captain seems even to have disordered your accounting of time. Oh, and you needn't look about for the children."

Sarah tensed in surprise when Ravensby took her arm in a firm, even relentless grasp.

"What do you mean?"

He gave her a polite smile she realized was not for her, but any audience they might have. It was his narrowed eyes gave the truer gauge of his temper.

"I have informed both the children and their estimable nurse that you will be departing with me and they need not wait for you."

Punctuating his announcement, Ravensby threw open the door to the library and marched Sarah outside. She considered resisting as he propelled her toward a smart gig waiting just down the street. She did not, however. To free herself she'd have had to fight in earnest, and Sarah was not quite up to having half of fashionable London look on while she wrestled with the Earl of Ravensby.

She would have fought had it been Kendall who had grabbed her up in such a peremptory manner. But it was Ravensby, and Sarah was not, at bottom, afraid of him. Unlike the captain, he would never dishonor her, only flay her with words.

Which did not mean Sarah was not furious. She was. The man had dragged her out of Hookham's as if she were a plaguesome child.

"You are the most arrogant, high-handed, insulting man!" Her imprecations were cast at him in a fierce, taut whisper, for there were dozens of pedestrians within earshot, many seeming interested in the elegant if grim-faced gentleman hurrying a lovely companion along the street. "I demand that you release me at once! Ah!" The sudden gasp came as Ravensby lifted Sarah by the waist and settled her with a thud she suspected had been deliberately punishing upon the seat of his gig.

"Beast!" she flung at him then, aware not only of umbrage at being treated with so little dignity, but of an infuriating warmth just above her rounded hips where he had held her. Ravensby did not hear her, of course. Sarah had muttered under her breath for one thing, and for another, he had stalked off to speak to his tiger.

After a few words the tiger darted a curious glance at Sarah, then trotted away. She watched him scamper off with no little envy. Ravensby's severe features were shuttered and forbidding as he swung up beside her.

Silence, natural enough while the earl was occupied with merging into the flow of traffic, stretched between them as they proceeded down the street, becoming, the longer it continued, heavier and heavier. At length Sarah could bear the tension no longer. "Where are you taking me?" she demanded gruffly, her hands curled into fists around the strings of her reticule.

"Home, of course," came the sardonic reply. "Where else, Miss Marlowe? Or are you accustomed to meekly accompanying gentlemen to unknown destinations?"

"Of course not!" Sarah tipped her chin up, the better to glare at him. "And I did not meekly accompany you anywhere, sir. You dragged me out of Hookham's. I shall have bruises on my arm tomorrow to prove it."

If she had hoped to elicit sympathy with the charge, Sarah failed miserably. Dominic did flick a glance at her, but it was decidedly unsympathetic. "I take leave to doubt that, unless you are more fragile than you appear. But I would not find a bruise cause for remorse, if it served to remind you how unsuitable Captain Charles Kendall is for a flirtation. He is a cad, Miss Marlowe. To be specific, he is the sort of man who would seduce an innocent girl without a qualm.

"Ah! I see I have put you to the blush," Dominic continued, remorselessly eyeing the line of pink coloring Sarah's cheeks. "I wonder why. Is it your innocence embarrasses you, Miss Marlowe? Is that the captain's attraction? He will gladly remedy the predicament, if you allow him. Or perhaps you continue to dally with him because you enjoy the challenge of playing with fire? You are adventuresome. There can be no doubt of that. But are you unpardonably foolish? Now, there's a question. Is it possible you actually believe the soft flattery he whispers to ulterior purpose?"

Sarah stared straight ahead. She told herself it was anger made her throat too tight to attempt speech. And it was, by heaven, for he'd no right to demean her with such questions!

Dominic glared down at Sarah when she remained stubbornly silent. A pretty leghorn bonnet framed her face charmingly, but

also hid her expression from him. "Well, Miss Marlowe?" he
barked. "What is the attraction?"

It was too much, that, addressing her as if she were some
minion of his. "I am not obliged to answer you on any subject,
my lord! I am aware you are arrogant by nature, but I do not
have to stand for being spoken to in that tone. Nor, may I add,
are my relations with Captain Kendall any affair of yours."

A muscle in Dominic's jaw tensed. "I saved your life, you
little fool. That gives me a right to an interest in your affairs."
Sarah opened her mouth to speak, perhaps to protest that by
his own account he had only saved her a broken limb or two,
but he did not allow her the courtesy of voicing her opinion.
"When I return you to Albemarle Street, I intend to speak to
your aunt and uncle. If they do not realize now how unsuitable
Kendall is, they soon will."

"No!"

"My, my, you do sound urgent, Miss Marlowe."

Cheeks stinging, Sarah wrenched her gaze away, unwilling
to suffer the mocking light in his eyes.

It did not help at all that she knew Ravensby had reason for
eyeing her so. She had sounded urgent, though of course not
for the reasons he imagined. It was conceivable she would never
need to speak to Charles Kendall again. Were she to come away
from the Whittinghams' ball with the Woodward necklace, she
would have no need to suffer his presence further. But Sarah
could not be certain of success. She might yet have need of him
in some scheme still undiscovered.

Briefly she considered confessing the truth, only to recall Sir
Adrian. She could not betray the proud old man's trust for purely
selfish reasons. Not then, when she felt she'd a good chance
of recovering the necklace soon.

"Please," she began, reaching out to touch Ravensby's arm
in her distress, with the unhappy result that the muscles beneath
her fingers tensed so that his team of matched chestnuts shied.

"Damnation!" Dominic swore in vexation, though in truth
he reined his team in with little effort. "Can you not even have
a care for a high-spirited team, Miss Marlowe?"

"I know nothing of high-spirited teams, as you know, and
I'll not allow you to make your usual analogy to Captain

Kendall! However ignorant I may be of horses, I am not a complete gudgeon. I have no intention of allowing Kendall to cozen me!''

"Why are you encouraging him, then?'' Ravensby flung back. "And do not think to say you are not,'' he warned grimly. "Those smiles you gave him were scarcely meant to put the rogue off.''

Sarah felt the heat rise in her cheeks again. How long had he watched her out that window? She wished he had not seen her play the flirt. She wished it very much. He'd reason for his poor opinion. Again she wished she could tell him of the Woodward necklace; wished she might confess she was only keeping the captain friendly on the chance she might not succeed at stealing an emerald necklace from him. Imagining the reaction that confession would bring almost made her smile.

"Have you some wager—with your cousin, perhaps—that you can wind the man around your finger? Is that it?''

"A wager?'' Sarah looked up in astonishment. "With Kitty? Good heavens, no!''

There could be no doubt of the sincerity of her denial. Sarah looked so taken aback, she appeared almost comical. Dominic gave her a dry look. "Very well, I accept that guess is off the mark.''

Sarah hurried to take advantage of the infinitesimal lightening of his expression. "I swear, my lord, that I have no ambition to entice Captain Kendall! Truly, it is the furthest thought from my mind.

"He . . .'' She hesitated a moment, aware Ravensby had turned such a piercing look upon her nothing would do but the truth. "He is amusing to a degree, his intentions are so obvious . . . and, too, my vanity is piqued a little.'' She flushed slightly, but held his gaze. "It is not, after all, such a difficult thing to hear one's praises sung even by a cad. But there is no more to it! Can you say I have truly played the flirt with him? No,'' she answered her own question with a grimace. "You cannot know. You would not have watched me so closely, but it is true! Can you not watch me a little and see if I flirt with the captain? I do not ask only for myself, but for my aunt and uncle as well, my lord. I would spare them the alarm and dismay they will experience, to no purpose, if you approach them.''

Dominic studied the blue eyes gazing at him steadily until the busy street called for his attention. It was as well he had cause to look away, he conceded, somewhere between rue and annoyance. She'd potent eyes.

But she was not trying to cut a wheedle. He'd endured enough of those from Jane and Ruth, and even Sophy, to know. Miss Marlowe had not allowed her eyes to mist over with affecting tears, nor had she batted her long lashes or cast him cajoling smiles. Her gaze had been entirely direct as she asked no more than that he be quite certain he'd real cause to warn her aunt and uncle, however tactfully, that they'd been dreadfully lax with their niece.

"Very well, Miss Marlowe. You have persuaded me to bide my time a little. But that is all, mind. If I see you flirting with fire again, I shall act.''

12

Sarah carefully breathed a sigh of relief, not least because Ravensby's agreement to ''bide his time'' meant her aunt would not have to suffer the mortification of being told by someone as top-of-the-trees as the earl that she had been remiss in her duties as guardian. Poor Aunt Vinnie! It would have been most unfair, had Ravensby raked her over the coals. She really had not been lax in regard to the captain. Though she did find him rather dashing, Mrs. Ponsby accepted him so readily only because she was quite confident neither Kitty nor Sarah was vitally interested in him.

Savoring her relief, Sarah only took in gradually that the congestion in the street had increased considerably. Glancing about curiously, she saw many conveyances had stopped to allow their passengers to disembark and join a steady stream of pedestrians proceeding down the street. She could not make out their goal, for they all turned at the next corner. As she turned to ask Ravensby what was occurring, her eye was caught by an entirely new and so amazing sight, Sarah stared, then chuckled aloud.

When Ravensby turned to her, Sarah glanced up half-guiltily, uncertain he would approve her levity, given how put-out he had been with her.

"It is that little fellow, there," she explained, gesturing across the street. "Oh, look! Now he has taken the woman's purse."

Dominic, following Sarah's prompting, was in time to see a brawny woman, hands balled into fists on her broad hips, charge after, of all things, a monkey. The little fellow had a master with some sense of humor, for he was outfitted as a gentleman, complete with tiny buckskins, a nattily cut burgundy coat, a white waistcoat, and a starched cravat. He was not, however, behaving as a gentleman, for he scampered away from his pursuer with her worn leather purse dangling from his fingers.

Just as it seemed the woman would catch up to him, the little rogue reached his master, who sat on a box with a tin cup placed strategically before him on the pavement. Chattering vociferously now, the monkey leapt into the man's lap and, emboldened, turned to face his outsize enemy.

A crowd gathered to laugh as the woman, querulously demanding her purse, reached to retrieve it. Quick as a wink, the monkey withdrew it from her reach, then swiftly dropped it down his master's shirt. The man gave a belch, as if he'd eaten it, and the crowd roared in appreciation. The woman, screeching that she was being robbed, beseeched the crowd for assistance.

The little monkey was not to be outdone. Standing upright on his master's legs, he assumed a stand in exact imitation of the woman's and began to harangue the crowd as well. When she gestured with her fist, the monkey did the same; when she shrieked threateningly, he chattered shrilly.

Finally, seeming to have had enough, the woman warned loudly, "I'll call the Bow Street Runners, see if I won't!"

At that dire threat, the monkey clapped his hands over his

ears, before, as if from an excess of emotion, executing half a dozen sommersaults in rapid succession. On the final one, when he landed upright still on his master's thighs, he lifted his arms in triumph, and to the wonder of the bystanders, the woman's purse once more dangled from his fingers. With a ludicrously graceful flourish, he then extended it to the woman, and when she held it up in triumph, everyone, including Sarah, clapped.

"You do realize it was all a show?" Ravensby remarked, amused.

Sarah looked up at him, eyes twinkling. "I believe you think me very naive, my lord. Of course I realize they were acting. Knowing that does not diminish the spectacle, however. I thought the little monkey wonderfully clever—a very taking fellow!"

"Taking indeed." Sarah's pun earned her a dry look that made her laugh. "So taking," Dominic continued the theme, "I imagine he's been known to fetch his master a real purse or two."

But Sarah only wrinkled her slim nose at him. "I'll not listen to such criticism, my lord. Not only is he the most charming of fellows, but anyone can see by his clothes that he is an utter gentleman."

Sarah managed a very sober expression, but the sparkle in her eyes gave her away, and Dominic laughed. "Impeccable logic, my dear. I am persuaded."

She glanced back at the monkey, afraid to look too long at the light gleaming so in Ravensby's golden-brown eyes, afraid she might end by staring foolishly. "Oh! And look now, not only is he amusing, but he is useful too!"

Sarah smiled, enchanted to see the monkey passing his master's tin cup about the crowd and according his more generous patrons an elaborate bow. "I have heard of monkeys, but never seen one before! But why are all these people here, my lord?" she asked, looking back to find Ravensby watching not the clever simian, but her. Confused, for she could not tell from the half-smile curving his mouth if he were laughing with her or at her, Sarah flushed.

She was not to receive an answer. Reminded by her question

of the congestion, Dominic looked about them with something less than pleasure, for they were only inching along. "I had forgotten, or I'd have taken another route, but there is a street fair ahead. Have you ever been to one?" he inquired suddenly. "If you've never seen a monkey, then I'll wager you've never visited a street fair."

Still uncertain if he were condescending, she said, very much on her dignity, "I have been to a country fair, sir." Then she could not keep from conceding truthfully, "But never a street fair."

"Where is your home, Miss Marlowe?" Dominic asked, curious and, too, a trifle astonished to realize how few details he knew about her.

"Cumberland."

"And you cannot ride a horse?"

Understanding the connection, she laughed. "My father is no horseman, you see, and believes we do very well with our feet or our gig or an old pony I have."

"And besides, you'd so many young men knocking on your door hoping to take you riding in their gigs, you didn't need a mount?"

"There were one or two, yes," she agreed with a smile that was neither boastful nor coy. "But I did not rely on them to get about. I am a hearty walker and a great hand with my pony."

Dominic gave her a skeptical if amused look. "He must be an old, staid fellow, then, but do you miss your home, Miss Marlowe, or has London's spectacle quite overwhelmed you?"

Sarah cast a wry glance over the throng that had brought them to a near-standstill. "London is a spectacle, certainly. I never know what will come next. One day I may happen upon a superb exhibition of watercolorists, and then the next be entertained by a monkey dressed as dashingly as any Corinthian. You will think me a goose for enjoying such a thing! Monkeys and art exhibits must be quite old hat to you."

"I would hardly mistake you for a goose, Miss Marlowe." For the merest instant something about the look in the earl's eyes reminded Sarah he had once remarked upon her beauty, but before she could revel in it, he was saying, "And so you wish to make your life in London? You did not mention the social whirl, but surely you have enjoyed that as well.''

''Yes, I have, but I do not think I would wish to reside permanently in town.'' When he looked at her in surprise, Sarah hurried to say, ''I know that sentiment seems at odds with the other, but London is like a very rich piece of cake. One slice is delightful, but I've a taste for contrasting fare as well.''

Dominic chuckled. ''And I take it you do not languish in isolation in plainer Cumberland?''

''By no means. My father has a wide circle of friends who come to visit. And we've good neighbors, of course.'' Sarah thought of Tom Woodward, but did not allow him to affect her mood. ''There are even assembly rooms in nearby Abberswater. So, you see, my lord, we are not so remote, and if there is some social whirl we do lack, why, we've lovely scenery to compensate.''

''You do,'' Ravensby agreed, rather charmed by her staunch pride in her home. ''I have been once to Cumberland on a fishing expedition.'' Before Sarah could ask where he had stayed, the earl looked beyond her, and a sudden extraordinarily boyish smile lit his face. ''Now, there is something you do not have in Cumberland!'' Sarah turned and saw a broad, ruddy-cheeked woman selling some sort of confectionery. ''Portugal cakes,'' Ravensby pronounced with unmistakable relish.

Without further ado he seized upon a wiry boy, who stood close by admiring the shiny, crested gig, and hailed him. ''Lad? There's a crown in it for you, if you can manage the horses for a few minutes.''

''Oh! Aye, m'lord.'' The boy nodded hastily, his eyes widening at the sudden turn in his fortunes.

In the space of a heartbeat, Ravensby was lifting Sarah down from the gig. ''You cannot say you've been to London until you've savored a Portugal cake. They are a city specialty.'' He laughed suddenly, seeing she was gazing at him quite bemused. ''I am being entirely high-handed, as usual. Let me begin again. Miss Marlowe, I have not enjoyed either a Portugal cake or a street fair in a very long time, and it would be the greatest pleasure if you would join me in strolling about as we sample the good lady's wares.''

Sarah did not protest he had mistaken the cause of her

expression. It would never do for him to know she had stared witlessly because she could scarcely credit the transformation his enthusiasm had wrought in him. Gone was the severely beautiful, formidable, arrogant earl, and in his place was a man so charmingly handsome he robbed her of her breath.

"Why, thank you, my lord," Sarah said, relieved to hear she did not sound too breathless. "I should like to join you very much."

The confectioner beamed broadly when Dominic purchased two of her cakes. "Aye, an' yer a fine gentleman, yer lordship." She grinned, eyeing him in such a way she left no doubt her description applied to more than the solid coin he gave her. "You'll turn yer lady up sweet with 'em, see if you don't."

Sarah flushed at being called Ravensby's lady, but the earl did not seem to make anything of it. After she took her first bite, he arched an inquiring brow at her and asked, "Well?"

Sarah bit back the impulse to say he did not need cakes to turn her up sweet. "Delicious," she replied with complete honesty; the concoctions, lightly flavored with rosewater, were as good as they were unusual.

"Shall we see the fair as we enjoy them?"

By way of answer Sarah slipped her arm through his, and with his smile to prompt her, set out to marvel without restraint at the range of sights to be seen at a London street fair. Several jugglers stood near the entrance, defying gravity with an amazing array of objects, while Gypsies called out promises to tell the most splendid futures. All along the street, vendors set up in temporary booths hawked an almost inconceivable variety of items, and an equally varied hodgepodge of animals performed tricks. Sarah continued to maintain that the monkey they had seen first was the most prepossessing of the creatures, but she conceded to Ravensby the point that the elephant they found midway along the booths made the greatest impression. She had not, she told him with some awe, ever imagined an animal could be so large.

"Oh, and look there!" Sarah so forgot herself in her excitement at seeing a contingent of fierce-looking men swaggering along in foreign uniforms, she elbowed Dominic in the ribs.

"Tartars, by the look of them," he enlightened her, then

grinned as an uncertain look flitted across her face. "I think you needn't fear, the Golden Horde has long since been tamed. They are in the Russian army."

"You are laughing at me, my lord, but I think my apprehension not so farfetched. Those men look as if they may have departed the great khan's retinue only a few moments ago."

He glanced down with a smile, and seeing a crumb of Portugal cake clinging to her cheek, flicked it off. "I will grant they are amazing horsemen still. I watched them display their abilities for Prinny at Windsor last year."

Unsettled by the degree of warmth that flooded her in response to Dominic's offhand but nonetheless familiar gesture, Sarah had to strain to recall the subject under discussion, and by the time she had, he was already steering her in a new direction, exclaiming with interest, "There is a skittles booth."

Now, skittles is a simple game, the object being, as in bowling, to knock down as many pins as possible, in this case with a flat wooden disk. And Sarah had had some practice with the game, for there had always been a skittles booth at the Abberswater village fair. After a slow start, she played rather well.

"I see you are not a female, Miss Marlowe, who believes she ought to cosset the consequence of her escort by allowing him an easy victory in a skittles match," the earl observed afterward.

Sarah grinned, seeing the twinkle in his eyes. "I am not, sir, and might even make a case that it would do the consequence of some escorts a deal of good to experience an occasional defeat."

"I do believe you are chastising me for my arrogance again. But surely you must concede now, Miss Marlowe, that I come by that arrogance honestly. I did win handily, your challenge notwithstanding."

He looked almost sinfully handsome then, with the breeze ruffling his dark hair and boyish laughter lighting his golden-brown eyes. "You did, my lord, but I shall learn that little trick you have of throwing the disk so it spins, and then we shall see."

He laughed aloud. "You noticed that, did you? You've too quick an eye, Miss Marlowe. I shall have to resort to challenging you to feats of horsemanship to keep up my consequence.''

Sarah giggled. ''Your head will swell to unseemly propor-
tions, you will win there so handily. Oh, look! What is that man
doing?''

''Not my ribs again!'' Dominic executed a sidestep to avoid
Sarah's elbow, with the result that her arm went around his back
and for a moment she lay across his chest, looking up at him.

It was a moment only that they were all but entwined. In the
next instant Dominic set her apart from him, but for that instant
a breathless awareness of their position held Sarah paralyzed
against him. She could feel his chest hard against her soft
breasts; could feel his lean waist with her arm, even his hips
just a little below. Gazing up, bewildered, really, by the way
his closeness made her pulses leap, she was further dismayed
to find his face expressionless, no trace of laughter remaining
to lighten it.

Then abruptly he set her away from him. ''You wished to
show me something, Miss Marlowe?'' he asked, his voice as
suddenly cooled as his expression.

''Only that man, there,'' Sarah said, her manner no less
constrained. And when she took a step, it was not toward the
man who seemed to be swallowing great bursts of fire, but back
in the direction of the entrance to the street fair.

Dominic followed her lead, stating the obvious only absently:
that the man was a fire-eater. Whereas she might have asked
in wonder how anyone could swallow fire, and he might have
teased in return that the secret was not known in his family,
they said nothing more at all. Only as they neared the entrance
to the fair was Sarah moved to speak again.

A ribbon on display at one of the stalls caught her eye, and
she moved away from Ravensby toward it, exclaiming quietly,
''Why, it is the perfect ribbon!'' Looking up from her inspection
of it to find Ravensby regarding her oddly, she insisted, ''Truly,
Anne will be delighted with it. It matches perfectly the dress
she's to wear to the Viscount Whittingham's ball. It is a silver
net with a blue satin underslip.''

Dominic had believed she desired the ribbon for herself. Half-
chagrined, but too, and more strangely, relieved to have judged
her unfairly, he reached into his pocket. ''You have convinced

me, Miss Marlowe. But how is it you know what Anne will
wear in a week's time to the Whittinghams' affair?''

"When we were at Richmond, Anne described the dress Lady
Sophia has chosen for the evening."

Dominic purchased the ribbon without further ado, but the
constraint that had set in when Sarah fell against him seemed
only to deepen with the mention of Lady Sophia Carrington.
The gay mood they'd shared at the beginning of the fair quite
gone, they attained Albemarle Street in silence.

Dominic lifted her down from the gig as if she weighed
nothing at all, and walked her up the steps, still without
speaking. Only at the top, before the door, did he meet Sarah's
eyes again. And smiled faintly, just enough that his severe face
softened a little. "Thank you for your company, Miss Marlowe.
I've not enjoyed a street fair so in a very long time."

"And I never, my lord. Thank you."

The Ponsbys' door was opening, but they stood before it as
if unaware. Then the earl lightly traced her smooth cheek with
a gloved finger. "You are out of the common way, Miss
Marlowe. Don't allow a rogue such as Kendall to turn your
sparkle into ashes."

And with that he was gone, leaving Sarah and the housemaid
at the door to watch him leap lightly onto his gig and guide his
team down the street out of sight.

13

Sarah received a note from Ravensby later in the week. In it
he thanked her for pointing out the ribbon. "Anne is very
pleased with it, which pleases me. I have enclosed a small token
of my gratitude. I hope you will accept it as such, but more.
I hope it pleases you. Yours, Ravensby."

The enclosed was a small pen-and-ink sketch of a monkey

lounging in a comfortable chair with his hands behind his head, watching with a distinctly jaded expression a parade of fashionably dressed humans. The earl had chosen well. Not only was the little sketch humorous, but it was exceedingly well-executed.

Mrs. Ponsby thought it a rather eccentric gift, but certainly within the bounds. "Of course you may accept it, my dear. It is a token of appreciation for your assistance," she reasoned, Sarah having explained to her that the earl had taken her up at Hookham's that she might assist him in selecting a ribbon for Anne.

It had been stretching the truth a bit to say that, Sarah knew, but she could not say the earl had taken her up to read her a scold over Captain Kendall. Nor, her aunt being the romantic she was, had Sarah believed it wise to inform her Ravensby had whisked her off to a street fair, for her aunt was likely to spin rapturous, impossible dreams from the simple thread of a chance outing.

Mrs. Ponsby had accepted Sarah's explanation readily enough, for as she said, gentlemen never had the least notion what to do about such things as ribbons.

Kitty, however, was not so easily fobbed off. After Sarah had given her the ribbon explanation, she shook her head slowly. "There is more to it, cuz! You will not persuade me that a gentleman seeming all but affianced to one lady would seek out an entirely different—if infinitely superior, to my mind—lady merely to ask the second lady to do what the first lady might just as easily have done in the first place." Kitty's lively grin appeared over the jumble of "firsts" and "seconds" she'd used, but she was not diverted. "Besides," she continued author-itatively, "you were in the earl's company longer than it would take to buy a ribbon, particularly as there is a shop just around the corner from Hookham's, with reams of ribbons."

"Oh, very well, Miss Nosy." Sarah made a half-laughing, half-exasperated face. "Ravensby took me up to read me a scold."

"A scold?" Kitty repeated, clearly surprised.

Sarah nodded. "He saw me with Captain Kendall ever so briefly and was most displeased."

"Do you know," Kitty observed thoughtfully after a moment, "I think it is vastly intriguing that Ravensby should concern himself with you and Kendall."

"He thinks the man's a rogue, that's all."

"Which he is, as I hope you do know." Kitty shot Sarah a questioning look that was answered by a faint smile.

"I am aware of the captain's character."

"Back to Ravensby, then," Kitty declared briskly. If Sarah wished to be mysterious about the captain, that was one thing, for he was, to Kitty's mind, negligible. But Ravensby . . . "The earl has not taken it upon himself to guard the virtue of any other young lady completely unconnected to him, and if he is looking for maidens in distress, I should say the captain spends more time flashing his smiles at Charlotte than at you."

"Miss Manwairing's purse is more marriageable than mine," Sarah remarked dryly. "But as to the earl, he interests himself in me, particularly, because he rescued me that day."

"Sarah, Sarah!" Kitty shook her head. "Really, my dear! Do you truly believe that if you were a drab, mousy thing, the earl would interest himself in your affairs merely because he snatched you up before you crashed headlong to the street? Don't be absurd!"

Sarah laughed. "I appreciate your confidence in me, but I am the one who has just been with him, Kitty, and I assure you he has no grand interest in me. He treats me like . . . a niece. A rather wayward younger niece," she added, not quite able to keep a wistful note from her voice.

Kitty smiled to herself. Hearing that note, she guessed at a little of Sarah's feelings, but knew better than to press where her cousin did not care to be pressed.

"He is an obtuse man, then," she proclaimed without in the least believing it. "And therefore we shall dismiss him in favor of considering an invitation we have received to take tea with Althea and Clarice Enderby this very afternoon. Shall we go? Althea's a dress she wishes to show me."

Sarah could scarcely believe her luck, nor that it held so nicely when they arrived at the Viscount Whittingham's, for not only were she and Kitty invited to the very house Sarah wanted to study, but it happened that Clarice Enderby was particularly proud of her home, a superb example of Palladian architecture, and was delighted to show Sarah over it, while Kitty and Althea stayed below to gossip.

Sarah learned not only where Kendall's rooms were but also that he had the corridor to himself, that there was another, unused room at the head of the corridor, and that inside the unused room, in plain sight on a table by the door, there was a candlestick conveniently placed in a light, portable holder. She need only bring matches, and she would have light when she searched the captain's room.

The night of the Viscount Whittingham's ball, Sarah strove for calm and succeeded to the extent that her plans for the evening began to seem almost unreal. She planned carefully, yet could not quite persuade herself she did, truly, intend to rob a man.

Yet, when the Marquess of Lisle came to greet her as soon as she entered the ballroom, Sarah realized her nerves were stretched much tighter than she had guessed, for she was wildly grateful his stolid presence would keep Kendall away. No matter how unreal her plans seemed, she knew she could not behave unaffectedly with the captain.

"Good evening, Miss Marlowe. I am delighted to remind you that you promised the first dance this evening to me."

"I scarce need reminding, sir. I have been looking forward to the pleasure of our dance."

"Not half so much as I, I assure you, my dear," the marquess replied with the blandest of expressions. "I have been in company with Sally Jersey, you see, and my ears long for a respite. It is the greatest misfortune, I believe, that no one of authority ever pointed out to the lady that only brooks should babble."

Sarah could not but laugh. Even her friends called Lady Jersey "Silence" for the way she rattled on. "I do hope you will not hesitate to warn me, should I begin to imitate a brook, my lord."

"Ah, but there is no danger of that, Miss Marlowe. You are not afraid of a little contemplative silence. It is one of your greatest attractions that you are more like a mountain lake. Very beautiful and very deep, I think."

The marquess's compliments had become gradually warmer over time, but still Sarah flushed. Each such remark, not to mention the admiration in his eyes, brought home to her that his interest in her was growing beyond the bounds of mere friendship.

Dominic, leading Anne out to join the set of which the marquess and Sarah were a part, saw that blush on Sarah's cheeks, and taking in Lisle's besotted expression, came to much the same conclusion as she had.

The marquess would be popping the question soon, as Richard had put it the night before at White's, where a wager concerning the marquess's intentions toward Sarah Marlowe had been entered in the betting book. "It's hard to say for certain with the old boy," Richard had observed, "but the signs are there. Dances with her twice every chance he gets, calls on her in Albemarle Street. Egad! The girl even brings him to smile. It's a pity to pair her off with a deadly thing like him, but unless someone else pops the question first, it's not likely she'll turn him down."

Of course it was not likely. In her wildest dreams a girl of Miss Marlowe's unassuming background could not have hoped to do better than a reasonably wealthy marquess. She would, as a marchioness, outrank him, Dominic realized. The thought did not make him smile, but not because he did not wish her to rise in the world. In fact, he wished her well, but at that moment Lisle had taken her hand in his, and Dominic had a vision of the pale, paunchy man caressing her.

It was an outrageous and rather detailed vision to have there on a crowded dance floor, but Dominic was not accustomed to apologizing for his thoughts. And he did know her body. He had held her close against him twice. He could recall as vividly as if they were at the fair, how full and heavy her breasts had felt against him, and how small, vulnerable even, her waist had been beneath his hand.

"Do say something to Sarah about my ribbon, will you, Uncle Dominic? I have thanked her, of course, but coming from you, she will know I was not merely being polite."

"Of course," Dominic replied to Anne, his thoughts returned to the ballroom in time for him to realize the ladies were moving to dance with the next gentlemen in the set.

Sarah's heartbeat increased when she realized her next partner would be Ravensby. She had not seen him since the fair. All she could think of was the constraint that had fallen between them after she had fallen across him. It had occurred to her that he might believe she had deliberately thrown herself upon him to catch his attention.

She feared she was blushing; knew she was, for her cheeks were warm.

And then she was being handed to him. "My . . ."

"Miss . . ."

When they spoke simultaneously, they both chuckled, and Sarah's tension eased.

"I thank you for the sketch, my lord. I expected no gift—"

"I am glad you like it," Dominic interrupted before she could go on about how little she had expected reward. He thought he knew that. "When I saw it, I thought of you." He swung Sarah lightly about as the other gentlemen did the same to their partners. "To be exact, Miss Marlowe, I thought of you laughing."

His eyes laughed down at her . . . an almost indulgent look in them. Her heart seemed to catch, and Sarch did not know what to say. She only knew she wanted to remain gazing up at him like that the rest of the night, an idiotic as well as impossible desire, she scolded herself. "Well, I did laugh, my lord. It was impossible not to, the monkey looked so very unimpressed with the *beau monde.*"

"Such an outrageous attitude, don't you think?" Ravensby asked, deliberately casting his glance toward a stout, corseted dowager draped in yards of puce satin, a turban of the same color sitting askew on her head. Sarah might have been moved to some levity at the picture Lady Adella Sims made anyway, but when the earl looked back at her actually grinning, she was quite helpless not to laugh aloud.

"Precisely how I thought you'd sound, Miss Marlowe," he remarked, but even as Sarah was registering the satisfaction in his tone, Ravensby, as he was obliged to do, handed her on to the next gentleman in the set.

Sarah was brought back to earth at the dance's end, when Lady Sophia Carrington came gliding elegantly forward to claim the earl and lead him off to some friends of hers. It was for the best, Sarah told herself. Like a brilliant light, Ravensby dazzled her, but he could burn her too, if she were not careful.

When he was safely across the room, she shook her head. Particularly on that night, she could not allow herself to be distracted by a quite hopeless cause. Glancing down at her card, Sarah realized how distracted she had been. The next two dances were the ones she had claimed for herself, scrawling so illegibly on the little card that dangled from her wrist that no one could know the names written there were entirely imaginary.

A rapid, very nervous glance around the room showed Mrs. Ponsby in deep conversation with a group of other matrons, Mr. Ponsby nowhere to be seen as usual, for he generally remained in the card room all evening, and Captain Kendall leading someone, it looked to be Charlotte Manwairing, in the direction of a servant serving champagne.

Her heart racing more than a little, Sarah slipped out of the ballroom. There were guests in the hallway, but nodding to those she knew, Sarah continued on as if she'd some urgent errand to perform. When she reached the stairs to the floor above, where the family's rooms were, she could see no one about, and lifting her skirts, dashed as fast as she could away out of sight. At the top, she did not pause, but hurried on to the captain's wing, where the single torch burning in the corridor revealed no movement at all.

Breathing hard, Sarah rushed into the room where she had marked there was a candle, seized it, and hurried on to Kendall's very door.

Hearing no one inside, she peeked in to find it deserted, and slipped inside.

Heart hammering painfully, she lit her candle and took an inventory. A large mahogany bed dominated the room, but it was the chest of drawers that drew Sarah. Her fingers shook as she opened the top drawer to inspect the captain's neatly folded shirts. She tipped them up, then felt along the back of the drawer but found no long velvety box. The drawer with his underthings she snapped closed before it was fully opened. She simply could not rifle through them. Another drawer held stockings and hose, but still no necklace. Careful to leave everything as she had found it, Sarah went on to the bottom drawer. His woolens took more time to search. She must be certain he'd not hidden the box inside a vest, but in the end, she came on nothing hard.

The wardrobe close by attracted her next. An enormous thing, it revealed carefully hung clothes. She was feeling along the bottom for a loose board when the sound she had been dreading came to her. A board squeaked in the corridor.

Strangely, in the moment when Sarah had the most to fear, a sort of calm descended upon her. There was naught to do but blow out the candle and scurry into the wardrobe.

She hid herself none too soon. As she pulled the wardrobe door shut, the door to the captain's room opened. Crouched, straining to hear, Sarah made out the sound of rapid steps coming directly toward the wardrobe.

Fear did overcome her then. She wondered if she could leap out of the thing and escape the room before she was recognized, but then, mercifully, the steps halted. She heard something, perhaps a drawer, sliding open. A bottle fell with a clink; then the sound was repeated, as if the drawer were being closed. At once the steps retreated, and she heard the click of the door with such relief, she sagged back in the wardrobe, hand to her throat.

Entirely unnerved, she almost gave up her search, but with an effort Sarah forced herself to recall that awful day Tom had pulled her lecherous, grasping cousin off her. She could not abandon her attempt. She owed him too much, and would never be given another such opportunity to recover his emeralds for him.

Wiping damp palms down the sides of her dress, she steeled herself, relit the candle, and turned to the captain's dressing table. It had been the object of the intruder. Sarah nearly laughed. She was the intruder, not whoever had come. The thought that whoever it was had come to snatch the emeralds from her grasp almost caused her to giggle again, and she put her hand to her mouth to stifle the bubble of hysteria.

Almost it rose again when she glanced into the glass above the dressing table. The clothes above her in the wardrobe had done damage to her hair. Several strands, catching on them, had been pulled loose from the coronet she wore atop her head.

Biting her lip, she forced her attention to the captain's toiletries. There was not the time to fix her coiffure then. She would do it later in the room where she had found the candle.

Quickly she searched through bottles of bay rum, shaving brushes, hairbrushes, combs, and a host of other toilet articles. One of the drawers contained a stack of letters. Sarah kept her eyes carefully averted as she felt the bottom for a box, but her nose told her more than one was heavily scented.

In the end, despite all her efforts and even a search of the upholstered furniture, Sarah found nothing. It was not easy to give up, not when she was so agonizingly close, but she knew that soon she would be missed from the ballroom.

Heavy of heart, she stepped quietly into the corridor, to find with a start the torch had gone out. Pausing to allow her eyes to adjust to the dark, Sarah thought she heard a muffled sound, a laugh, from a room somewhere behind her. Though she half-suspected her mind was only playing tricks on her, she hurried away as lightly as she could.

Like a wraith she entered the small guest room from which she'd purloined the candle and carefully closed the door behind her. Only one more thing to be done, and she would be away. She lit the candle again, and turning to the glass above the table, lifted her arms to repin her hair.

She was in that posture when, without warning, the door to the room swung open.

Ravensby! Sarah stared speechless to see him arrested there on the threshold, one hand behind him on the door handle as he stared in his turn, seeming slow to take in the picture she made, the light of the candle bathing her as she attended to her hair.

He stepped forward in the next moment, sending his gaze winging around the room. Sarah felt her stomach knot when, having ascertained she was alone, Ravensby rocked back on his heel and closed the door behind him with the softest, most ominous of clicks.

He filled the room. It was not large anyway, and seemed to shrink as he stepped forward, his broad shoulders completely erasing the door, the room's only exit, from Sarah's sight.

She could see his severe, beautiful face all too well. The

candle stood between them, flickering, true, but illuminating the earl's expression clearly. "My lord—" Sarah began, her voice rendered high and thin by the cold fury in his eyes.

"You were seen with our good Kendall," he cut in flatly. "Don't waste your breath with more lies."

Sarah felt her breath escape her in a rush. She opened her mouth, but no sound came out as he stepped close enough to touch her.

Dominic glanced to her hair and followed the disarray down to where several strands lay on the swell of her breasts. Her skin, though she could not know it, gleamed pearly in the candlelight.

Sarah did know her skin heated beneath his gaze, and her hand lifted unwilled to shield the bared flesh he studied, but already he impaled her again with his eyes. Gleaming, impenetrable obsidian they seemed, for there was not the faintest hint of gold to warm them.

Sarah stumbled a step back, shrinking from him. It was quite the wrong move. Dominic caught her bared shoulder.

He did not grasp her hard, but his touch felt unnaturally hot, and she shivered beneath it, all the while staring into his eyes.

"You said you could manage him, that you'd no thought of enticing him. All true, it would seem, but not in the way you led me to believe with those blue eyes opened so very wide. You did give me some warning, though. I admit it." He smiled, a cold, mocking travesty of a smile that did not reach those hard eyes. "You said you were a capable actress. You fooled your aunt and uncle, you said, into believing you could ride. Ah, but, then, you can ride, can you not? Does he like these?"

Sarah gasped when lightly, ever so lightly, Dominic trailed his fingers just above the edge of her bodice on the swell of her breasts. She tried to shrug free of him, but his hand on her shoulder tightened its grip.

"Hmm?" he asked, piercing her with his eyes as he trailed his fingers back along the pearly skin of her breasts.

"My lord, please!" she begged, her voice shaking. He was so angry, and yet he left a trail of prickling fire where he touched her so lightly as to tease. Her breasts seemed to swell, almost lifting into his touch.

She grasped his arm to stop him. "Please!" His fingers did cease their teasing, but did not desist touching her. So aware of them lying weightless just on the curve of her bared flesh was she that Sarah could scarcely choke out coherent words. "Please, there is some mistake!"

"Where were you, then, Sarah?" he almost whispered, his voice silky. "How did your golden hair come loose?"

He lifted his hand from her décolletage to wind a silky strand of her hair around his finger and caress it with his thumb. His eyes, however, were on her flaming cheeks.

When Sarah could not seem to find speech to explain where she had been and why, Dominic spoke, his tone disarmingly casual. "A servant saw you running to him, you know. You were too eager. You forgot to look both ways before you tripped into the captain's eager embrace. You played me for a fool, Sarah Marlowe."

The accusation followed so quickly the other completely incomprehensible remarks, Sarah only had the time to gasp and shake her head before Dominic's fingers landed on her lips.

"No! You'd have done better to tell me the truth from the first, you know. Had I known you were entirely lost to the captain, I'd have let you be. It was your seeming innocence— and your quite remarkable beauty, of course—kept me . . . interfering. Tell me," Ravensby went on curiously, "does he value these adequately?"

His fingers traced her lips with the same tantalizing feather touch he'd applied to her breasts. Sarah opened her mouth to protest, but no sound emerged. Her lips were so dry, she wet them.

At the sight of her tongue darting out to caress her lips, Dominic uttered a low, harsh curse, and then, before she could guess what he intended, took her parted lips with his.

Sarah's mouth tightened as she jerked stiff, but Dominic seemed not to notice as he tasted where he would, his mouth firm, hot, and demanding upon hers. He gave her no opportunity to gasp for breath even, as he held her securely, one large hand cupping her head, the other fastened upon the small of her back.

The bodice of Sarah's dress was low, the lowest of all her

evening gowns. The coat Dominic wore was of silk, the waist-coat too, and as his clothing slipped sensuously across her exposed skin, all Sarah's madly careening thoughts suddenly focused there.

He'd prepared her, she thought wildly. He'd made her skin, her breasts, sensitive. They felt aflame, and aching to meet his hard chest.

Perhaps he guessed, for he crushed her to him, creating a sensation in her breasts almost too intense to endure.

And suddenly and entirely unexpectedly there was fire between them.

Blood pounding in a wild, urgent rhythm, Sarah no longer strained against Dominic. She strained into him, lifting her arms around his neck, as his kiss became fiery, hungry. Shuddering, she felt his hand caress the satiny skin behind her ear, then fall that it might trace slow, sensuous circles at the nape of her neck.

When he urged her closer to him, she stretched to meet him, opening her mouth to him as he nipped her lightly with his teeth.

Heat, liquid and searing, leapt through her. His hand was stroking the slender indentation of her waist, then trailing lower, feeling the rounded curve of her bottom.

Sarah trembled, and her knees sagged. Dominic caught her tighter to him, groaning as a hot surge of desire shook him.

She was his.

Any man's!

He jerked himself up straight, ripping his mouth from hers.

Even as her mouth protested the loss of his plundering lips, Sarah's eyes flew wide. Her first thought was for how heavily Ravensby breathed and the next was for the expression in his eyes. They were no longer black. But gold or not, they flung contempt at her.

Sarah read Dominic's mood aright for the most part. Only some of the derision blazing in Dominic's eyes was for himself. He had meant, he knew not what, but perhaps to satisfy himself she was, indeed, a lying, wanton witch with an actress's ability to play at innocence.

And he had made her whimper, had made her groan even, with desire. He'd laid her bare, only he had not held aloof.

He had not so lost himself in an embrace since he was a

stripling and sensuous pleasures, being new to him, had the power to overwhelm him.

But still her eyes were trained as seemingly guileless as ever on his face. The witch! To look so fresh and innocent!

Oh, there were the signs of passion. Even now, her lips looked bee-stung and rosy pink. Her tousled hair lay tumbled over breasts that rose and fell more urgently than before. Nor were her eyes quite as wide as usual. Passion had made their lids heavy . . . God! He wanted her even now.

Kendall had taught her well. Dominic's hands tightened upon Sarah's shoulders as his mouth twisted in a derisive grimace. ''By God! You've a need for men, don't you? Your plan suits your proclivities nicely, does it not? How simple it will be for you to do your duty to Lisle in licit and so-profitable union, and still have all the energy you'll need to dally with Kendall whenever you can get him.''

Sarah struck him. Before either of them realized what she intended, she reacted, striking out as hard as she could, the sound of her palm against his cheek echoing like a gunshot in the still room.

Dominic's mouth tensed, going white, even as color flared bright on the skin stretched taut over his high cheekbones, and such a light blazed to life in his eyes, Sarah flung up her hands to protect herself.

And it was his first impulse to deal her a blow in return. But he had never hit a woman, and no matter that he'd provocation aplenty, Dominic held himself very still.

Then, in the next instant, he turned on his heel, putting her behind him as if she disgusted him, and quit the room without another word or look or gesture. Outside, he closed the door behind him, leaving her there quite alone.

14

"Why, Mama, the Selbys have invited us to a dinner party!" Kitty glanced up from the cream-colored invitation she read. "Do let us go! We have scarcely seen a thing of them since we came to town."

"We've been traveling in different circles, my dear," Mrs. Ponsby replied, not without a hint of pride. "But when is the dinner party? I should like to see how Maria Selby is getting on."

"Tuesday."

"Tuesday? But that is out of the question, Kitty! Have you forgotten we are invited to Lady Sophia's soiree on Tuesday?"

"I suppose I had forgotten. I've looked forward to it so little. Oh, I know it will be a very elegant affair! I don't doubt that, but Lady Sophia is so very high in the instep! I can't recall ever seeing her really smile." Kitty looked hopefully at her mother. "The Selbys' affair will be much more enjoyable."

Sarah sat before the room's largest window, using its light to sketch a bowl of fruit she had arranged on a small rosewood occasional table. A little distance from her aunt and cousin, she had not taken any part in their discussion over which invitations to accept and which to reject. Indeed, she had not much listened to what they had said, but now she glanced at her aunt.

Mrs. Ponsby was regarding her daughter disapprovingly. "Kitty, we have already sent our acceptance to Lady Sophia. It would be unthinkable to cry off at this late date. And even if we could, I should not care to miss her entertainment. Why, Lady Sophia is known for her soirees! Besides," she continued, a more cajoling note in her voice, "as I understand it, dear Anne is to be the guest of honor that evening. I am certain you would not wish to disappoint her."

Sarah had not harbored much hope that Kitty might somehow

pull off exchanging Lady Sophia's soiree for the Selbys' dinner, but the little hope she had entertained died with a pang as she acknowledged her aunt's position to be unassailable. Kitty could not say Anne would not be disappointed. The poor girl had made it clear she counted on Sarah and Kitty to support her through the soiree to which Lady Sophia had deigned to invite only a very few persons of Anne's age.

A surge of panic threatening her, Sarah bent her head over her sketch, making erratic, random lines upon it. She must cling to the hope Ravensby would not attend. It was not the most groundless of hopes, she tried to assure herself.

The earl was not in London, after all. He had been called away from town shortly after their encounter in the smallest of the Viscount Whittingham's guest rooms. According to Anne, the earl had gone posthaste to Kent to the bedside of an older man he considered almost a father.

Sarah sent a prayer winging heavenward. Though she knew it was wretchedly self-centered to beg the heavenly Father to busy Himself with her affairs, she did ask if only this once He might not arrange it that the old man, though entirely free from pain, would continue to demand Ravensby's company.

It was not so much to ask, really. Some powerful intercessor had already seen to it that Ravensby had no reason to rush back to London. Anne was being looked after superbly. The messenger who had delivered the summons to Kent had been the earl's sister, Lady Ruth Dacres. With her husband recovered from the gout, she intended to remain in town the rest of the Season.

Given luck and a little divine intervention, it was just possible Ravensby would not return at all, or would not join the social round if he did, and Sarah would never see him again. She had not seen him since that night.

That night. Two weeks had passed. Yet it was still so horribly fresh in her mind. How desolate he had left her! How alone, with only the click of the door shutting behind him for company.

And ashamed. She had looked in that glass and seen herself with a cry of horror. Her lips swollen and red, her hair tumbling wantonly, her bodice sagging low over her breasts, she had looked precisely what he thought her.

Sarah's hand made a slashing diagonal line across her page. He had done it deliberately. Why else would he have kissed someone he despised? He had set out to make her blood sing hot and wild in her veins, had intended to bring her agonizingly near something magical; then, by design, he had broken off their embrace to fling that very magic in her face. She was glad she had slapped him back.

And why? Why had he done it? Over some wretched misunderstanding she might have untangled, had he only given her time. Time and the room to think clearly. But he had not. He had fired his questions at her, after taking care to confuse her mind with mysterious, tantalizing sensations she'd no defense against.

She ought to have had, though! Sarah squeezed her eyes shut. He had not forced her. That was her shame. He had held her, true, but she had made only a most feeble protest against him. Had she struggled in earnest . . . But she had not. She had stood breathless and still before she had caught fire and not merely yielded, but pressed urgently against him.

Sarah's hand, hovering over her sketchpad, wavered. Her knuckles turned white as she clenched her hand around the pen she used. She could see his eyes. How cold they had been, how devoid of all feeling but contempt. She could not face them again, could not endure that scathing look knowing she deserved at least a measure of his aversion.

"Dominic, darling! You are back!"

"Perceptive as ever, Ruth." Dominic smiled faintly as he returned his sister's embrace.

A handsome woman in her mid-thirties, Lady Ruth paid no heed to her brother's smile at her expense. "And Lord Langston?" she asked. "Was it as serious as the old boy thought?"

"His condition has not greatly improved, but he lives." Having poured himself a glass of claret, Dominic dropped into a wing chair commodious enough to support his length. A deep sigh signified his relief to be home and freed from the confines of a rattling carriage. "He'd matters with his will he wished me to attend to, but he sent me away before, as he put it, he 'gurgled his last.' "

Lady Ruth shook her head. "That does sound precisely like him! Langston has ever striven to shock. But he does dote on you, and so I forgive him."

"He was a great help after Father's death. I shall miss him."

"As shall we all."

Lady Ruth waited tactfully a few moments, but when Dominic did nothing but moodily study his glass of claret, she stirred. It was not like her brother, this abstraction. He was normally the most reasonable of men, if hardheaded.

Having been with Langston two weeks, he must know the old man was ready to go. Langston had lived a good, rich life, and was departing his mortal coil with his faculties intact. She'd have thought Dominic would be the first to agree it was all one could ask for an old friend.

Sooner rather than later, the gloomy silence became more than Lady Ruth had the least intention of bearing. "Enough of the sickroom, my dear!" She broke the silence, waving her hand decisively. "Langston would not wish us to dwell on his illness. In fact, I believe he would detest the thought. And besides, we've happier matters to discuss. You've timed your return perfectly, as I am certain you are aware. You will just have a moment to wash off the dust and change before it is time to depart for Sophy's soiree."

"It is tonight?" The look on Dominic's face made it quite clear he had not thought of the soiree in a long while. "Damn! but I've no desire to go. I'm weary as the devil."

He did look weary, Lady Ruth could not but agree. However, she did not believe brooding alone would help to lighten his mood.

"You will simply have to rouse yourself, darling!" she protested. "Sophy would suffer the greatest disappointment were you not to put yourself out for her affair. She's bound to learn you are back, you know. And Anne is in a great fret over the evening." Lady Ruth studied her brother, weighing whether to speak further, and decided, in the end, in favor of a full accounting. "Sophy rather awes our niece, you know."

His reply was casual, and the more startling therefore. "Yes, I'd some suspicion of it."

Lady Ruth blinked, but did not surrender. "Well, in that case, you must have some idea how anxious the child is. She's certain Sophy's company will be entirely above her. . . ."

As his sister cataloged the myriad anxieties Anne entertained, all to the end of assuring that he spend his evening enduring the chatter of a soiree rather than enjoying the rest his bed promised, a sense of fatalism overtook Dominic. He would go. There was no way around it unless he wished to feel a cad for disappointing Sophy and a worse one for denying Anne his support.

There were not to be many young people present. When she had first told him of her notion to have a soiree for Anne, Sophy had explained she did not wish to invite merely "the same mindless young things one sees everywhere. It is time Anne learned to mingle in all sorts of company. I shall invite an amusing group, though. You needn't worry that I mean to invite only Papa's circle of friends. I know you found them somewhat antiquated that Sunday." Before Dominic had been able to decide whether he wished to protest her more-accurate-than-not observation, Sophy had gone on, "You'll enjoy this group. I shall have people of refinement, of course, but also people who are known for their conversation, and even one or two artists. They can be so amusing, and I've some acquaintance with a gentleman who is all the rage just now. I shan't leave Anne entirely without company of her age, however. Indeed, I shall be particularly magnanimous and invite the Marlowe child and her cousin, as Anne is so fond of them."

At the time Dominic had applauded the notion. Anne would need the support of close friends if she were to face with any equanimity at all the sort of evening Sophy had planned.

And so the die was cast. On his first evening in London, he would be faced with Sarah Marlowe.

Dominic downed the remainder of his claret, then departed his sister's company for the soothing, undemanding ministrations of his valet.

From experience Dominic knew only solitude would do when thought of the girl overtook him. He scowled darkly. What balderdash that was! She had seldom been out of his thoughts. Even when he was not thinking of her directly, she lay like a silent weight upon his mind, keeping his mood dark as pitch.

There was one moment in particular pricked at him. He'd been angry with himself, infuriated he could feel desire for such a devious jade, and he'd lashed out.

She had been a little wary. He had just pulled back from her, and she must have seen in his eyes he was not in the best frame of mind. But she had not shaken off the effects of their passion yet. Her mind had been sluggish; her thoughts disoriented.

And it was then, while she yet felt soft and languorous beneath his hands, that he had attacked. In his most cutting voice, in so many words, he had called her a whore. He believed his charge true, that it was her plan to wed a wealthy title while she continued to indulge her passion for Kendall, but she'd been defenseless at that moment, and he brutal.

Just for one instant, before anger had overtaken her, he'd observed the effect of his words. Once, on his estate, Dominic had seen a young boy, playing with a knife, cut himself badly. The same shock had registered in Miss Marlowe's eyes as in that young boy's when he'd looked down to see the slash across his hand. The dark pupils of her eyes had dilated in the same way, and her jaw had sagged, lifeless.

She'd recovered. She'd slapped him. But, still, he found it impossible to rid himself of the memory of her ashen face and of her wide, stricken eyes.

Abruptly Dominic sat up, flinging a spray of water onto the floor as he reached for the glass of claret he'd had the foresight to order.

Damn! It was more than time he saw Miss Sarah Marlowe again. He needed a reminder how she could act the innocent, how she could appear so fresh and untouched, even as she planned to run with wanton enthusiasm into Kendall's arms.

There could be no doubt she did dally with the captain. Dominic had proof other than the heated nature she had displayed in his arms. More claret was required as, with a grim effort of will, he turned his mind from the way she'd suddenly caught fire beneath him.

He would concentrate instead upon how he had watched her leave that ballroom, thinking little of her departure until, a short time later, Kendall had slipped out as well after looking slyly about. Dominic had stilled an impulse to charge after the man.

Should Miss Marlowe need an ally, there were certain to be at least one or two guests within hearing. But as the minutes went by and still she did not return, he became increasingly concerned. Kendall knew the house. Perhaps he had maneuvered her into a secluded corner.

In the end he had murmured some excuse to Sophy and taken himself off to save Miss Marlowe once again. What a laugh!

A cursory check of the rooms near the ballroom had revealed more than one couple entwined, but not the couple he sought. Frustrated, he'd taken a servant aside. Perhaps it was the look in his eye, or perhaps it was his promise that the man would be rewarded handsomely the next day if he presented himself at the Earl of Ravensby's home in Bedford Square, but the servant had been most forthcoming. He had seen the captain.

"With a lady, 'e was, in the 'allway, to 'is rooms, yer lordship. I'd not 'ave seen 'em at all, sir, but the lady went runnin' with a laugh to meet 'im. She was waitin' for 'im, and then they went in 'is sittin' room."

The man had even given directions to the particular door, and Dominic had bolted away up the stairs.

There had been no logical reason to go after her. If she had run laughing to Kendall, she was past rescue or even consideration, but something had compelled him on. Perhaps he wanted to verify with his own eyes that the girl he'd escorted to that street fair, who had seemed so unguarded and true, could be such a deceiver.

Or perhaps he had only wanted her to know that he knew what she was.

Whatever, he had made haste to the captain's wing and found the hallway light doused, a most telling thing, he thought. The pair would want to creep about in the shadows, unseen. He also realized he had not listened to the servant's directions, deafened to such details, perhaps, by the thought of Sarah Marlowe running delightedly to her lover. Would they laugh together when she related how Ravensby had agreed there was no need to warn her aunt and uncle about Kendall?

Incensed by the thought, he'd plunged into the first room he came upon. And there she had been, a vision of loveliness, her hair gleaming a soft gold in the light of the candle, her skin

a pearly pink, her firm breasts straining against the tiny bodice
of her gown. A lady at her toilette, arms lifted, hands busy
smoothing away any trace of her interlude with her lover.

15

"Mr. and Mrs. Ponsby, Miss Ponsby, and Miss Marlowe. I
am pleased to welcome you this evening." Sarah curtsied with
a lightness that she had not felt in some time. She doubted Lady
Sophia was so pleased to see their little party as she said, and
it remained a mystery to her why the lady had invited them at
all, as she was not one, Sarah suspected, to honor her guest
of honor's preferences over her own.

But nothing, nothing at all, mattered to Sarah just then except
that the Earl of Ravensby was not standing in the reception line
between Lady Sophia and Anne. He is not here! He is not here!
He is not here! A smile so vivid lit her face as she looked up
at her hostess that Lady Ruth, standing a few feet further on,
found herself smiling with pleasure.

"You know Anne, of course," Lady Sophia continued in her
cool, authoritative way. "And Lady Ruth Dacres, Anne's dear
aunt."

Sarah turned away from Lady Sophia's aristocratic beauty
and looked with pleasure to Lady Ruth. Anne's aunt was a dear.
She did, distressingly, remind Sarah of Ravensby, for he was
tall and dark and handsome, but she possessed such hearty
warmth, Sarah was able to forgive her the resemblance.

"My dear, you are a pleasure to the eye," Lady Ruth
exclaimed, taking Sarah's hands in hers. "I really do not think
I have ever seen a more infectious smile."

"I am anticipating a most interesting evening," Sarah replied,
adding only to herself: and carefree! He is not here! "May I

say you look very handsome tonight, Lady Ruth? And you, Anne, delightful?''

"If I do, it is, as usual, on your account, Sarah, my dear. 'Twas you advised me to choose this shade of rose, you may remember.''

"I do." Sarah nodded, then grinned. "But it is you who wear it so well.''

"A shameless and dear flatterer!'' Lady Ruth applauded. "But go in, my dear, and enjoy yourself. We shall be here only a little longer, I think, and then Anne may join you.''

As her aunt and uncle and Kitty passed into the room ahead of her, Sarah paused on the threshold to look for them. About the large, well-proportioned room, numerous tables, armchairs, and couches, most showing Sheraton's superb influence, were arranged in some half-dozen groups, that Lady Sophia's guests might carry on their conversations in comfortable circumstances.

Sarah scanned the groups nearest her, recognized several familiar faces, acknowledged their greetings, then lifted her gaze beyond them. And looked, all unprepared, directly into Ravensby's amber eyes.

The breath went out of her in a soundless gasp. And the blood draining from her face, she swayed, staring like one mesmerized.

"Sarah! Sarah Marlowe! Good Lord, my dear, are you well?''

Sarah turned dazedly in the direction of the concerned voice. She felt cold all over, and yet her palms were horribly moist. A familiar face swam into view. Mr. Aubermont! He was her father's friend and her sometime tutor in watercolors.

"Mr. Aubermont!'' Her tutor seemed an anchor at the moment she needed one most, and Sarah held out both her hands to him. "I am so very glad to see you.''

"You look exceedingly pale, my dear,'' Mr. Aubermont observed with concern.

Sarah managed a feeble smile. "I did feel a little faint just then, but the moment has passed. The delightful surprise of seeing you here has quite restored me.''

Martin Aubermont beamed as he patted the slender hands he held. "I cannot convey, my dear Sarah, how gratifying it is for a man in his fifties to be told by a beautiful girl that his mere presence is a restorative. I shall savor the thought all night long, I assure you. But why do we not sit down upon this lovely settee that has been so fortuitously placed directly by us? In that way we may both be comfortable while you gather your energies and I simply enjoy looking upon you.''

Sarah's smile strengthened under the influence of the older man's courtly charm. ''I fear Papa would scold you for excessive flattery, my dear sir,'' she chided softly.

He saw her settled with a glass of ratafia to fortify her before returning to the subject of Sarah's father. ''I am well aware that Ivor has ever maintained, particularly in your presence, my dear, that what truly matters is not the outer arrangement of a person's countenance but rather the mind animating that countenance. And I quite agree with him. However, perhaps because I am an artist, my dear, I cannot but note that Ivor, when it came time to choose a wife, selected a very beautiful lady, and now quite dotes upon his even lovelier daughter. But perhaps the explanation is that you possess, as did your mama, a mind equal to your countenance.''

''You are too kind, my dear sir. And are putting me to the blush.''

''I cannot apologize!'' Mr. Aubermont beamed fondly at Sarah. ''I am delighted to see the color return to your cheeks. But I shall not insist upon embarrassing you. If you would rather, I shall change the subject to ask when it is you intend to visit my studio. Your papa has advised me that I may give you a lesson or two, if you wish it.''

Sarah chuckled. Her father would have done no such thing, for he knew very well that as Mr. Aubermont's reputation as a watercolorist had grown, so the time he had to give to his students had diminished. ''Merely seeing your latest work, sir, would be a lesson. And I would come for it tomorrow, if my aunt will permit.''

''We shall apply to her as soon as may be, then, for I am excessively proud of the home and studio I am able now I am 'the rage' to afford. Your good father would scold me for being, how does he put it, 'awash in the world.' '' Mr. Aubermont's eyes twinkled. ''Ah, but, my dear, I've little remorse, for it is the greatest pleasure, after all these years, to be awash in good fortune.''

As her old tutor recited the advantages of his rise to fame, Sarah calmed a little. She no longer felt so desperately ill as she had in that moment when Ravensby materialized before her very eyes, like some brooding, dark, accusing Lucifer. She did not know what she had expected. Perhaps that he would step forward, finger pointing at her, to accuse her of wantonness, to cry for all to hear, "She's hot blood in her veins!"

Sarah clenched the hands she held in her lap. She could not run from the room, nor sit shaking like a birch all night. She would not. She would not give him the satisfaction of seeing her defeated.

From the corner of her eye Sarah could see Ravensby. He still stood as he had been when she entered, his broad shoulders propped casually against a handsomely carved chimneypiece, a glass of claret dangling from his hand. Now she saw he was in conversation with Lord Richard and an older gentleman seated in a large chair by the fire.

He was not striding across the room to denounce her. How could she have been so stupid as to fear he would? Sarah smiled bitterly. He'd not chance a scene with Lady Sophia's cool eye upon him.

"Have you seen Anne, Sophy?" Frightfully nearsighted, but too vain to wear spectacles, Lady Ruth peered ineffectually around the room.

"Yes, I have." Lady Sophia smoothed an imaginary wrinkle from her sleeve. "She is speaking with Mr. Aubermont, the watercolorist."

"Ah, then she is with Miss Marlowe. What a lovely creature that child is! And so very generous to Anne. Curious one of her age should know an artist like Aubermont so well."

When no one in the small group gathered around Lord Matthew Beresford's chair seemed inclined to explain or perhaps to know the explanation to Lady Ruth's question, the Viscount Malthorpe, who prided himself on knowing everything, spoke up. "It would seem Mr. Aubermont is a friend of Miss Marlowe's father, Mr. Ivor Marlowe, and once taught—"

"Ivor Marlowe is her father?"

Lord Malthorpe flushed to be interrupted so rudely. But he

answered. Lord Ravensby was not one he would presume to reprimand for discourtesy. "That is the name Mr. Aubermont gave. He said Mr. Marlowe is something of a scholar or philosopher. He writes an occasional essay, I believe."

"I've read one or two."

When it did not seem to her that her brother intended to amplify upon his remark, but only to stare rather broodingly across the room at the daughter of the man in question, Lady Ruth prompted him. "And what did Sarah's father have to say?"

"Marlowe? Marlowe?" Lord Matthew echoed before Ravensby could respond, if he had intended to do so. "He's the fellow recommends simple living, isn't he? Fewer luxuries are good for the soul and all that?"

Lord Matthew, Ravensby did not ignore. "Yes, sir."

Lady Ruth thought it a pitifully thin reply, but before she could demand amplification, Lady Sophia spoke, a faintly derisory note coloring her tone. "Is he a Quaker, then?"

Ravensby shrugged negligently. "No, I don't think so. Merely an Anglican who believes overindulgence corrupts the soul."

"Corrupts the soul? What an odd notion! I must declare I am devoutly grateful that you, Papa, are no such ascetic." She leaned down to brush her father's cheek with her lips, seed pearls in her hair, larger, more lustrous pearls in ropes about her graceful neck, and still more of the gems enhancing the sumptuous beauty of her satin dress. "I should languish for want of your shameless indulgence. Poor Miss Marlowe! Now I suppose I understand better why it is her dresses are invariably so simple."

"Simple, yes," Lady Ruth agreed, glancing off in the direction she thought Sarah Marlowe to be, "but vastly becoming. Of course, the child would look well in most anything." She turned to smile innocently at her hostess. "Don't you agree?"

Lady Ruth nearly crowed with pleasure when Lady Sophia's eyes narrowed ever so briefly. So! Sophy was jealous of the child. Lady Ruth had begun to suspect as much from one or two other remarks the beauty had let drop over the last two weeks, but now she was certain. Had Dominic given her reason to fear a rival in that quarter?

Lady Ruth glanced at her brother. There was no way to know, drat the man! He was tossing off the last of his claret, his expression as remote as if he had not heard a word said. But she could bide her time, Lady Ruth thought to herself, and with some relish, for, quite like her sister, Jane, she had always thought Dominic lucky to have escaped the cool, self-centered daughter of Lord Matthew Beresford.

Not nearly so remote as Lady Ruth believed, Dominic finished his wine and looked for more. He had heard every word spoken and had detected Sophy's reluctance to agree that Sarah Marlowe would be riveting in a sack. And why should she not be reluctant? he addressed that part of his mind that faulted Sophy for her pettishness. Most females did resent rivals.

He shot a brief glance in Sarah Marlowe's direction. She and Anne were part of a group around the watercolorist Aubermont, or they were a group around her. She was encouraging Anne to tell a story. Catching a gesture Anne made, he guessed it had to do with the parrot, of all things, that Anne and Miss Marlowe had encouraged Ruth to purchase. They were all the rage, Anne had explained to him, when the thing had startled him nearly out of his wits by screeching, "Pretty boy! Pretty boy!" as he had joined Anne and Ruth in the drawing room before leaving for Sophy's.

Ruth had screamed with delight, and confided proudly the rogue not only could tell men from women but could swear in three languages. Anne was blushing now. Likely she was describing, if not the oaths themselves, then the talent.

Miss Marlowe, of course, was not blushing. Oaths must be little to her, and too, he admitted, she had not recovered all her color, though she was no longer as white as she had gone at the door.

He had refused to be in the welcoming line, though Sophy had implored him. To her he had made the excuse he was too weary from travel to be so convivial, but the truth was he'd balked at the thought of exchanging bland politenesses with a woman he'd held in a scorching embrace, then called a whore. Had it been a matter of life or death, he'd have carried the thing off, but as it was only Sophy's receiving line, he had chosen to stand well back in the room with Lord Matthew. Occasionally his gaze had strayed to the door, and therefore he had seen her the moment she crossed the threshold.

His memory had played him false. What he knew of Sarah Marlowe had colored his image, and as a result she was lovelier and fresher and more unspoiled than he had been prepared to find. Her hair was pleasingly arranged in a knot of loose golden curls that framed her face and trailed lightly along her neck. Her dress, for all it was simply adorned with only a flounce of Belgian lace, was nicely cut, suggesting her curves without displaying them immoderately. A light flush stained her cheeks, the veriest hint of a smile curved her mouth, and a sparkle lit her eyes. In short, she looked a beautiful girl preparing to enter a room full of people she expected to enjoy. Certainly nothing at all about her betrayed the least sign of her sordid relations with Kendall.

Dominic had given some thought to what her reaction would be when she saw him. He had expected surprise, embarrassment, dismay, or any combination thereof, but he had not once considered she might faint. When she had turned pale as a ghost, he had nearly started up to try to catch her before she cracked her head on a table, when the artist, Mr. Aubermont, her father's friend, had stepped in to clasp her hands, look anxiously at her, and take her to a seat.

Under the older man's appreciative gaze, she had, not surprisingly, recovered quickly enough. She'd almost all her color back. There was an adoring group about her. She was smiling and chatting as securely as if everyone in the room thought what she wished them to think of her.

Dominic only just kept himself from scowling. It did not suit him at all that she, the evildoer, should appear in such good spirits, while he, the almost entirely innocent party, fell into a blacker and blacker mood. Had she sat chastened in the corner, he'd have felt differently. He might have been able to forgive her, or failing that, to ignore her.

As it was, his awareness of her was intense. He could not be pleased, was not pleased, and he determined to put the little strumpet in her place. She seemed to have forgotten there was one present who knew her for what she was, and could, at any time he chose, have her sent from London in complete disgrace. He would remind her.

* * *

It was Mr. Aubermont, in the end, who united Sarah with Dominic. After a musical interlude Lady Sophia had arranged for her guests' pleasure, Sarah had become separated from her teacher, a condition he remedied not long after when he sought her out expressly to present her to Lord Matthew Beresford.

By then Sarah knew the identity of the older gentleman before whom Ravensby was again standing, but she could arrive at no excuse to avoid being taken to him. Her heart tripping almost painfully, she went forth, like a lamb being led to slaughter, determined she would ignore Ravensby completely.

A small group was gathered around the old man with the bristling brows. Lady Ruth was there, the Viscount Malthorpe, who seemed to be everywhere, a paunchy gentleman with a loftily inclined nose named Sir Percival, and, of course, Lady Sophia standing by Ravensby.

Sarah grew so wretchedly aware of the earl, as Mr. Aubermont brought her forward, she'd the wild notion the whole group would guess her preoccupation. He stood across from her, tall and formidable as always. She thought his darkened gaze was upon her, and strangely, though she had dreaded the thought of meeting his eyes ever again, now she was so close to him, it was all she could do not to look up at him.

When Mr. Aubermont presented her, Lord Matthew said something gruff about having read a paper of her father's. Sarah replied honestly that her father would be pleased to know a man of Lord Matthew's standing had shown an interest in his work.

Sarah searched for some excuse to depart after so little time, but the Viscount Malthorpe spoke first, clearing his throat and remarking in his oily way, "My dear Miss Marlowe, Mr. Aubermont tells us you yourself work in watercolors."

Her thoughts on Ravensby, Sarah almost missed the remark. Watercolors. The viscount had mentioned watercolors. She made herself nod. "Yes, I do enjoy working with them, though I've none of Mr. Aubermont's genius."

"Genius, my dear! That is too much. You pay me back in my own coin." Sarah could smile a little at Mr. Aubermont as he shook his finger at her. "And you must not diminish your

Emma Lange

efforts. You are my pupil, after all, and you record nature with a rare sensitivity.''

It was high praise. Sarah inclined her head, as she felt her cheeks heat. "Thank you, sir."

Lady Sophia's eyes narrowed. It had not been her plan that Sarah Marlowe would receive acclaim that evening. She had made the decision to invite the girl to her gathering after a "friend" had reported seeing Dominic driving Miss Marlowe in his gig. She could not confront him, demand to know his intentions toward the ambitious chit. She'd not the right to question him yet, but she could expose the girl for lacking entirely the depth and assurance to mingle easily with truly discriminating people. That Miss Marlowe was not only at ease but also shining among them was enough to make Lady Sophia unreasonably angry.

"Is it nature inspires your efforts, Miss Marlowe?" she inquired, her high voice sounding rather more bored than not.

Sarah nodded, a little surprised Lady Sophia would condescend to address her. "I work on other subjects as well, but it is when I am attempting to capture a natural scene I feel the strongest communion with my work."

"Communion?" There was the faintest amazement threading Lady Sophia's languid echo. "My dear, that is a strong term, indeed. I don't doubt you subscribe to Rousseau's theories, then, perhaps even believe in the noble savage?"

With the merest flicker of frustration darkening her eyes, Lady Sophia ignored Lady Ruth's demand to know who the devil "that man" was, and waited, her eyes upon Miss Marlowe, for an admission of ignorance.

"Rousseau, my lady?" Sarah inquired as expected, but did not wait for a reply. "No. I find Jean-Jacques Rousseau rather too single-minded. In my estimation a person's character is formed by a variety of forces, proximity to or distance from civilization being only one. However, I am certain there are noble savages, just as I am certain there are savage nobles."

Mr. Aubermont smiled widely, while Lady Ruth exclaimed in congratulation, and even Lord Matthew hrrmphed, "Well said! Well said!'' Lady Sophia's response was to cease smiling the superior smile that had put Sarah's hackles up.

But Sarah scarcely noticed. It was beyond her powers not to look to Ravensby. Chin up, she met his dark gold eyes and knew with an explosion of gratification her hit had registered. Something leapt in the air between them, and Sarah could not have looked away from him had she wanted to. No one else seemed to exist as she watched the earl lift his glass to her.

"You've the point, Miss Marlowe. Rank is, indeed, a superficial attribute and no more a guarantee of character than . . . why, than a person's outward appearance."

Holding her gaze effortlessly as he mocked her, Dominic then lifted his hand and set to slowly, deliberately, even sensuously stroking the rim of his glass.

Sarah stood as if rooted to the floor by his suggestive gesture. Just so had he caressed the nape of her neck.

The hot sting of color rushing to her cheeks reminded her they'd an audience. Abruptly she turned to Lord Matthew, and curtsying, mumbled some excuse to flee.

But though she succeeded in putting the room between her and Ravensby, Sarah seemed to see his hand everywhere, drawing lazy circles around and around, and his eyes! Triumph had flashed in them, mocking and hateful, when she had gone red as a beet, her little victory over Lady Sophia ashes in her mouth.

16

"Yes, Sarah! The gray now has precisely the pearly, luminous quality of an overcast day in Cumberland. I am amazed you could capture it so exactly."

Sarah looked from Mr. Aubermont, who was bending over

her easel studying the work he had given her to do that afternoon, to the window. "The view from your window was of considerable assistance." She summoned a smile as she glanced back at her teacher. "The sky has been heavy with clouds for days now."

"And one can see them marvelously from here." Mr. Aubermont's expression of intense concentration became a broad smile. "Is not this spacious, airy attic a grand benefit of becoming 'all the rage'? Imagine! I, who have never had more than a room to call my own, have now three floors and a garden! And three servants to augment my faithful Crevins. All male, of course," he added with a twinkle in his eye. "Crevins cannot abide females, as you know."

Sarah's mouth turned up. "Maddie calls him a 'dour devil.' "

"Your faithful Maddie enjoys the old devil's tea cakes, however, and the nap she invariably takes after eating them." They both glanced down the length of the room to Maddie, who dozed in a high wing chair that had been brought in especially for her. "I am afraid her nap is nearly at an end. If you are to meet your aunt and cousins in time to see the marvelous balloon ascension, you must go soon."

"I've only this outlining to do," Sarah replied, returning to her work. "And I would finish it, as I'll not be able to return for several days."

"Your Season is as enjoyable as a beautiful girl's Season should be, then?" Mr. Aubermont asked from across the room, where he fished out a small framed picture from among several others.

Grateful she was not being observed, Sarah made no effort to smile and only answered a succinct, "Yes, we are very busy every day," as she carefully edged the trunk of a tree with a thin, dark line.

"I have heard that no less a gentleman than the Marquess of Lisle is paying you marked attention, my dear." Sarah looked up then, meeting Mr. Aubermont's eyes, and her teacher smiled mischievously. "You look surprised, but I assure you it is quite the *on-dit* that you may soon be a marchioness. I shall even tell you who told me: Lady Ruth Dacres."

"Oh! I . . . I did not . . ."

"Realize you were a subject of interest to the lady?" Mr. Aubermont supplied as Sarah groped for a response. "Allow me to assure you that you are. You befriended her niece, I believe, and that has quite put you in Lady Dacres' good books. She could not sing your praises strongly enough when her brother brought her one day."

"Ravensby?" Sarah asked, as if Lady Ruth had dozens of brothers.

Mr. Aubermont nodded decisively. "A very interesting man, that one. Strong and forceful, but with a sense of humor too, and sensitivity." The older man laughed. "He admired my work, so you see I can be assured he'd a sensitive eye. And he admired yours as well, my dear."

"Mine?" Sarah went very still. "What do you mean?"

"The earl found this by the wall there." Mr. Aubermont produced the watercolor he had found earlier. It was a portrait of Becky Ponsby that Sarah had painted as a gift for Mr. and Mrs. Ponsby. "He recognized little Becky at once, and appreciated how well her character was captured. You cannot imagine his surprise when I told him it was not I had done the work, but you."

A fierce thrill of pride seized Sarah. So! Ravensby had been brought up short to find he did not know everything about her. Would he, as a consequence, be prompted to question his current demeaning assumptions about her? She swung back to her easel. No! He was too certain and too arrogant to admit himself wrong.

A knock on the door heralded the arrival of Mr. Aubermont's man, Crevins. "A Mr. and Mrs. Martin are below, sir. Will you see them?"

"The Martins?" Mr. Aubermont demanded of Crevins' impassive face. "But they were to come tomorrow. It is the Earl of Ravensby who made an appointment for today."

"Ravensby?" Sarah's question was sharp enough that Mr. Aubermont looked at her in a little surprise.

"Did I not say he was coming to choose a gift for his mother's birthday? He should be here at any moment. But now I've these . . ."

He waved his hand vaguely, and taking his cue, Crevins supplied, "Martins."

"Well, I must go," Sarah announced, standing at once.

"But I thought you meant to finish your work." Mr. Aubermont looked bemused. "And as you know the earl, you could entertain him a moment while I see to the Martins. I cannot afford to ignore the pair, you see, for though they are exceedingly fatiguing, they are, as well, exceedingly wealthy."

Sarah gave her tutor a sympathetic smile, but she remained firm. "I am sorry, sir. I cannot stay today. You remember I am to meet my aunt."

"Heavens! I did forget. I cannot say what is happening to my mind. The balloon ascension. We were only just speaking of it."

Sarah, having already glanced to see that Maddie had been roused by Crevins' advent, nodded briskly. "And I've just time to reach St. George's Parade in North Audley Street if I depart now. Crevins, will you find a hansom for Maddie and me?"

"And, Crevins, do tell the pair below I shall be with them as soon as I can." Swinging about as Crevins departed on his various missions, Mr. Aubermont gave Sarah an apologetic look. "Would you mind seeing yourself out, my dear? If I wash up quickly, it is possible I can have the Mervins on their way before the earl arrives."

"The Martins, dear sir," Sarah corrected him with a grin. "And of course Maddie and I can see ourselves out."

"Good. Then I shall see you a few days hence, and don't forget Becky's picture. I may find myself selling it off, if you leave it."

Even before Mr. Aubermont was gone, Sarah began unwrapping the voluminous apron she wore to protect her clothes. "Have you my reticule and parasol, Maddie?" she asked from within the folds of the thing. "And shawl?"

"Aye, they're all here." Maddie, still a little foggy from her nap, looked vaguely around at the items tossed upon a nearby table. "But I donae see your hat, lamb."

"Perhaps it fell off the table," Sarah called out over her shoulder as she washed her hands. Maddie shook her head, after a look, however, and Sarah dried her hands quickly to join the search. "Blast it! Where did I put the thing?" she muttered, when she did not find it on the hatrack or beside Maddie's chair.

"Calm yourself, now. There's no need fer swearin'. It's here some'eres." Maddie lowered herself ponderously to look under a rough table by the door. "At least I think 'tis," she amended beneath her breath.

Sarah felt a rising panic. She had not seen Ravensby since the night of Lady Sophia's soiree. Evidently he believed his sister's presence at Anne's side left him free to do as he pleased. And what he pleased to do was not to attend the bland entertainments to which his niece was invited. Anne said he had been once or twice to Lord Matthew Beresford's, but most evenings he went out with Lord Richard and stayed out with his friend until well into the next day.

A bitter expression darkened Sarah's face. He could spend night after night steeped in debauchery, and what was the result? The young ladies to whom Anne described his late hours and vague destinations tittered with approval. But let Sarah allow or respond to one kiss, and she was considered fair game for public mockery.

Sarah bit her lip. How well he had put her in her place. He had not only sent her flying in cowardly retreat that night with his double-edged words, his suggestive gestures, and that unholy, mocking gleam lighting his eyes, but every time she recalled the scene, he succeeded anew in piercing her to the quick. Oh, but she did not want to encounter him again. Would not!

"Ah, here 'tis."

"Oh, Maddie! Thank you."

"There, now, lamb." Maddie looked rather startled by the fervency of Sarah's gratitude. " 'Tis only a hat, after all."

Urgency moving her, Sarah clapped her hat on her head and gathered up her other possessions. Becky's portrait was nearly forgotten and had to be rushed back for as Maddie muttered something grim about haste, Sarah did not listen. Jerking her hat ribbons into a bow, she flew out the door and down the stairs.

"Wait, now!" Maddie called out. "I canna take the stairs like a young . . . Ah!"

"Maddie!" Sarah spun at the sound of a great clattering on
the narrow stairs to the attic. "Maddie! Oh, Maddie!" she
exclaimed in dismay when she found the old woman in a heap
on the narrow landing, her leg turned at an odd angle and her
eyes closed fast. Ravensby forgotten, Sarah knelt by her, and
untying Maddie's hat, threw it aside. "Maddie! Do you hear
me?" When the maid did not respond, Sarah jumped up to go
in search of assistance.

"Sarah? What has happened?" It was Mr. Aubermont,
Crevins behind him.

"Maddie slipped upon the stairs! She has lost awareness, and
oh, look at her leg!"

"Now, then, calm yourself, my dear," Mr. Aubermont
cautioned as Crevins knelt by Maddie and in expert fashion lifted
her eyelids, then examined her leg. "Crevins knows what he
is about. Many's the time in foreign places I have relied upon
him rather than trust a local quack."

"She's bumped her head a bit and twisted her ankle, no
more," the wiry servant turned to say.

"Let us take her down to the guest room, then, where you
may attend to her, Crevins."

Maddie was no lightweight, and it took the men some little
time to get her to the Spartan but clean room Mr. Aubermont
kept for guests. When Crevins was once again attending to his
patient, Mr. Aubermont pulled Sarah out into the hall. "It will
be best if you await results in my sitting room, my dear. It is
just here." He showed her into a modest, simply furnished room
situated at the front of the house. "Crevins does his best when
he is quite unhindered. Here, I believe a little of this would not
be amiss." He poured some brandy from a decanter into a glass
and handed it to Sarah. "You look so pale, my dear, but I wish
you would not worry. Crevins is excellent with sprained ankles
and mild concussions. Alas, I cannot stay!" he exclaimed,
suddenly recalling his guests below. "You will be well, if I
return to the Marvins, Sarah? They are on the point of
purchasing a less-than-favorite work that I admit I deliberately
made as expensive as I could in the hope the ridiculous price
would impress them."

His little joke succeeded in making Sarah summon a smile.

"Please do go down," she urged. "I shall be quite fine. But you will ask Crevins to give me a report?"

"I will," Mr. Aubermont assured her.

Sarah swallowed a portion of the brandy, scarcely aware, in her agitation, what she did. It was her fault Maddie lay hurt! Heedless of anyone else, she had rushed to escape Mr. Aubermont's before Ravensby came, and now Maddie lay in pain.

The sound of a carriage drawing up before the house interrupted Sarah's self-recriminations. Heart in her throat, she took care to stay back in the shadows as she peeped out the window. It was Ravensby. Her heart began to pound painfully, though all she could see was the top of his dark head and the strong, powerful set of his shoulders.

He spoke to his coachman briefly, then turned. Sarah drew back sharply, but not so far she could not examine his harsh, arrogant features. She looked for signs of dissipation and was disappointed. His strong face was as arresting as ever, his expression as dauntingly cool.

Agitated, Sarah resumed her pacing. He was not so like Lucifer by day, more like the archangel Gabriel, flaming sword at the ready to rid the world of sinners. She was being absurd. She knew it, and downed the remainder of the brandy, seeking some warmth. A rush of heat seared her throat but did not wash away Ravensby's image. She could see his hand making those lazy circles on his claret glass that night. It was the sheerest luck no one else had followed her riveted gaze and guessed the significance of the gesture. Just as it was her good fortune Ravensby himself could never know his gesture had, despite everything, the power to make the skin at the nape of her neck prickle.

The sound of the door opening sent Sarah whirling about, expecting Crevins and news of Maddie. Instead it was Ravensby's piercing gaze she met. And the glass in her hand cracked.

"Oh!"

"The devil!"

Sarah stared blankly down at the jagged cut marking her palm. She was not wearing her gloves. They lay forgotten on a table with her hat, reticule, and shawl. There had been nothing to protect her from the sharp glass, and now blood began to well from the cut.

Half-stunned, she was scarcely aware of Ravensby striding quickly across the room and collecting the fragments of glass she held, but she flinched when he took her hand to examine it. "Don't be ridiculous," he growled curtly. "You need assistance. Sit down before your knees give way." They gave way, and Sarah sat. "Are you on the point of swooning?"

In truth Sarah did not know. She felt light-headed, but she was not certain that feeling stemmed from the cut to her palm. She had never fainted at the sight of blood before.

She met Ravensby's intent gaze and shook her head. "Very well, then. I am going to pick out these bits of glass before going for a basin and water. Hold still. I cannot get them if you shy away. Look out the window."

She did, biting her lip at the stinging pain. He worked quickly but carefully, holding her hand in a strong, firm clasp. Did he believe the pain she experienced was as much as she deserved?

She shot Ravensby an angry glance. No. He was not that cruel. There was not satisfaction in his expression. He looked rather grim about the mouth, in fact.

"I want you to press here." He glanced up to find her watching him, and gestured to the lower part of her palm. "Hold tightly while I go for water and bandages. You must do it to arrest the bleeding. Can you?"

Sarah nodded again, then Ravensby showed her precisely where to hold and how firmly. "Don't let up." He rose, then paused. "And lean back." He nudged her shoulder, tipping her against the back of the chair. "You stand less chance of fainting like that," he told her.

Sarah watched him stride from the room, then closed her eyes. Her palm had begun to hurt, and she concentrated upon the sensation. Better that than to think how the mere sight of Ravensby had caused her to snap a glass in two.

It seemed only a moment before he returned, carrying a tray laden with a basin, towels, soap, bandages, and salve. Sarah wondered why Crevins did not come, but was too drained to ask. Ravensby did seem to know what he was about. Carefully and efficiently he set about washing her hand first. When her blood turned the water in the basin pink, she did not need to be told to look away. The soap stung, and he said nothing when she curled her hand into a fist, waited only a moment, then gently nudged her hand open again.

She resolved to be braver and held her hand almost stiff as she concentrated on the window ledge, where a sparrow was hopping about. A sudden burning, however, overcame her determination. Catching her breath, she jerked back to him.

Dominic looked up, gaze level. "It is the salve. Aubermont's man said it would burn at first, but would help the cut to heal. The discomfort shouldn't last long."

Perversely, when he offered some sympathy, Sarah rejected it. "It's nothing," she told him stonily.

He gave her a long look, but said nothing before returning to his task. In only a little, he had wound a clean bandage around her palm and tied it off. "That should do you. The bleeding has stopped, and as the cut was not overly deep, I think it will heal quickly enough."

Sarah concentrated on the pattern of the bandage, not the hand cradling hers. Still, she registered that beside her skin, his looked bronzed; by her fine-boned hand, his looked large, if no less well-kept. "Thank you, Lord Ravensby."

Her eyes fixed upon her hand, Sarah did not see the earl look at her, only felt his eyes on her. "It was the least I could do." He paused, perhaps waiting for her to look up, but Sarah kept her lashes lowered. As they were long and thick, there was no possibility of their gazes meeting. "I did not mean to startle you so."

Still Sarah resisted the impulse to meet his eyes. By way of response she lifted her shoulders negligently. "I was upset over Maddie." Her voice sounded hoarse, and she cleared it.

"Aubermont's man said your nurse is resting well." That brought her gaze up. She was pale, her eyes dark and wary. "As it is his opinion she must rest, Aubermont has suggested that I convey you to your aunt, while Maddie, I believe it is, remains here. She—"

"No!" When one of Ravensby's eyebrows arched, Sarah shook her head. "I do not wish to leave Maddie."

"She has been given laudanum and will not know whether you are here or not. Your aunt, I have been given to understand, on the other hand, is awaiting you at St. George's Parade and will worry where you are."

That was true. There was no denying Aunt Vinnie would be overset when Sarah did not appear for the balloon ascension at the time and place they'd arranged. "I shall send her a note," Sarah declared, stubbornness tingling her voice.

Perhaps it was that tone that pricked Dominic into returning firmly, "You need the air. The ride will do you good, and you will enjoy the spectacle."

"I don't want to go!"

A light flashed in the earl's golden-brown eyes, and it was not an amused light. "You mean you do not wish to go with me. Isn't that it, Miss Marlowe? There's no need for ceremony between us, I think. We may as well speak plainly, and therefore, I shall reply by assuring you that I make it a practice to refrain from ravishing wounded girls. You will be quite safe with me—if you can trust yourself."

Dominic derived a grim, harsh satisfaction from the scarlet that flooded her cheeks. How telling her reaction was.

But then the excessive color receded, leaving her paler than before. No less beautiful, though, in her high-necked muslin of fresh periwinkle blue.

Aware suddenly that he was staring, Dominic wrenched his gaze away. "My carriage is waiting, Miss Marlowe. I imagine you will wish to speak to your maid a moment, and then I shall meet you below."

Eyes sparking at his arrogance, Sarah opened her mouth to say, simply, no, but once again the door swung open abruptly. "You are not badly hurt, Sarah?" Mr. Aubermont rushed in looking anxiously at Sarah. "Crevins has only just told me you cut yourself. I hope it is not your right hand!"

Sarah smiled a little at his artist's concern. "No, it is my left. I have broken your glass, however."

"That is nothing! As long as you are not permanently damaged. How lucky that you came when you did, my lord." Aubermont looked to Ravensby, and if he wondered why the earl did not rush to agree, he did not remark the man's lapse aloud. ''Sarah will set the style at the balloon ascension with your bandage, it is so well done. Speaking of which, you had best go, my dear. I am concerned your aunt be beside herself.''

''Miss Marlowe was just going along to bid her maid farewell.''

Ravensby looked to Sarah. His features were impassive, but she thought she detected a faint gleam at the very back of his eyes. He knew, as did she, Mr. Aubermont's arrival had tipped the balance in his favor. To anyone but Ravensby it would have been a sign of madness had she maintained she would prefer to send her aunt into a paroxysm of worry rather than abide the earl's company.

Still, Sarah did not have to like the only choice she had, and so she informed the earl with her eyes as she stood. Then, turning to Mr. Aubermont, she summoned a smile. ''Maddie and I have placed quite a burden on you, sir, and I am grateful for the care you've given us both. You will convey my thanks to Crevins?''

''Of course, my dear. And think nothing of it! Keeping your good Maddie for the night only means I shall have the pleasure of seeing you tomorrow when you come to fetch her.''

Sarah did not need to stand on tiptoe to reach his cheek. Mr. Aubermont was not overly tall. Like some gentlemen. Her kiss made him beam as he professed himself delighted he could aid a beauty in distress, and flushing a little from his praise, Sarah excused herself to look in on Maddie.

''The old devil'll care for me,'' Maddie assured her charge. ''Don't ye worry. And get on, lamb! Yer aunt'll be worried sick.''

Sarah finally accepted how useless she would be to Maddie when the old woman promptly nodded off. Giving her maid a final kiss on the cheek, Sarah murmured something about needing her more than the reverse, then went down to find Ravensby striding impatiently about the entryway.

17

Sarah allowed Ravensby to hand her into the carriage, but took care to settle herself as close as possible to the far window. He made no attempt to crowd her. Indeed, as they rolled smoothly away from Mr. Aubermont's town house, he laid Becky's portrait between them.

"You forgot this, I think."

She glanced at him. In the confines of the carriage he seemed more overpowering than ever—and that even though he was not attending to her. He was studying the portrait.

It agitated Sarah that she wished to know his thoughts. "Thank you," she said coolly, and determined at least to appear unconcerned, she turned to gaze out the window.

"I like it very much." Sarah clenched her good hand, hidden in her skirts. There. She knew, and it did not matter. He complimented her almost grudgingly. "You've managed to convey how the child can be at once older and younger than her years."

Sarah had worked hard to capture that very dichotomy in her little cousin. It was what had made Becky an interesting subject to attempt, and it could not but be immensely satisfying to know she had succeeded in conveying her thoughts.

"I admire the quality of the light as well," Ravensby continued, seeming unaffected by the fact that Sarah stared mutely out her window. "You've caught the subtle intensity of colors at eveningtime without overdoing them."

The coloration was another aspect of the work upon which Sarah had made a great effort. Inspired by Turner, she had tried to make her colors vivid without rendering them garish.

"Thank you." She flicked Ravensby a brief glance and immediately looked away. He was regarding her now, and with an intensity that would have unsettled her anywhere, but did so particularly when she was already desperately conscious of being alone in a small space with him.

"Who the deuce are you, Sarah Marlowe?" Surprise jerked her gaze back to him. "Are you the fresh, unguarded beauty I rescued that first day?" Caught despite herself, Sarah waited warily to hear who else she might be. It was as well she prepared herself. "Or the passionate woman who went readily from Kendall's arms to mine, or yet, the skilled, sensitive painter of this work?"

When Ravensby gestured to the portrait, Sarah followed his movement with her eyes, unable to hold his gaze while her cheeks were aflame.

"I do not know why you ask your question." She addressed Becky's likeness, her voice somewhat thick. "You have decided against the first possibility already, and of the final two, while you may allow them both, only one, the former, is of real significance to you."

Swiftly she looked a challenge at him. He did not deny what she said was true, only continued to stare broodingly at her, as if he were considering how he might stamp out those traits of which he disapproved.

With a frustrated groan, Sarah turned her back on his scrutiny. It galled her he did not, now he had her before him and they'd the time, bother to inquire further whether his version of the events of that night was, indeed, correct.

Silence settled heavily between them, but though the tension strained her nerves, Sarah resigned herself to enduring it for the remainder of their trip. There was nothing more to be said.

Oddly, then, given the keenness with which she felt that silence, when Ravensby did speak, she did not at first take in what he said and had to ask him to repeat it.

"I said that if it has concerned you, you may give up worrying whether I intend to reveal your indiscretions to Lisle. I do not."

Sarah stared. She had not considered the possibility. "Why, thank you, my lord!" she spat out so bitterly, his brow shot up. "Thank you so much for not repeating what is, in all, the merest speculation on your part. How gallant you are! Thoughtful, too, gentlemanly, even decent!"

"You were seen!"

"I could not have been!" she protested, equally adamant. "I was not with Captain Kendall."

"There is no point in lying! I have seen no other girl so infatuated with him she would sneak up to his rooms."

"I tell you I did nothing of the sort!" Sarah slapped her good hand on the seat for emphasis. "I am not infatuated with the captain, nor do I have the least intention of taking him as my lover, if I marry . . . whomever I marry! I repeat, sir. I did not meet Kendall that night."

"You would have me believe that you were in Kendall's wing of the house by mistake perhaps?" Dominic shot back. "Good God, I am not such a fool! Nor am I so naive as to credit that an innocent girl could possibly respond as you did in my arms."

She wrenched her gaze away, biting her lip as she felt another wretched blush give her away. Always on that point he had her. She had responded to him! Only she was innocent. She had never responded with anything approaching abandon to anyone else. He would never believe that, though . . . and if he did, there would be the question why she responded uniquely to him.

Dominic watched Sarah wrench her gaze back to her window with something less than the triumph he ought to have felt at having the last word. Perhaps it was that she had lifted her bandaged hand to push irritably at a stray golden tendril that had come loose from the ribbon she wore. Watching, he was reminded how he had felt when he heard the glass she held crack in the stillness of that room. And then, dear heaven, the sight of her blood welling from the cut!

Would a jade, even a newly turned jade, react so violently to his mere appearance at her door? Could he be wrong? The servant had said . . . Abruptly Dominic banged his hand hard against his fist and growled aloud, "I don't know what the deuce to believe!"

And he did not. Whittingham's footman had not said the girl had golden hair and was . . . beautiful. Very beautiful, Dominic amended, looking down into the startled sapphire-blue eyes Sarah had turned up to him. Beautiful and beguiling, and unable to deny she had been in Kendall's wing of the house pinning up her loosened hair.

Sarah made no move to plead her case. Arrogant as he was, he would decide for himself, and if his thoughts upset him as they seemed to do, so much the better. He deserved to suffer. She had. And for what? For the good opinion of a man who, it seemed, had been half set against her from the first.

"What does it matter anyway?" Sarah heard with astonishment the question tumble from a tongue she had directed to be still. "You intend to marry Lady Sophia, and I . . ." She waved her hand, intending to indicate she did not know her precise future, but paying scant attention to what she did, she slapped it against the side of the carriage.

"Oooh!" She caught it to her, then uttered a short, telling, "Blast!"

"Is it bleeding again?" Dominic demanded, leaning across her and simply taking possession of her hand as if he'd some right to it. A few drops of fresh blood glistened brightly on the white linen. "Damn."

The gruffness of the single syllable affected Sarah despite herself. "It is only bleeding a little. Nothing to be concerned over."

Ravensby seemed to study the stained bandage a long moment. When he looked up, his expression was exceedingly grim. "It does concern me that you sustained a painful cut because I walked into that room. I'd not have you score your hand every time you encounter me."

Sarah's fingers curled involuntarily at the thought, and Dominic, as if to protect her, encircled her balled fist with both his hands. Sarah could not seem to pull her eyes from the sight. "No," she said slowly. "No, I suppose I cannot be breaking everyone's crystal."

She knew she must pull her hand free of him. His touch unsettled her, as had the low, rough note in his voice when he told her he'd not have her hurt herself on his account.

Almost against her will, it seemed, she lifted her gaze to his. And caught her breath. His eyes had turned a smoky, dark gold. She knew he was aware of her. As she was of him. Heart pounding hard, as if compelled by his eyes, she leaned forward. His eyes were alight now . . .

No! Oh, no! Sarah shrank back abruptly, uncertain whether

she cried out aloud or not, but it did not matter. Her retreat
had shattered the moment.

She dared not look at Ravensby as she held her breath, waiting
for she knew not what. But nothing happened. No attack came,
nor spate of recriminations. He settled back in his seat silent
as a judge.

When she darted a glance at him, Sarah found he sat with
one foot resting on the seat opposite, his arm draped over a bent
knee, looking out his window as if he had forgotten her
completely.

Though Sarah had been telling herself for days all she wanted
was for Ravensby to ignore her, she'd an urge to pound his
chest, engage him, establish she was worthy of consideration,
even an angry consideration. Anything would be preferable to
being dismissed as easily as if she were merely another one of
the lightskirts in whom he and Lord Richard had undoubtedly
indulged that week.

"And you are certain Maddie is not badly hurt, my dear?"

Sarah nodded reassuringly. "Yes, Aunt Vinnie. Mr. Aubermont's man, Crevins, is very capable. She only needs rest
now."

Satisfied, Mrs. Ponsby turned to lay a plump hand upon the
arm of Sarah's escort. "My lord, we do thank you! What a
marvelous bit of luck that you happened to go along to Mr.
Aubermont's house at that very time. We were becoming
anxious over Sarah's whereabouts, as you can well imagine,
for she was some half of an hour late, and Sarah is always so
punctual."

"I am glad I could be of service, Mrs. Ponsby."

"It is a miracle Thompkins found you!" Kitty exclaimed from
where she stood beside Johnny Carstairs despite a warning look
from her mother. "With this throng, he might as easily have
missed you as not."

"Thompkins was sitting above the crowd on the carriage
box," Sarah explained to the group that included not only the
Ponsbys, as she had expected, but also Johnny Carstairs and
the Marquess of Lisle, who had, it seemed, arrived together.
"He recognized my parasol."

"We're lucky the man's a good eye," Mr. Ponsby remarked. "I never imagined so many people would come out. Had we not chanced into Lisle, here, we'd have been stuck in the crowd below. He sent out a man this morning to stake out this spot on the rise."

As it was the highest point all around the parade, and most of it was covered with dense bushes, the small clearing in which they stood comfortably apart from the throng was the only really good vantage point for watching the ascension unless one cared to stand in the forefront of hundreds of jostling people.

Sarah, as a result, thought the marquess could be pardoned for the rather smug bow he gave to Mr. Ponsby. "I was on hand for the ascension in 1807, and learned then how little I care for a crowd. Were one thing to go awry, they would trample everything in their path." Deliberately he lifted Sarah's hand, patted it, and settled it in the crook of his elbow. "Couldn't have that."

Dominic watched Sarah reward the marquess with a warm look, and heard her say something to the effect that she had not expected to see Lisle at all. Lisle replied that he had not known she meant to witness the ascension until Mr. Carstairs had made mention of the Ponsbys' plans the evening before, after Miss Marlowe had departed whatever entertainment it was they had all enjoyed together.

Dominic considered making his farewells, though the balloon was still filling with air. It had not been his intention to join the Ponsbys. He had meant to leave Miss Marlowe with her party and depart. But she had not been met by her party, only a thin, stooping, elderly coachman, and he had not trusted the man to see her through the crowd safely.

"Have you seen a balloon ascension ever before, Lord Ravensby?" Charles Ponsby, excited beyond his ability to contain himself, bounced up to tug on the earl's coat sleeve, a liberty he felt it perfectly within his rights to take, as they were, in his estimation at least, fast friends.

His mother, unaware of the depth of the bond that can be established when a maze is conquered, cried in dismayed tones, "Charles!" but Dominic found the boy's enthusiasm a pleasant antidote to his mood and smiled.

"No, Charles. It has never been my pleasure to watch an ascension before. Have you seen one?"

"Never! And Johnny knows Mr. Sadler!"

Dominic looked to Johnny Carstairs, who was smiling at Charles's seeming non sequitur. "Sadler is the balloonist, my lord. You can just see him. He is the one in the green cap."

Out of the half-dozen men milling about the enormous billowing, brightly colored piece of fine linen struggling to stand upright, Dominic could discern that one wore something green upon his head.

"Johnny says he will need the cap and the coat, because it will be cold in the sky." Ravensby glanced down to see Becky Ponsby had come to insert herself between him and Miss Marlowe. He did not object. He was not crowded in the least. There was ample room for the child between them, for, of course, Miss Marlowe stood close to the marquess—and as far as possible, given the limited space on the hill, from him.

"Is that why there is a fire in the basketlike part?"

Sarah asked the question of young Becky, but it was Lisle who said, "The fire is to warm the air in the balloon and lift it."

Becky, finding the explanation insufficient, added gravely, "Hot air rises, Sarah."

"Ah, yes. Thank you, Becky."

Dominic could hear the smile in Sarah's voice, but he could not confirm she did smile, for she had tilted her parasol in such a way that her face was hidden from him. It was entirely probable she had deliberately blotted him from her sight.

Jaw tensing, Dominic thought of the chance they had missed to arrive at some understanding. He had thought it time to extend an olive branch, that they might banish at least some of the tension between them. He could not want her so agitated she hurt herself on his account, nor did he, for his part, wish to chance putting on another performance like the one he'd given at Sophy's. Not only had he taken Miss Marlowe down a peg, but he had sent her packing in such a way, he'd found Ruth considering him interestedly.

But they had not cleared the air. They'd magnetized it, instead.

He'd only had to take her hand in his to become aware of

her: the petallike softness of her skin, the sweet fragrance of her hair, the enticing curves of her body—and then she had looked up, her eyes flared wide, their depths turned a deep and liquid blue. It had taken all his power of will to keep from sweeping her up in his arms. Only the need to have her admit, aloud, her desire for him had held him back.

But she had resisted. Pulling back of a sudden, as if from a fire, she had pricked the bubble of desire, and he had subsided into his corner to brood upon the attraction over which he seemed to have no control at all.

What was he to do? He felt helpless and did not care for the feeling. He could not force her to be his mistress, could not even, seriously, consider that course. The Ponsbys were good, decent people, whatever she was.

Ask her to be his wife, then? Take her to his bed anytime he wanted? And then wonder how many others did the same when he was not about?

Great God, what a life that would be, to wonder of every man he met: has he enjoyed my wife's charms?

"Oh, look!"

Sarah's voice startling Dominic from his thoughts, he swung around to look at her. She had lowered her parasol completely as she, like the others, strained to watch the balloon shudder, then lift.

Suddenly, feeling his regard, Sarah turned and met Dominic's eyes. The interchange was brief, but nonetheless left her shaken. Everyone else disappeared from her awareness. Even Lisle, whose arm she held, could well have fallen off the face of the earth. Only Ravensby, tall and compelling, stood there, the breeze ruffling his dark hair, his amber eyes unreadable as they stared down at her. His jaw, alone, gave an indication of his thoughts, and it was set hard against her.

18

"Ah, here you are!" Lady Ruth greeted her brother and niece upon their return from a ride in the park with a wave. "I am glad you did not dally, my dears. As you can see, Sophy has dropped by to take tea with us."

"I was in the neighborhood." Lady Sophia addressed Dominic.

He lifted the languid hand she held out to his lips. "A happy coincidence, my dear."

Lady Ruth rang for the tea tray but did not allow herself to become so intent upon her hostess's duties that she neglected to watch her brother greet their unexpected guest. How polite he was, she mused, smiling to herself, and how very restrained.

Sophy seemed to think much the same thing, for there was the faintest flicker of impatience in the fashionable beauty's pale-blue eyes. But she had composed herself by the time Dominic was settled comfortably in his wing chair and turned to greet Anne. "You are looking well, my dear," she observed.

Lady Ruth found her guest's tone, laden with world-weary *ennui,* particularly grating at that moment, for it had the effect of unsettling Anne and making her, as she stammered her thanks, seem painfully unpolished.

But Lady Sophia's attention did not linger on Anne long. She looked back to Dominic as the tea tray was rolled in. "You and Richard have been quite the pair this fortnight and more, Dominic. I vow you seem like a married couple, you've been together so often!"

"He's a good fellow, Richard," was all Dominic seemed inclined to say before he looked off to accept a cup of tea from his butler.

Lady Ruth took her cup and settled back with enthusiasm. There was nothing like a good cup of tea, while being entertained by a polite sparring match, she thought. Dominic had been in Sophy's company only two or three times since he had returned from Langston's bedside, and it seemed the beauty had come to determine what he had been up to, if anything.

She did not waste much time returning to the subject. As she stirred her tea she gave Dominic a cajoling smile. "Richard is the worst tease! He will never satisfy my curiosity. Every night it is the same, 'Oh, we are only going round to White's, my dear.' "

Dominic chuckled. "That is Richard to the inch, Sophy."

Lady Ruth came within an inch of ruining her fun with outright applause. The entirely pleasant smile with which Dominic punctuated his evasion was perfect theater.

Lady Sophia was not so amused, and assumed a slightly pouting expression. "I declare, all you men are tight as clams! But I've a suspicion you smile so mysteriously because you have been nowhere more interesting than a dusty dull club every night."

All night? Lady Ruth appended in fascinated silence.

Dominic, however, smiled in agreement with Lady Sophia. "And all the while we desperately hope the world will think the worst of us. Now, tell me of you, my dear. I'm certain you have been much in demand."

Match to Dominic! Lady Ruth looked with approval at her brother, though Lady Sophia was not quite rolled up.

"Well, Percy Kitely has been very gallant, escorting me about," she said with studied indifference. "He was a friend of Neil's, you know."

"He's the fellow who thinks Richard's taste in dress is too plain?"

Lady Sophia looked rather blank. "I don't know that he's ever commented on Richard's taste in clothes to me, but Percy is always dressed to the nines."

"Will he be escorting you to Lady Sefton's birthday ball, Sophy? Or are you planning to go at all? Anne's dragged a promise from me that I put in my appearance. She'd a rather powerful inducement."

He smiled at Anne, who blushed. "Uncle Dominic!"

Dominic only grinned at her embarrassment and explained

with obvious pleasure, "Anne has met a young man who has taken her fancy."

"And who is this paragon, my dear?" asked Lady Sophia as Anne dragged her mortified gaze from her uncle to their guest.

"Uncle Dominic is speaking of the Viscount Evensham, my lady. Sarah Marlowe introduced us." Unable to think what to say when Lady Sophia's brow lifted, Anne added inconsequentially, "She thought we would suit, as the viscount is an enthusiastic hunter."

"A most generous girl, Sarah Marlowe!" Lady Ruth exclaimed to see what entertainment the remark might provoke. "And a prodigious matchmaker."

"I rather think Miss Marlowe herself may be in need of matchmaking services just now." Something in Lady Sophia's tone caused Lady Ruth's gaze to sharpen. "You were not at the Averlys' last evening, Ruth, and have not heard the latest *on-dit,* I think?"

Lady Ruth shook her head, wary of the knowing smile playing around Lady Sophia's mouth. "No. What is the latest gossip?"

Lady Sophia paused to smooth the long sleeve of her afternoon dress before she glanced up. "It would seem that Lisle has thought better of paying the girl his addresses. Though they both attended the Averlys' soiree last evening, the man noticeably kept his distance. It caused quite a buzzing, everyone being so certain he was on the point of asking for her. He was queried on his change of heart, but Lisle's a gentleman and brushed off the questions, even left the affair early. The general agreement is, however, that he must have discovered some scandal about the child."

"Scandal?" Lady Ruth snorted contemptuously. "I take leave to doubt that. A more charming girl I have never met. "No, no. Sophy, if Lisle's decided against paying his addresses, then he did so because she advised him his suit was hopeless. He was the one smitten there, not she."

Lady Sophia gave a light, dismissive laugh. "You do not think she was smitten with Lisle's title, Ruth? Why would she undertake the expense of a come-out in town if she did not desire to marry a peer? If she'd only wanted a simple Mister, she could have found him wherever it is she hails from."

"Cumberland," Anne said in a strained voice. "Sarah's home is in Cumberland. And though I cannot say why Sarah came to town or anything about her relations with Lord Lisle, I . . . I never thought they suited very well."

"Monstrously, in fact," Lady Ruth cried, saving Anne, who had begun to wilt before the faintly incredulous expression Lady Sophia turned on her. "The boy's not without his merits, I know, but he wasn't up to her."

Lady Sophia laughed, astonished. "Not up to her, Ruth? I see you are determined to be eccentric." Giving up on Lady Ruth, she turned to arch a delicately plucked brow at Dominic. "But what of you, my dear? You've not weighed in with an opinion. Think you the girl threw over the marquess, or that the marquess discovered some past stain as yet secret from the rest of us?"

Dominic had been studying his tea perhaps in the hope a stray leaf might reveal whether Lisle had, indeed, discovered the very real stain on Miss Marlowe's character of which Dominic knew too well. He'd have thought she would be exceedingly careful not to lose such a golden goose, but perhaps her passionate nature had overcome her sense.

Preoccupied, he met Sophy's eyes and discovered there was an avid, eager glitter animating them. Unexpectedly, he wondered, should the circumstances be reversed and the gossip swirling around Sophy, whether Sarah Marlowe's eyes would reflect such ill will. The thought that they would not surprised him.

"I've not the slightest notion, Sophy." He shrugged negligently. "And in truth, I must say I've scant interest in speculating about them. Gossip has never been my strong suit, particularly since I nearly lost my estates on account of it. Had there not been such exaggerated speculation about our straitened circumstances after father's death, I'd have found sources of credit a great deal easier to come by, you see."

Lady Ruth wanted to crow aloud. Sophy put to the blush was an unexpectedly delightful sight, but she was not allowed the time even to open her mouth and exclaim, "Hear! Hear!"

Already Dominic was addressing Sophy as smoothly as if he had not just delivered her a deservedly stinging set-down. "So, let us leave the affairs of Lisle and Anne's friend Miss Marlowe to them, and discuss our own instead. Tell us of your plans for tomorrow. Will you accompany us to Lady Sefton's?"

"I shall look forward to seeing you there, of course—" Lady Sophy flicked an invisible piece of lint from her skirt—"but, ah, Percival is to escort me."

If it was Lady Sophia's intent to punish Dominic by according her hand to another for an evening, neither she nor Lady Ruth was to know whether she succeeded. His expression remained entirely unchanged as he inclined his head casually. "I hope you will save a dance for me, my dear."

Sarah stood a little apart from the Ponsbys. Old friends of theirs from Sussex had pounced upon them at the door to Lady Sefton's ballroom, and as she knew the Ramseys only a little, she preferred to gauge the mood of the gathering.

The ball was in full swing. Perhaps fifty couples were dancing to a minuet, the ladies' tiaras sparkling in the light of the candles blazing in their sconces.

Despite the considerable heat the candles put off, however, Sarah found the air in the ballroom less than warm. She was not taken by surprise. Kitty had warned her that when it got about Lisle was no longer seeking her hand, many of the gossips would assume he had cried off because he had found some scandalous fault in her history.

An unexpected twinge of amusement curved Sarah's mouth when she caught sight of a small knot of ladies glancing her way and whispering behind their fans. What would they say, she wondered, if she were to drop down by them and cry, "I do believe that dratted necklace is cursed, the way it has haunted me for the entire Season!"

They would regard her as if she were mad, and if she told the full story, they might well pack her off to Bedlam.

As usual it had all begun with Tom Woodward. She had received a letter fromm him, written some month after he arrived in the Indies, but before he had received her letter asking for advice on what she might do now she had met Kendall.

In his letter Tom had sober news. He described again the inhospitable climate of the island he lived upon. With the approach of summer the heat had become more stifling and had brought fever. Many Englishmen had fallen ill, and one, a good man Tom had met on his trip out to the islands, had died only the week before.

The greatest alarm had gripped Sarah. An uncomfortable environment was one thing, a deadly one quite another. Were her friend to contract fever and die, she would consider herself, in part, to blame, for she had made but one attempt to recover his necklace.

All that day she had pondered what more she might do, but to little avail. Another search of Kendall's rooms seemed pointless. She had nothing to give him in exchange for it but perhaps a kiss, and he would have more than a simple kiss, she knew. Playing him at cards seemed a possibility, but, again, she'd nothing to put up as stakes.

When the Marquess of Lisle came late in the afternoon to take her for a drive, Sarah did try to throw off her preoccupation, but it was difficult, for the concern that Tom might even then have the fever preyed on her mind.

Eventually, despite her best efforts to be convivial, Lisle asked if something were amiss, and even as her lips formed a polite, "Oh, no," Sarah hesitated. Sir Adrian's prohibition weighed against sharing her burden with Lisle, but the death of Tom's friend had rattled her severely, and she wanted to consult a man she considered a steady friend.

If, at the back of her mind, Sarah hoped Lisle might offer to take Kendall on at cards, she did not admit as much either to herself or to the marquess.

After explaining that she spoke in the strictest confidence, she told the story of the Woodward emeralds in its entirety, omitting only her search of the captain's bedroom.

"And so, you see," she sighed rather glumly at the end, "I cannot think what to do. Kendall's no right to the necklace, for he won it unfairly, but retrieving it from him poses such difficulty!"

The marquess did not reply at once, but Sarah did not fault him for taking time to consider what she had said and what she might do. However, when Lisle spoke, it was not to voice a suggestion but to observe, "Your quest for this . . . young man's necklace seems exceeding important to you, Miss Marlowe."

Sarah subdued a spurt of irritation at his merely remarking the obvious, and nodded. "Yes, it is. As I explained, Tom performed me a great service, and I feel an obligation to help him."

"To help him retrieve a necklace he lost in a fair game."

"But it was not a fair contest!" She looked at Lisle in dismay. "Captain Kendall deliberately encouraged Tom to drink beyond his capacity for clear thinking."

In a ponderous tone quite devoid of any humor, Lisle said, "It was Mr. Woodward's responsibility to keep a clear head, not the captain's to look after him. Mind, I do not approve what Kendall did. There is little sport winning over a green boy three sheets to the wind, but it was not his duty to keep your, ah, your friend sober."

He was cutting it rather fine, Sarah thought. "Were we speaking only of the captain's having won a sum of money from Tom, then I could not agree with you more. But he took"—she paused for emphasis—"a great deal more. The Woodward necklace is the family's pride. It was both cruel and dishonorable to strip it from them."

Lisle was obliged to attend to his driving then, to maneuver them around a wagon stopped before a dry-goods store, but Sarah could tell from the set of his jaw he was not well pleased with her answer. Whether he was displeased more by her willingness to gainsay him or by her demonstration of interest in another man, she could not tell then, but received some answer when they had left the obstructive wagon behind.

The marquess turned upon her then a rather narrowed and in all unfriendly gaze. "It occurs to me to wonder, Miss Marlowe, exactly how important this gentleman, Mr. Woodward, is to you. For example, would you still believe yourself under an obligation to him if you were joined in matrimony to another man entirely?"

"Yes, my lord." Sarah held his gaze easily, if a little sadly. It had never occurred to her Lisle would not be able to offer even a word of advice or encouragement, only think of himself.

"I would continue my efforts on behalf of my friend were I wedded. And I would even go a step further, sir, though I imagine I may be accused of romanticism. I would actually expect my husband to add his efforts to mine."

When the marquess returned Sarah to Albemarle Street, he failed to assure her he would see her again. Two nights later, the breach between them was brought into the open when they both attended the same soiree and Lisle failed to acknowledge her in any way at all.

Sarah regretted the complete break. She had enjoyed his dry flashes of humor, and come to rely on his stout presence to give her a little respite from the younger, more excitable bucks pressing their attentions upon her.

Looking about Lady Sefton's ballroom, Sarah caught sight of Arthur Farquahar, one of the young bucks who'd often besieged her. The young man's mother was holding him by the sleeve as he inclined his head in Sarah's direction. The sight made her smile wryly. It seemed even in absentia the marquess was performing the service of keeping the young bucks away.

"Dominic! I was only just coming to the card room to fetch you. You must do something!"

"Ruth, you've that look in your eye I know to beware. The Woman with a Cause." Dominic folded his arms across his chest and tipped his head. "Well, what is it you wish me to do? Slay a dragon?"

"You were ever a rascal and have grown no better with age." Lady Ruth looked at her brother with the greatest affection. "And I do have a cause, the beautiful damsel in distress. Just look at Sarah Marlowe standing all alone in the doorway with hundreds of eyes variously scorning, condemning, or, perhaps, in fairness, only questioning her, and tell me you are not affected."

His first thought, even before her beauty struck him afresh, was how assured Sarah Marlowe appeared standing there quite alone. She held herself confidently, not defiantly, and certainly not defensively. A cabal of dowagers whispered behind their fans, but she only looked on, seeming almost amused, as if they were actors in some play put on for her amusement.

"Why is she alone?"

Lady Ruth eyed Dominic, but her brother's expression had closed, and she could not read it. "The Ponsbys are a little behind her there, greeting some friends. She could go to them, but I suspect she would rather not involve them in whatever unpleasantness there may be tonight. If she judges the atmosphere too cool, I imagine she intends to make some excuse to depart and leave them to get on without her shadow over them." Lady Ruth paused, but Dominic said nothing, only shot a glance across the way toward Arthur Farquahar, who was engaged in an argument with his mother, evidently over the beauty in the doorway, for it was to her they looked. "Her pose is affecting, and not merely because she is beautiful. She looks very brave and certainly entirely blameless."

Blameless. Dominic knew she was not that. Whatever the reason for Miss Marlowe's parting with Lisle, she had intended to play the man false. The punishment of cutting glances was not unjust.

Frustrated that Dominic did not seem as affected as she had expected, Lady Ruth exclaimed, "You must go to her, Dominic! Her brave pose may win this evening for her, but she will almost certainly face the same gauntlet another night, if the gossips have their way."

She glanced up slyly, hoping the mention of gossip might set him off, but Dominic continued only to stare at the figure in the doorway, aloof as ever . . . no, perhaps not so aloof, she decided, really looking at him. With a spurt of hope, she imagined there was something rather intense about the way Dominic studied Sarah Marlowe.

"Your cachet, my dear, would be the very thing to put this unpleasantness behind her. Anne will go to her, and Lieutenant Stevenson. They are both looking anxiously toward her, bless them, but they are trapped upon the dance floor at the moment, and besides, their cachet is naught at all to yours. Really, I think it is absurd the way even the highest sticklers fawn over you, but I suppose it is because I knew you in short pants and they did not! But that is beside the point here. I myself shall take the girl around in a moment and be certain she is seen with Sally Jersey and Emily Sefton at the least. I firmly believe you and I owe her our support, Dominic.

"Anne has told me a little of the first weeks of the Season, and they were rather ghastly for her. She did not know how to go on, and the more she faded into the background, the easier it became to fade further, until finally Miss Marlowe took her in hand. By Anne's account, the girl simply said it was high time Anne enjoyed her Season. Oh! Can you credit that? Adella Sims, of all people, snubbing her like that? Well, I'll not wait for you . . . Dominic?"

But her brother was gone, lifted from immobility by the sight of Lady Adella Sims, fat and ugly as a spoiled pug, and her thin, whippetlike daughter trailing along behind, marching by Sarah, their noses raised as if, like the dogs they resembled, they'd caught a scent they did not care for.

Dominic did not stop to analyze why the sight incensed him. He'd an image in his mind of Anne returning from a tea with Lady Adella and her daughter cast down, because the harridan had loudly exclaimed she was far too plain to take in society.

Little surprise Lady Adella would seize such a golden opportunity to quash another rival to her daughter. Miss Marlowe would never be cowed by a few cruel words as Anne had nearly been.

Nor was she cowed even by the woman's public cut. As Lady Adella waddled by, she stood, a memorable foil for the malicious toad who would do her ill before the most select members of the *ton,* quite still and poised and beautiful as a lily.

19

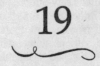

"Come in, girls! Help yourselves to chocolate from the extra pot Demarice has brought up."

Sarah smiled upon her aunt, delighted to see her looking so cheerful. Poor thing, she had been quite cast down by Lisle's defection.

Unable to tell Mrs. Ponsby the whole, Sarah had distilled her disagreement with Lisle to what she did honestly believe was at least a part of its essence. Explaining that Lisle had asked whether she believed a wife ought to conform to her husband's opinion entirely, Sarah told Mrs. Ponsby she had replied she thought a wife ought to take her husband's opinion into account—while she arrived at her own, quite independent conclusions.

Mrs. Ponsby had clapped her hands together in distress. "Dear girl! No gentleman would care to hear such a thing! No gentleman at all. They've a wish to think of themselves as . . . captains of a ship, in sole command, don't you see?" Her aunt had not waited for Sarah to indicate whether she understood that the emphasis was upon "wish" to be in sole command. She went on at once. "It can never do for a lady to be forthright on the subject of a wife's independence. She must be tactful and circumspect. Oh, I do believe your notion that you must be so . . . so honest comes from being raised by your father alone. Ivor is a good man, don't mistake me. I know my brother-in-law, but he is a man, after all, and he holds a man's lofty notions of honor and truthfulness. Your mother, I am persuaded, would have had the good sense to teach you the necessity for delicacy in dealing with gentlemen."

Even now the little speech made Sarah want to smile. Poor Aunt Vinnie! She had suffered a grievous blow, yet she had not cut up shrilly at her niece for losing a relatively wealthy marquess. Instead she had offered advice she thought entirely reasonable upon men in general.

Now, the morning after Lady Sefton's ball, she looked quite recovered, ensconced in her bed, a nest of pillows supporting her as she breakfasted from a tray upon her lap.

"Dear Sarah!" she said as Kitty and Sarah sipped their chocolate. "I was too exhausted to say much after the ball, but upon awakening, I could scarcely wait to see you. I did not wish to worry you before we left for Lady Sefton's, but I can confess now that I was most concerned about your reception last evening. For a *parti* as obviously taken as the marquess was to cool so suddenly . . . well, people will often put the worst possible construction on such a thing!"

Kitty rolled her eyes at Sarah, while Mrs. Ponsby paused to

choose between the two sugared buns remaining upon her plate. Neither girl saw any need to shatter Mrs. Ponsby's cozy illusion that they were too young and innocent to recognize treacherous social shoals.

"And there was some unfortunate speculation, my dears!" Mrs. Ponsby admitted, a frown creasing her brow. "Emily Manwairing confided that even she, for the briefest moment, you understand, was uncertain what to think of Sarah. Of course, it is only because we know so few people in town . . . but that is of no moment!" Her brow clearing, she beamed happily. "Everything turned out quite splendidly in the end. I vow, I never was so delighted as when I turned and saw Ravensby at your side, Sarah. The Ramseys had distracted me. I had no notion they would be at Lady Sefton's, and to see them like that, our best friends from home! Well, it was the greatest pleasure, but I did lose sight of you, child, though only for that moment, you do realize?"

"Aunt Vinnie, I will not hear you apologize for anything," Sarah said at once. "I might have stayed speaking with the Ramseys, had I wished."

"Emily said you were quite alone for a moment, my dear, and I felt very badly to think of it."

Mrs. Ponsby looked so anxious, Sarah rather wanted to rap Mrs. Manwairing's knuckles. "You must not tease yourself a moment more, aunt! Truly. I felt in no difficulty. Mrs. Manwairing was speaking quite out of turn."

"No, no! You must not think it. In truth, Emily was remarking favorably upon you. She thought your brave pose helped to turn the evening in your favor. All the ladies around her were deeply touched by how very calm and unaffected you seemed.

"And then Lord Ravensby recognized you with everyone looking on! But I am grateful to Lady Ruth too. It was very kind of her to make such a show of her support and take you around that you might be seen in conversation with Lady Sefton and Mrs. Drummond-Burrell and Lady Jersey too. My dear, had I been able to plan the evening, I could not have done better."

"I did feel rather as if Lady Ruth were my guardian angel,

she spent such a lot of the evening shepherding me about.''

"And the earl, cuz?'' Kitty's eyes sparkled with interest. "Was he not like your personal St. George, slaying the gossiping dragons with his cachet?''

A loose thread caught Sarah's eye, and she removed it from her sleeve before glancing to her cousin. "I was and am most grateful to Lord Ravensby for lending me his support, of course, Kitty. But you make more of his actions than there is. He himself gave our kindness to Anne as the reason he rallied to my side.''

It was the truth. Ravensby had given her generosity to Anne as his motive. She had asked what it was, for she had been dumbstruck that he, of all people, should have been the one to come to her when she needed someone the most.

Sarah had failed to see him approaching. Lady Adella Sims had just paraded by, snubbing her blatantly. The gesture did not much prick her, for Sarah did not think highly of the woman. Still she knew it had been witnessed by the entire ballroom. Were she to receive no show of support, Lady Sefton's guests were likely to follow the only lead they had. Thinking of her aunt and how miserable Mrs. Ponsby would be to see her niece given the cut direct, Sarah began, slowly, to turn and give some excuse to depart.

Half-poised for flight, she had almost missed Ravensby's "Miss Marlowe,'' and, unwilling to credit her ears, had looked back only slowly, making a play at indifference lest her eyes confirm that her ears were playing devious tricks upon her.

But they were not. The one man she had expected would derive satisfaction from her public fall, the one person who did know of at least one indiscretion that would certainly have turned Lisle against her had the marquess known of it, stood before her. Tall, harshly handsome, powerful, Ravensby blocked out the whispering matrons entirely.

"We danced the waltz once before, Miss Marlowe, and did so well, I hope you will consent to stand up with me again.''

He did not smile as he threw out his lifeline, and though she tried to penetrate his thoughts, Sarah found his eyes unreadable. Stunned, unable to account for his display, she could not seem to form the proper words to accept him.

"Your dance card is not full, I think?" he inquired, when she stood mute, but then he did not wait to see if his attempt to prick through her bemusement succeeded. Taking matters into his own hands, literally, Dominic lifted her hand onto his arm and strolled with her toward the floor.

It was then Sarah realized the entire ballroom had gone still. Or perhaps it was only a trick of the lighting made it seem Lady Sefton's ball stopped, that no one spoke or laughed or drank champagne, but froze in place, watching the Earl of Ravensby accord Sarah Marlowe his mark of approval.

After a moment, it seemed the guests gave a collective nod, then the ball resumed, and the dance floor filled. They were only one couple among many as the music began, and released at long last from the scrutiny of the room, Sarah steadied again.

She looked up, and their eyes met. "Thank you, my lord."

"For what?" He shrugged his broad, elegantly clad shoulders negligently. "Cadging a dance from you before anyone else could?"

"You know very well why I am grateful, my lord," she said quietly, eyes holding his. "You . . . surprised me."

Dominic did not answer at once; indeed he regarded her so long in silence, Sarah was not certain he would reply. But then he shrugged again. "My niece means a great deal to me. It would have been a shabby thing, after the generous way you have dealt with her, to abandon you to the gossips."

Sarah stifled a feeling of disappointment almost before she recognized it. Absurd, given how greatly she had needed support, to regret the reason the support had been given; to wish it had been given on her own account, alone.

Her eyes slipped. "Anne is my friend. I do not believe I have done anything extraordinary in her regard, but I am grateful, nonetheless. I was at the point of surrender."

"You did not look it." He said it without inflection, so that she could not tell if he complimented or faulted her. Her throat dry, she wished to demand how she had looked to him, but then he told her. "You looked very beautiful."

Sarah felt her heart leap. He had told her once before she'd beauty. But his look had been admiring then, she reminded herself. Now it was inscrutable.

"And blameless," he added, voice cooler. "You looked quite blameless, Miss Marlowe."

"I am blameless!" Sarah said it before thinking. Rushing to defend herself, she forgot they both knew her statement to be quite, quite untrue.

His brow lifted mockingly. "I recall a certain embrace in a guest bedroom at Whittingham's, if you do not, Miss Marlowe."

"Oh!" The caustic reminder stung the more deeply because she was not quite prepared for it. "Will you always throw that embrace up to me? Why did you lend me your support, if you insist upon thinking the worst of me? Very well, then! I did behave scandalously once—in your embrace. There! That much is true. But naught else is! And if I looked blameless just now, it is because in the matter of the Marquess of Lisle, I most certainly am blameless. You and the other gossips might well be amazed were you to learn the reason we parted, but you would certainly not be scandalized!"

Sarah flung a final, flashing, defiant look at Dominic before giving him the top of her head and finishing the remainder of the dance so achingly aware of him she wanted to bolt from his arms. It seemed unfair he should be so arresting. It was impossible to be stiff in his arms and simply endure his presence until she could be released. So much she wanted to fling up her head and demand that he believe her! Or to remind him at the top of her voice that he himself had been a most involved party in her one scandalous act.

Or simply to plead that he say something, anything, to break the fraught silence between them. And Dominic did, eventually, but not before he had studied the top of her golden head a time.

She had asked a fair question. Why had he lent her his support? The answer came clear, if unbidden.

He admired her. He admired her courage. And he admired her beauty.

Her courage he had not discovered that night. She was one of a very few had ever stood up to him. And she had done it consistently. He had only to think of the dressing-down she had given him at that art gallery when she'd informed him he had been hateful to her.

As for her beauty, it had affected him from his first sight of her, when she was only one rider among many on a busy street. Had she been homely, he'd still have tried to save her a bruising. He was not entirely self-centered. But surely he would not have interfered in her affairs as much as he had.

No, and certainly he would not have told her she was beautiful as he had just now in a tone that rendered the compliment close to an accusation. But he had been angry.

Dominic smiled grimly. How interesting introspection was, if not uplifting. He had been angry with himself quite as much as her, and why? Because despite everything, he had wanted to protect her, to defend her.

Let Lady Adella Simms snub her or the Ponsbys seemingly abandon her, and he felt almost murderous. It seemed only he might cut up at her, mock her, use her . . . harshly.

That embrace was, in fact, the only thing he knew with certainty he could hold against her. And though that moment of abandon had cost him a great deal of self-recrimination, he could not say he regretted it. At all. And he had been responsible for it.

What an absurd coil! Perhaps he ought to try a new tack. He could accept her protestations of innocence. She certainly sounded sincere when she protested she was, but for the one embrace, quite blameless.

Her eyes had fairly blazed with righteous indignation. But as he'd the occasion to remark before, hers were potent eyes.

He expelled a long breath. At least he could be honorable enough to concede what was no more than the truth. But he still hesitated, uncertain, given all that had gone between them, quite how to begin or precisely what to say once he did. It was the realization that their waltz was coming to an end that goaded him to make some, any, beginning.

"I feel a fool."

As an opening, it was effective. Sarah found him smiling wryly when her eyes flew up to his. "I thought that would get you to look up." He paused a moment, and she remarked, her heartbeat quickening dramatically, that his expression seemed softer than it had been in a long, long time. "I do feel a fool, and more, for cutting up at you again about that embrace."

Sarah nearly stumbled over her own feet, but almost as if he anticipated her reaction, Dominic caught her up before she did and continued, "If you are not blameless in the matter, certainly I am not. Forgive me. I'll not throw it up to you again."

He heard her breath catch as she stared up at him, arrested but a little wary too, as if his confession and apology might be cruel ploys. Dominic could not much blame her for her doubts.

"I am not in the habit of apologizing, Miss Marlowe, but I invariably mean what I say, when I do." She was still absorbing that when he added as softly, "The music has ended, I fear, and for the sake of the onlookers, I think you would be wise to make the requisite curtsy."

Sarah sank down at once, a step behind the other ladies but in time to murmur her thanks for the honor done her, all the while she wondered dazedly if she ought to be adding her thanks for the apology he had made.

But when she rose, Dominic did another unexpected thing. He lifted her hand to his lips, saying, "The honor was mine, Miss Marlowe. While I was cutting up at you as per usual, it occurs to me I neglected to say not only did you look very beautiful tonight, but you taught us all an exquisite lesson in courage. I wish you to know, you have my admiration for it."

The expression about knocking someone over with a feather had never had meaning for Sarah until then. She felt quite that astonished by his remarks.

Dominic actually chuckled when she stood too dumbfounded for words. "I think I have never reduced you to speechlessness before, Miss Marlowe. But I shall take advantage of your temporary loss for words and deliver you to Ruth forthwith. She admires you enormously, you know, and would, I fear, side with you in an instant if she heard you cutting up at me."

It was the last thing he said to her that night, but for the *adieu* he murmured before leaving her to his sister. In the end, Sarah had departed the ball exonerated before the gossips, but completely uncertain over the cause of Ravensby's change of heart, or more important, its extent.

"Sarah? Sarah?" Sarah blinked and found her aunt smiling at her. "You have been woolgathering, my dear. I believe you did not hear Demarice come to say there is a gentleman below to see you."

"A gentleman? No! I did not." Sarah flushed, discomfited that the Earl of Ravensby could absorb her so. "Who can have come at this hour?"

"He gave his name as Captain Steward. I can see by your expression you know him no better than I. Only wait a moment, my dear, and I shall make myself presentable to go down with you."

"Captain Steward, ma'am," the squarish man smartly dressed in a blue uniform announced himself when they entered the drawing room. "I apologize for the hour, but I only got in last evening and hope to make my family in Suffolk by tonight. It was on my ship young Tom Woodward sailed to the Indies, and he asked if I would bring you and your niece, Miss Marlowe, word of him."

"Tom is well, Captain?" Sarah asked anxiously, and was at once reassured by the captain's broad smile.

"The lad's in good health, if that's your question, Miss Marlowe, though he would rather be in England than the Indies." The captain searched in his pockets and withdrew a small, neatly wrapped package. "He asked if I would assure you he thinks of you and give you this." Sarah took the gift with a word of thanks, and again the captain smiled. "He'll live, lass! You needn't worry over him. He said it was the climate troubled him most, but now I've seen you, I doubt it is only England's cool temperatures he longs for so."

Sarah's smile came with effort. She did not like to think of Tom pining for her. They had talked of marriage once, but ages ago, and in only the vaguest terms. To her now the thought of marrying Tom seemed as old and stale as a biscuit that has been left out too long on a plate.

At Kitty's urging, when the captain had departed Sarah opened the package and found a very handsome coin purse of worked leather inside. She held it out for her aunt and cousin to admire but not to hold. The purse was suspiciously heavy, and she thought it would be very like Tom to hide something in a gift.

He had. When she went into her room, Sarah found a letter and five one-hundred-pound notes neatly folded inside.

Five hundred pounds! Sarah had never held such a sum in her hand and was gazing dumbstruck at the fortune when she heard a tapping at her door. She just had the time to tuck the notes into the sleeve of her dress before Kitty swept into the room.

"Was the purse all you received from Tom, cuz? It seems such a . . . well, a useful gift!"

Sarah laughed. "You are the veriest romantic, Kitty. Did you expect a leather rose, perhaps?"

"A gold one!" Kitty returned with a grin. "Or one of those darling birds such as Anne and Lady Ruth have. But what does he say in his letter?"

Sarah shrugged casually, as if she had read the missive. "Now it is getting toward summer, the weather is hotter and less bearable. There are more insects too. Poor Tom! He even writes in praise of England's mists."

Kitty giggled at that. "Poor thing, indeed! He writes in praise of them because he does not suffer them. We've not had a sunny day this week. Ah, well, I am certain Sir Adrian will bring Tom home soon. And in the meantime, we've an entertainment for which to plan!"

"What?"

"We're to visit Vauxhall!" Kitty announced with an excited giggle. "Mama thinks it would be the very thing to get up a party and take the Ramseys. She even agreed we might forgo the pleasure of Westphal's company just this once, when I said naught of inviting Johnny to accompany us. I think you were half right, Sarah. She does not care for the thought of forcing the earl upon me—she thinks to sweeten me into accepting him instead!" Kitty sniffed in affront. "As if my feelings for Johnny could be so easily got around! Or my intention to stroll down one of those famous walks with him." A mischievous sparkle lit her eyes. "Little does Mama anticipate that while the earl languishes at home with all his daughters, Johnny will happen along at Vauxhall!"

"You don't think Aunt Vinnie will happen to guess you arranged the coincidence?" Sarah asked.

Kitty tossed her brown curls. "She may, but it will not matter. I will have had a walk with Johnny in the world's most famous—or infamous—pleasure gardens, and with any luck at all, we shall manage to be discovered in such a shockingly compromising position Papa will rush me forthwith to the altar, Johnny at my side!''

"You would not play your mother such a trick!" Sarah protested, but there was a question in her voice, and Kitty laughed.

"Alas, no! I am not so bold. But I shan't allow you to look so relieved, Sarah Marlowe. You would do it, in my place. When your mind is set upon something, you will risk almost anything to achieve it. I remember that time you learned Devon Carstairs was setting traps for foxes in his home woods. You went out alone in the dead of night and freed one! The Carstairs' game warden even shot at you! But no one suspected it was you did the deed.'' Kitty shook her head resignedly. ''I think it is because of your beauty people never imagine you capable of anything the least outlandish.''

Sarah did not point out that she had, in that instance, confessed to her deed and even threatened to repeat it, because, although she understood foxes could be a menace to domesticated animals, she thought trapping them the cruelest way to control their population. She made no reply at all. She was thinking of Ravensby again, and wondering if it was because of her looks he'd found it so easy to think the worst of her. Or was it on account of her appearance he'd decided to acquit her of at least one of the charges he held against her? Oh, she had no idea, because he had left her hanging so!

20

The group that set out for Vauxhall the next evening included, besides the Ramseys, all the young people included in the Richmond outing except Charlotte Manwairing, who was indisposed. Her absence could not dampen the general gaiety, however, for the weather had changed dramatically, and though it was early May, the night felt delightfully warm.

As they strolled through the pleasure gardens, Sarah laughingly announced she felt as if she'd crossed to some magical isle. No hard, grimy streets existed there, no gaslights destroyed the warm dark of the night, nor did she feel the constriction she experienced sometimes with only heavy town buildings crowding in on all sides of her. The walks on their isle were of giving gravel, the lights were soft, rosy-colored lanterns, and the air was scented with the earthy smell of trees and grass.

Once settled in the Ponsbys' box, they were served champagne and the shavings of burnt ham that were the specialty of the house. They had only just raised their glasses in toast to the evening when the music began, and everyone, even Mr. and Mrs. Ponsby, danced.

After a little time, Kitty's face lit, and following the direction of her cousin's gaze, Sarah caught sight of Johnny Carstairs amid a group of friends entering another box. Mrs. Ponsby did not notice, however. She was smiling delightedly in quite the opposite direction.

At the same moment, Anne cried, "Oh, good! It is Uncle Dominic. He did say Sir Percival's party might come to Vauxhall after their dinner."

Mrs. Ponsby was in alt when the earl strolled away from his group. To be greeted cordially by a gentleman of such standing and presence, while her dear friend Carlotta Ramsey looked on, was an unalloyed triumph. Ravensby further obliged her when he readily accepted a glass of champagne.

It seemed to Sarah that all the ladies preened a little as the earl greeted them; even Kitty, who was devoted to Johnny, smiled rather besottedly and sought to keep his attention for a little by exclaiming, as had everyone else, upon the pleasantness of the evening.

Sarah concentrated upon her glass of champagne. She could not blame Kitty. Ravensby was striking in coat and trousers of midnight blue with a waistcoat as snowy white as his cravat. In the light of the bandstand area, it was no difficulty to admire his severe, beautiful features and even to remark his compelling eyes. She knew that because she had met those eyes, when, startled by Anne's announcement, she had looked around unprepared.

And glanced away again as quickly, almost frightened by the stab of pleasure she felt to find that, of all the people in the box, she was the one upon whom his gaze was fixed as he approached.

Eventually, her glass holding only modest interest, Sarah gave in to a longing to glance at Ravensby again. Standing outside the box, his shoulders propped casually against it, he discussed horseflesh with the gentlemen, while the ladies looked on, smiling and laughing, their spirits elevated as much by the striking gentleman in their midst as by the free flow of champagne.

He'd an appealing laugh too. Rich and genuinely amused, it made one want at least to smile.

Only Sarah remained unaffected. Or rather she was so affected by Ravensby, she felt stretched taut as a wire. How could she not be, uncertain as she was of what he thought? And, having received one concession, wanting more, wanting him to believe her blameless entirely; wanting, at the least, some indication what he was thinking at that very moment; thinking she might scream if she did not get it. Sarah shot him a dark look, willing him to return to his box and quit cutting up her peace. Lady Sophia awaited him. Sarah could see her beplumed head.

"And do you still find Vauxhall like an enchanted isle, Miss Marlowe?" Sarah blinked. She'd been far too lost railing at Ravensby to follow the conversation. Now, caught by his golden-brown gaze, she was unable to think of anything but that he was smiling at her. He gestured to Kitty. "Miss Ponsby reported that was your fancy."

No, you are my fancy. Sarah bit her lip. It was an unwelcome thought come at a quite inconvenient moment. "Yes, ah, there was the crossing by boat, and now here it is very beautiful."

To Sarah's ears, her voice sounded absurdly breathless, but mercifully the musicians, rested from their interval, had struck up again, and no one seemed to notice. No one but, perhaps, Ravensby, who, eyes still on her, said softly, "Very."

Sarah had to think what was "very" before she recalled they

had been speaking of Vauxhall, and by that time she had lost the opportunity to reply. Lieutenant Stevenson was holding out his hand to her, reminding her he'd bespoken the dance.

Sarah heard Mrs. Ponsby say to the earl that they had enjoyed his company and would miss him greatly now he must return to Sir Percival Kitely's group. But Ravensby surprised her, and everyone else, saying the other box would get along well enough without him. "I was hoping you, Mrs. Ponsby, would honor me with a dance—that is, if Mr. Ponsby does not object."

Sarah actually giggled at Mr. Ponsby's reply. " 'Pon my word, Ravensby, it would mean my life if I did!"

"William!" Mrs. Ponsby scolded, but only lightly as she tripped out the door of the box to place a small, plump hand on the earl's arm. "You are too kind, my lord!" She beamed up at her partner.

If Sarah had found occasion to fault the earl's manner toward her aunt in the past, she forgave him everything then. A single dance was a small thing to him, but Mrs. Ponsby would live on the story for months. Sarah, watching her with a smile, thought she looked as dazzled as a girl while she danced with the Earl of Ravensby.

He did return to his group after that, but came back after a little to lead Anne out. Sarah tried hard not to waste her time wondering if he meant to ask her to dance as well. The earl had danced with her only twice all Season, after all. Just because he'd admitted he was no less blameless than she in the matter of their embrace did not mean he found her worthy of greater attention.

Still, Sarah found it hard to tear herself away from the dance area when Kitty suggested the young people depart for a stroll in the gardens.

She went, nonetheless. She'd have felt too foolish for words had she not, and sorely lacking in cousinly devotion.

The group happily welcomed Johnny Carstairs and his friends when they appeared. Some pairs formed, but everyone remained together as they strolled about enjoying the night and the gardens, laughing, talking, and giggling, too, when they passed entwined couples.

Eventually a fountain decorated with plump cupids drew them.

The girls sank onto its edge to rest, while the young men took turns tossing coins into it, claiming they would make the girls' dearest wishes come true.

It seemed such a charmed night, no one was much surprised when Captain Kendall appeared with two friends, but only Sarah was truly pleased to see the man, though she controlled her enthusiasm. Charlotte Manwairing missing, he worked his way to Sarah, and after a little, she allowed him to wheedle her apart from the group into the shadows.

He was not satisfied, however, with the distance he had achieved, and entreated, voice purring, "Come, Miss Marlowe! We'll not be missed if we slip off around this hedge. A night such as this deserves a few stolen moments. You'll not regret it, I promise!"

"Ah, but I think I would, Captain Kendall." Sarah's voice was low but emphatic. "You see, I've no wish to compete with Miss Manwairing for your favors."

With a spurt of pleasure she saw the captain's eyes widen, confirming the accuracy of her guess. "How . . . ?"

He caught himself, but not before he had revealed more than he meant to. Sarah shrugged. "It does not matter. And anyway, it is not your embrace I desire."

If she had surprised him before, Sarah caught the captain completely off-guard then. "I'm afraid I don't understand," he said, straightening.

"What I desire of you is something you possess—the Woodward emeralds."

"What?" Even in the flickering shadows, it was possible to make out the man's surprise. "You are not a Woodward, are you?"

"I am Tom Woodward's friend, and I wish you will return his necklace."

The captain's laugh was soft but nonetheless derisive. "Even your wishes, my beauty, are so much air, unless they are feasible. I've uses for that necklace."

"You have your heiress, Captain," she returned, but went on before he could speak. "But I do not expect you to surrender it. You enjoy games of chance, Captain Kendall, and that is what I am proposing."

"You would play me for the necklace?" Kendall could scarce believe his good fortune. Any game between them would have to be in private. "What have you for a stake?"

"Five hundred pounds."

Tom had had no specific purpose in mind for the money he had sent Sarah. In his letter he had said only that he wished to contribute to her efforts on his behalf, and it had occurred to him she might have need of some pocket money. What better to do than challenge the captain to a game, if only he would accept! She knew piquet well, having played it with her father for years.

Kendall almost laughed aloud. He valued the necklace far more highly than a paltry five hundred pounds. It might seem a vast sum to a girl, but he had lost more than that in one round of cards.

He controlled his expression, however, as he allowed his gaze to drift over Sarah Marlowe's seductive figure. She would be the prize. "And when do you propose we engage in our game?"

"The Ramseys have invited us to a theater party tomorrow. My aunt and uncle will go, and Kitty. If I plead illness, it will be a simple matter for me to slip out of the house unnoticed. They will dine out after the play, and I'll not need to return until two o'clock at the earliest."

"You have thought the thing through." The captain's smile flashed in the dark. "Shall I suggest the place?"

"Please do."

"You are deuced cool, Miss Marlowe." He bowed slightly. "Allow me to tell you how much I admire that quality in you, and to add I hope it will sustain you when I say the only place I can think of is a gaming establishment. A very elegant one, I assure you, in St. James Square. I can make arrangements for a, ah, conveyance to meet you around the corner from your uncle's house. From there it would be a simple thing for you to enter the gaming house, fully cloaked, by a back entrance. Someone will be there to lead you upstairs."

"How thoughtful you are, Captain." Sarah gave him an ironic smile, knowing he was as desirous as she of discretion. He would not want any word of a rendezvous with her to get back to Charlotte Manwairing. "I shall be there by ten o'clock. If I am not, then something has occurred to keep me home."

"Until then, my beauty."

Kendall had her hand to his lips before she knew what he was about, then he slipped away around the hedge into the night.

Sarah thought his precipitate departure odd, to say the least, but, relieved to have done with the captain, she shrugged the matter off as she turned back to join her party. Only to stop stock-still. The area by the fountain was entirely deserted.

She blinked, a silly tactic that was not the least effective. Having lost sight of her, the others must have assumed she had returned to the dance area with Kendall.

Sarah shivered of a sudden, realizing she was quite alone in the shadowed gardens that were known for a certain amount of wickedness. It was part of Vauxhall's charm, when one was well-escorted, that sense of license.

Unescorted, however, she found the warm night full of menace, and when she heard a step on the gravel behind her, Sarah whirled with a frightened cry, thinking she must defend herself.

The man approaching was much closer than she had realized. She bumped into him as she turned, crying out again and raising her hands to push at him. "Oh!" Her cry turned to a sob of relief as the hands that had lifted to ward off an attacker clung, instead, to a midnight-blue coat. "I am so glad it is you, my lord!"

She sounded so frightened, Dominic could not but clasp her reassuringly to him. Still, he had seen Kendall disappearing around the hedge. It stunned him that the man would leave her to her own devices. It seemed impossible, looking down into her lovely face, that anyone, even a cad like Kendall, could demonstrate such carelessness for her. Perhaps the captain had seen him approaching? It was possible. There was more light upon the walk than back of the fountain where the pair had been trysting.

Dominic's jaw set as he leaned back. "Did you not hear your group depart, Miss Marlowe? All twenty pairs or so of feet crunching in the gravel? Could it be you were distracted by your *tête-à-tête?*"

Sarah did push off from him then, straightening slowly and stepping back. Of course he would find her with Kendall and put the worst construction possible on their *tête-à-tête*! But in the next moment her anger fizzled. It would be asking a great deal of anyone to put a good construction on a meeting in the shadows with Kendall.

"I think it is pointless for us to attempt to speak about this, Lord Ravensby." Hearing her voice waver, Sarah stopped to master it before she continued. "You will not believe me when I say that though I was, indeed, distracted with Captain Kendall to such an extent that I did not hear my party leave, still there is nothing romantic between us. And, truly, I cannot say I blame you!"

Dominic could hear the catch in her voice; could see her bite her lip. "What is between you, then?" he bit out roughly, impatiently.

Whether he meant to give her a fair hearing, it was impossible for Sarah to say. But it did not matter. She could not make an explanation, satisfactory or otherwise. Frustrated, she made a sharp gesture. "I said it was pointless to speak of this. I cannot explain anything. I would betray a trust if I did, and I have learned nothing good comes of that. I wish you would be good enough to return me to the boxes. I am certain your party awaits you."

"My party is out strolling in the gardens."

Later Sarah would consider the point that Lady Sophia had gone for a walk without Ravensby. Just then she could only think of the wretched tears that had risen suddenly to prick her eyes. She had felt relatively controlled until it occurred to her that, having seen her again with Kendall, Ravensby might not care even to offer her his protection to the boxes; might believe she deserved to be abandoned to her element, the night. A sudden shiver shook her at the thought.

"Good Lord, can you be cold?" Dominic reached for her, perhaps to ascertain if there were goose bumps on her arm, but Sarah jumped back before he could touch her.

"No! I am not cold."

That the thought of his touching her made her overheated sent Sarah away abruptly. Seeing the fountain, she made for it.

Anything to put some distance between them, that she not be tempted to throw herself into his arms and beg him to believe her.

A frustrated groan escaped her. Why did she not wish for immortal life or the discovery of a pot of gold at the end of the rainbow?

"Sarah?"

He had come to stand just behind her, to tempt her with the warmth of his body; the sound of her given name, even. Why did he not just let her be!

She hunched a shoulder at him, refusing to turn or answer. She would not be cozened by him, only to have him cut up at her in that ice cold voice.

In a most uncharacteristic gesture, Dominic raked a hand through his hair. He had had only good intentions when he came out into the gardens, after encountering her group and finding both Sarah and Miss Ponsby missing from it. He had felt no alarm, thinking Miss Marlowe with her cousin. He'd sought her to speak to her in privacy, but then he'd seen her with Kendall, and anger had routed all reason.

Reminding himself why he wished speech with her, he said quietly, "Sarah, I wish you to turn and look at me." Again he reached for her, and again she shrank from his touch, fearing it, or rather her response to it.

"Please, let us have done with this! Only take me back, if you will."

"I don't wish to take you back just yet. I've something to say, now my temper's cooled, and I wish you would turn. It is difficult to be humble to a back, however slender and fetching."

Unfair! She could feel her resolution melting. How could it not, when he spoke of humility so arrogantly? And told her she'd a fetching back, of all things.

With a sniff, Sarah did turn, but to hold his effect upon her at bay, she demanded in cool tones, "Well?"

He smiled. Damn him.

"Thank you. Here." She took his handkerchief with a nod, drying her eyes, while Dominic, watching her, began his speech.

"As I say, my temper's cooled, and I've recalled why I came

out to find you in the first place." He smiled, more at himself than at her, she thought. "When you put me in my place the other night, I was moved not only to admit, as I said then, that I was party to our embrace, but also to recall a suggestion you made long ago. Perhaps you will remember you once advised me to stand back and observe you and Kendall. I am afraid I believed I had done just that, yet it would seem all this while I have observed only one of the two of you. You will, I think, not be astonished if I admit it was not Kendall drew my eye?"

He smiled dryly, and not seeming to expect an answer, went on. "I disciplined myself at Lady Sefton's. While you made your triumphal tour of the room with Ruth, I watched Kendall. He does have an eye for you, but that is scarcely damning or startling. Most men do. It was to whom he looked when he did not feast his eyes on you that interested me. I can assure you, as well, Charlotte Manwairing was foolish enough to return the regards he gave her. Indeed, when her mother was not watching —absorbed, I fear, with you—Charlotte went a step further and contrived to meet Kendall in one of the alcoves Lady Sefton was so unwise as to include in the design of her ballroom. Was it Charlotte Manwairing he met that night, Sarah?"

Her tears quite forgotten, feeling almost light-headed, Sarah cried, "I cannot say! I did not see anyone except you. I did not go to his wing of the house on his acount, you see. It was something else entirely! Oh, can you believe me? I understand how it must have looked to you!"

Dominic broke his promise. He took Sarah by the arms and drew her to him. She did not seem to mind at all, perhaps because it was the eaiser to gaze up at him entreatingly.

"I do believe you. I want to, at any rate. But I desire you to tell me what this business is. It is what brought you to meet him tonight?"

"Yes! But I cannot tell you of it. Truly. And it does not signify, for I will soon be done with it."

Dominic shook her a little, impatience tightening his mouth. "I would know what it is! I'll not have you going near that man's rooms again, or making assignations with him in the dark at Vauxhall." The entirely arrogant, quite possessive remark did not have the effect of vexing Sarah. Quite the contrary, the half growl had the effect of making her heart leap in her throat. "I . . ."

But Sarah was not to know what he meant to add. Absorbed in each other, they had not seen the pair hurrying along the path behind them, and both started in surprise when a voice cried, "Sarah! But where are the others?"

Sarah jumped around, breaking free of Ravensby's clasp. "Kitty!"

"Lord Ravensby!"

Not without a touch of irony, Ravensby continued the litany of names. "Mr. Carstairs."

The earl's amusement did not register with Johnny, who appeared, Sarah realized, oddly strained for a young man returning from a tryst with his beloved. "Lord Ravensby, I would ask that you escort Miss Ponsby back to the boxes. I . . . must go."

"Of course," said Ravensby, and watched impassively as Kitty, seeming about to throw herself on Mr. Carstairs, put her hand to her mouth while he stiffly bowed to her and her cousin.

"Sarah!" Miss Ponsby did throw herself upon her cousin as her young man stalked off. "Johnny has had an offer of a position. But it is in Scotland!" Seeming oblivious of her audience, she wailed, "Mama and Papa will never allow me to marry him if he must go so far away. Never! Oh, what shall we do? He is so brave, but I cannot be!"

"Kitty, Kitty." Sarah rocked her a moment. "You distress yourself unduly. It is only the first offer, I am certain." Gently Sarah disentangled herself. "Here is a handkerchief." Dominic noted she gave up his to her cousin's cause. "Good, that's better. Now, we must get back. It would be the worst of times to have Aunt Vinnie put out with you, you'll agree?" Kitty, mopping her eyes, nodded mournfully. "Come, then, and take the earl's arm."

Sniffing, Kitty obeyed, and after they had walked a little way, she asked whether the others had been gone long.

It was Dominic replied. "Not overlong, but I imagine your parents will be relieved to see you."

Sarah could not give thought to the others, only to the man whose arm beneath her hand felt so strong and steady and warm.

Ravensby believed her! Or wanted to, which was almost the same thing. She was certain she'd have floated at least a foot above the path, were she not holding to him. The feeling was so blissful, Sarah wished they might walk along in the fragrant gardens forever.

Their walk could not, of course, last forever. As will happen, they came to their destination, to lights, questions, and considerable relief upon the Ponsbys' part at finding "their girls" had wandered off with the earl.

It was near midnight. Time to watch the fireworks with their separate groups.

"Good night . . . Miss Marlowe."

"My lord." She curtsied, her mouth curving at his hesitation over her name. "Thank you for the escort."

"It was my pleasure."

And for once Sarah believed the politeness no more than the truth.

21

Sarah listened carefully at the door to her room. The house was quiet.

The servants were belowstairs enjoying a brief respite from their duties, and Maddie, her ankle yet weak, had retired some half-hour before, having accepted Sarah's contention she was not ill so much as fatigued.

Quickly Sarah tied the ribbons of the gray wool cloak she had not worn since leaving Cumberland and took up her reticule. It bulged with Tom's five hundred pounds. And with a little lady's pistol.

Despite her tension, she smiled, recalling how furiously she had complained to her father when Tom Woodward had expressed shock at the notion that she should wish to join him in target practice. Why, she had demanded of her father, ought young men be given the means to protect themselves, while young ladies were not? Unable to find a satisfactory answer, her father had made her a gift of the pistol and had taught her how to shoot the dainty thing.

Quiet as a shadow, she hurried down the stairs. No step groaned beneath her slight weight, nor did the door sigh as she opened it. When an inspection of the street assured her no one loitered there, she gave herself no time for thought, but closed the door behind her and flew down the steps.

At the street, she slowed her pace to a brisk, authoritative stride, straining her eyes for sight of the conveyance Kendall had said would be waiting at the corner. Her reticule clutched before her, she told herself she was indeed prepared to slip the catch and withdraw her pistol, if need be.

The need did not arise. There was a hansom cab waiting just back from the corner out of sight of the Ponsbys' house. The coachman touched his fingers to his hat brim when Sarah looked up at him. She supposed that meant he was the one to meet her, and climbed inside.

She had no more than settled herself when the hansom lurched forward. A little cry escaped her, but she calmed herself. She had acomplished the first step of her plan successfully. It was not the time to lose her nerve.

Peering out the closed curtains, she marked their progress and knew when they turned into a wide mews. She did not need to be told what to do when the hansom rolled to a stop before a closed gate. Pulling her hood close about her, she made haste to it, rapped softly, and stood back as it swung noiselessly open. Taking a deep breath, Sarah stepped through.

Inside she found a cadaverous older man in livery. He never acknowledged her as he slipped a bolt on the gate and stepped around her to lead the way. She'd an impression of a small yard, a gravel path, a wooden door; then they were inside the house. The kitchen was nearby. The smell of food was strong, and in the far distance Sarah could hear the muted babble of voices.

The elderly man chose a steep set of narrow stairs to their left. They climbed only one flight before her guide stopped and held up his hand for Sarah to do the same. He cracked the door, only to close it quickly in the next instant.

Sarah listened tensely as several people passed. Two gentlemen were speaking, and another laughed uproariously as a lady squealed. A door opened, then closed, and silence returned.

The second time her guide peeped out the door, there was a different result. Hearing no one, he stuck his head through, looked both ways, then let go of the door altogether, and making a hurrying motion with his hand, stepped quickly across the corridor, leaving Sarah to follow. Two doors down, he stopped, rapped softly on a door, and opened it before Sarah, at least, heard a reply. Eyes downcast, he allowed her to pass by him, and the moment she had crossed the threshold, he shut the door soft as a whisper behind her.

"Miss Marlowe!" Captain Kendall, standing directly opposite her beside a table, swept her a courtly bow. "I am delighted. I confess I doubted you would have the resolution to come."

"Captain."

Sarah threw back her hood and glanced around. The room was not large, but ornately decorated. Crimson satin was draped about the window, and the same sumptuous material covered the gilt chairs as well as the couch in the corner. It seemed particularly large and wide, and Sarah averted her gaze from it to look to Captain Kendall.

"Shall we begin, Captain?"

"Tsh, tsh! You are in such a hurry! Won't you have a glass of champagne with me, my pretty? Drink to our game?"

Sarah shook her head. "I am not so foolish as Tom Woodward, Captain. If you win tonight, it will be because you deserve to win."

The captain went still. "Are you accusing me of cheating, Miss Marlowe?"

Sarah flung up her head, her eyes meeting his without flinching. "I cannot say if you cheat, sir. Tom did not accuse you. But I do believe you set out deliberately to take advantage of a green young man."

"You are not complimentary, Miss Marlowe."

Kendall's dark, sleek brow arched above black eyes that glittered suddenly. Sarah's heart raced in reaction, but she told herself it was better to do business with a wolf when he was in wolf's clothing.

"We understand one another better, I think, Captain Kendall," she said, managing a level tone.

Her manner impressed him. He laughed unexpectedly. "You are a cool thing, Sarah Marlowe! Such a surprise in one so young. Well, then, be seated, my dear, and let us see who reaches one hundred points first."

While he poured himself champagne, Sarah removed her cloak and took her seat, being careful to keep her reticule in her lap.

Kendall dropped into the chair across from her, stretching his legs out to the side. For a brief moment Sarah had the sense she was in some mad dream. Could it really be she, primly turned out in a serviceable long-sleeved blue dress that buttoned high at the neck, sitting in a luxuriously appointed gaming-house room quite alone with a dissolute cavalry officer? At least Kendall made up in splendor what she lacked, his brilliant scarlet regimentals sporting the gold epaulets that made the most of what she had always considered rather narrow shoulders.

"As time is of the essence, Miss Marlowe, shall we play a practice rubber to get the feel of the other's style merely, then decide the winner of our match in the subsequent rubber?"

She nodded. "That arrangement would suit me nicely, Captain Kendall."

"And I do wish to suit you nicely, Miss Marlowe."

His wolfish smile, greedy and knowing, flashed out as he pushed the cards to her, that she might cut them. Restraining an impulse to lay her pistol on the table between them, just to wipe that smile from his lips, Sarah cut and returned the deck to him.

Sarah had been playing piquet since her mother's death. Her father, bored during the winter, when they'd few guests and the distance to their neighbors' was lengthened by cold and snow, had taught her, and they had spent many an evening playing. Mr. Marlowe had been, as well as a challenging opponent, a strict teacher, who did not believe in allowing a young student to win merely to bolster her confidence.

Kendall's brow lifted in unfeigned surprise when she took

the first rubber rather easily. "I do believe, Miss Marlowe, that should you ever need employment, you could take up card-sharping. You'd make a handsome living."

"I don't think I would care for the hours, Captain Kendall." He was sitting slouched in his chair, coat unbuttoned, legs carelessly arranged, and she added to herself: Nor would I care to sit with such as you forever.

Kendall seemed to read her thoughts. "Wouldn't care for the company either, eh?" He tossed off his champagne, then gave her a narrowed look from beneath the lock of hair that Sarah suspected he encouraged to fall so boyishly across his brow. "Your tune's certainly changed, my dear Miss Marlowe, or were you only pretending an interest in me because I had the necklace?"

Sarah managed to curb her tongue. His expression had hardened, giving her caution. "I received a letter from Tom Woodward only a few days ago." It was no lie. "And then I saw you at Vauxhall the next night."

Kendall reached around behind him for the bottle of champagne resting in its silver cooler. "Vauxhall!" He laughed harshly as he poured. "Damn, but Ravensby's a way of turning up at the least expected moment. He's an eye for you. He must have, no matter that he's all but affianced to that haughty block of ice."

"Cut, Captain?" Sarah tried distraction rather than reprimand. After all, and regrettably, she had derived a certain satisfaction from hearing the elegant Lady Sophia disparaged.

The captain cut, but returned forthwith to his former subject, grinning wickedly as he studied his cards. "I do wonder what the earl would think could he see you—us—now."

"Captain Kendall, I did not come here to speculate upon or to discuss the Earl of Ravensby. Shall we play?"

"Oh, by all means, Miss Marlowe." His eyes gleamed with silky satisfaction. "It was a most moot question anyway. This once, at least, the earl will not appear from out of the dark to come between us."

Sarah concentrated upon her cards, trying to stifle a frisson of unease. Surely he was not threatening her, suggesting she would need rescue. But even if she did, she had her little pistol.

Her cards were not good. Perhaps Kendall guessed, for when he looked up he'd a rather smug smile on his face. "And so we begin our real game, Miss Marlowe, our deciding game. Your play, I believe?"

Sarah exchanged the full five cards, as Kendall had dealt, but when it came time to lay their cards down, he'd the rest of the points.

The next hand was not quite so bad. She did earn a point for longest suit, but he'd all the others.

The tension mounted as the rubber progressed. Sarah's palms turned damp. With every play she studied her hand intently and repeated the litany that she was doing the best she could, the very best. Oh! But she must win!

Then it came to the last game. How many cards, and which to discard? He seemed to have an uncanny knack of estimating her hands. She chose to discard her face cards, hoping for *carte blanche*.

As the captain made his discards, Sarah slowly examined the cards she'd chosen from the eight betwen them. One was a nine, the next a lowly seven, and the third . . . a king!

She groaned aloud, and his cry, in response, was exultant. "I have won! You are mine, by damn!"

Sarah's eyes flew wide. "I beg your pardon," she snapped tensely. "You are five hundred pounds richer. That is all!"

"Five hundred pounds?" Kendall gave a contemptuous laugh. "You did not believe I would accept a wager of five hundred pounds against a priceless necklace! You're no fool, tantalizing little Sarah." His dark eyes glittered hotly as he leaned across the table toward her. "You know very well what you put up against my emeralds!"

Her heart began to pound. "Oh, no, Captain Kendall! I know nothing of the sort. And you are aware of it." As she spoke, Sarah worked her reticule open. "I said I'd five hundred pounds to wager." She flung the notes upon the table, and laid her hand upon her little pistol. "There they are."

"And how do you propose to elude me? Return as you came? My dear, did I neglect to mention the hansom does not await you in the mews? That you would be obliged to trip home on foot all alone in the night unless I take you when I leave?"

He laughed again, an evil sound, as he gestured to the couch that was nearly the size of a bed. "I shall taste you there first, my luscious prize. You can't escape. The back door of the house is locked fast, and the front door is surrounded by more than a few gentlemen known to you. If you believe you had difficulties after Lisle's defection, think what you would encounter when it got about you'd been seen exiting Maude O'Neil's gaming house. Come, now, resign yourself, my pet. You will not regret it.''

"I would rather wither away a disgraced spinster than suffer the touch of one of your fingers, Kendall! You are a cad and a rogue!''

The ill-considered speech sent Kendall leaping to his feet, cursing as he made to grab her by the shoulders, but Sarah shoved the table at him and surged to her feet as well. Before he could seize her, she had her pistol leveled upon him.

Face contorted with fury, Kendall went rigid until he examined the barrel trained on him. Then, seeing its size, he began to laugh.

Sarah lifted the little thing so that it pointed at his heart. "I'll not miss you entirely, Captain Kendall. You'll suffer, if you are not killed.''

"And have half the gentlemen in this gaming house come running to see what's afoot?'' He sneered. "By the devil, I'll have you!''

Sarah could have gotten a shot off. She had a split second, and her finger was on the trigger. But she had not, in her heart, truly expected she would be obliged to fire a bullet into a flesh-and-blood creature. And Kendall was quick. While she stood in shock, unable to comprehend that a man she had seen behave within the bounds of civilized norms could really be the creature springing upon her, Captain Kendall captured her wrist.

The instant he touched her, she was galvanized to resist, gripping the pistol as tightly as she could while he tried to wrest it from her. They hit the table, struggling fiercely. A chair crashed to the floor. Sarah scarcely heard it, all her energies concentrated upon keeping the pistol in her grasp. He had got her arm between them, twisting her wrist so she feared it would snap.

Then a sharp crack reverberated about the room, taking them both so by surprise, they froze, staring, each waiting for the other to stagger back clutching a pistol wound.

22

Upon taking her seat in the Ramseys' box, Kitty cast a surreptitious glance toward the pit and soon found Johnny's auburn head. She smiled, if painfully. He had said he would not attend the play, that seeing her would only be punishment now there was so little hope they could marry.

Biting her lip, she stared at him, willing him to look up and see how glad she was he'd come. Johnny did not turn, however, from his companion. Kitty frowned, studying the young man, but did not recognize him, which surprised her, for all Johnny's friends were known to her.

It was just as the play was to begin that Johnny turned abruptly to scan the boxes. A little late, Kitty thought rather peevishly, but she did straighten to attract his attention. To her surprise, chagrin, and some annoyance, his expression did not soften when their eyes met. Indeed, no sooner her had recognized her than he looked behind her, to examine, or so it seemed, the other occupants of the box. Kitty frowned in confusion at that, and was no more enlightened when Johnny glanced back to her, an urgent look animating his expression.

The possible meaning of that look nagged at her through the first act of the comedy, and she was quick to leap up when Johnny came to their box at the intermission. The expected courtesies performed, Kitty smoothly preceded him into the corridor, confident Mrs. Ponsby would not stop her and hazard a scene with the Ramseys looking on.

Kitty had told herself Johnny did not mean to inform her he'd a new, more attractive offer of a position. His expression had not hinted at good news, but still she was taken aback when he grasped her hands in his and asked in a low undertone where Sarah was.

"Sarah?" Kitty repeated.

"Why is she not at the theater tonight, Kitty?" he queried urgently.

"Well, she isn't feeling quite the thing. Said she'd a megrim and wished to rest."

"Has she ever had a megrim before?"

Kitty thought a moment, then shook her head, a puzzled frown creasing her brow. "No, I cannot remember that she ever did. But what is your concern for Sarah?"

"Deuce take it, love, but I may be mad! Come with me where we can speak more freely."

Uneasiness pricking her, Kitty allowed Johnny to hurry her away from the people crowding into the box to welcome the Ramseys to town. Not coincidentally, they also managed to avoid the Earl of Westphal.

"This is far enough, Johnny!" Kitty dug in her heels when she thought they were well away. "I shall go mad if you do not explain."

"Kitty, the strangest set of coincidences has left me . . . unsettled. Did you see the fellow I was with in the pit? That was Jason Woodward. You won't know him. I scarcely do. He is Tom Woodward's older brother. We met earlier today at . . . well, at a drinking house." When Johnny gave her a rueful look, Kitty bit her lip, but they bravely ignored the topic of Scotland. "At any rate," Johnny continued, "Jason, having returned from Ireland, where he was inspecting some of his father's estates, asked me to join him in celebration. I did, and eventually got around to asking how Tom fared in the Indies, saying it had surprised me that he had chosen to go, for my old school fellow had never struck me as an adventurer. His tongue being a trifle loosened by that time, Jason mumbled something about Tom's having no choice in the matter. I suppose I started in surprise, I can't say, but eventually I had the story. Kitty, you'll not credit it, but Tom lost the Woodward emeralds in a game of cards!"

"Sir Adrian's necklace?" Kitty gaped in astonishment,

knowing of the necklace from a time when she had visited Sarah, and Sir Adrian had proudly displayed his pride and joy for her.

"Can you credit it?" Johnny shook his head in amazement. He, too, upon a visit to Cumberland in Tom's company, had witnessed Sir Adrian's pride in the illustrious necklace. "Sir Adrian has taken the loss so bitterly, he has forbidden any in his family to tell of it, as Jason admitted most sheepishly. That is why no one knows it was lost, or understands Tom is in the Indies, because his father has virtually banished him from England."

"But who won the thing from Tom? And why has he not broadcast his feat?"

"You will not countenance who won it, though I think you will understand why he has not made his possession of the necklace public, when you do know."

"Who is it?" Kitty cried, almost past the point of civility, she was so curious.

"Charles Kendall."

At the announcement a dozen different thoughts and questions occurred to Kitty, but the one she voiced, though she could not have said precisely why, was, "Does Sarah know?"

"You're a gem, Kitty!" Johnny beamed, looking as if he might embrace her on the spot. "That was the very question to ask, or so I think. No need to dwell on Kendall. Of course, he'd desire so spectacular a victory over a green boy kept quiet. There are too many questions about his play as it is. If this got out, doors would begin to close to him. There was . . ." Johnny chuckled when Kitty tapped her foot impatiently. "All right, enough of Kendall! As for Sarah, she has known all along."

Immediately Kitty grasped the significance of the announcement. All the time Sarah had been, if not precisely encouraging, then certainly not discouraging Kendall's attentions, she had been harboring a strong grievance against the man.

"Oh, dear!" was all she could think to say.

"There's more, Kitty! In the pit just now Jason was telling me of a mysterious note he received from Tom a day or so ago, advising him to look in on Sarah, as she'd some hope of recovering the necklace with a sum of money Tom sent by some sea captain.''

"The purse! Oh, he could not have encouraged her so!''

"He did," Johnny confirmed in the tone of one who sees some unbelievable thing, a mountain move, say, and cannot credit it. "Five hundred pounds of encouragement, to be exact. I cannot think what he imagined she would do with it, but that does not signify. The important thing is to consider Sarah. First"—he ticked off his point on his fingers, ''she knows Tom is suffering because Kendall won the necklace from him. Second, she can behave idiotically in support of a cause she believes just. We both recall how she traipsed off into my brother's woods in the night to free wild foxes from steel traps.'' He shook his head briefly before continuing, "And third, when I asked one of those two fellows Kendall goes about with all the time where the captain could be found tonight, he smirked suggestively and said Kendall was involved in quite deep play this evening. Kitty, I've the worst suspicion Sarah has challenged Kendall to a game of chance, staking Tom's five hundred pounds against the necklace.''

"But it is worth much more! Surely—''

"I've seen the way Kendall looks at her when he thinks he's not observed.'' The young man's cheerful countenance hardened. "If he thought he could get her to a private room, he would say anything she wanted to hear. He'll have his way with her, and she will have no recourse. She cannot threaten him with a duel, nor can she decry him publicly.

"Oh, Johnny! But you must find them!''

When Kitty put her hand out imploringly, Johnny took it in his. "I will, of course, if it comes to it, but, Kitty, love, I've the most painful admission to make.'' Johnny looked so dreadfully shamefaced of a sudden, Kitty squeezed his hand tightly, with the result that he gave her a rueful smile. "The truth is, I'm no match for Kendall. I can bring down a partridge, on a clear day, but he's a crack shot; and while I have lifted a sword perhaps once in play, he's spent half his adult life becoming proficient with one. As to fists . . .'' Johnny shrugged, allowing his short, square—and entirely dear to Kitty—figure speak for him. "If our confrontation could be played out at cards, I might give him some challenge, but I doubt I could force him to meet me on that field.''

"What are we to do, then? Sarah must be with him. I've no doubt of it now, for she has never been sick a day in her life. I cannot think why I suspected nothing, except that I was distracted over . . . over you. Oh, Johnny, what are we to do!'' Kitty cried, when the warning bell for the second act chased her own difficulties from her mind.

"I've a thought, but I would not act without your approval, love,'' Johnny said quickly, mindful of the bell. ''It involves someone outside your family. I had thought to speak to Ravensby.''

"To Ravensby?''

Johnny nodded. ''I know it seems farfetched, but—''

"No!'' Kitty gripped his hands, beginning to smile. ''No, it is not farfetched at all. I think there is something between the two of them, though Sarah denies it. They are always turning up together, and have you noticed how the very air between them seems charged, somehow?''

"Rather,'' Johnny replied dryly, thinking how intent upon each other the two had been in the gardens at Vauxhall. ''But the best of it is Ravensby's here tonight and without Lady Sophia.''

"Go quickly, then, before the interval is over.''

"First, my dear, I must return you to your mama. She will be livid if I do not, and I shall send in a note to the earl. It will be for the best if we speak after the play's begun, when no one is about.''

Johnny's note brought Dominic out at once into the deserted corridor, but it took the young man a little time to convince the Earl of Ravensby of the merit of his concerns. First, he had to explain about Sarah, how loyal she was and how nobly foolish she could be. In other circumstances he'd have been amused by Ravensby's reaction to the story of the fox traps. ''Little fool!'' he distinctly heard the man growl.

Dominic asked a spate of questions. Johnny took them in good part, answering readily, but did not wait to be questioned on Sarah's regard for Tom Woodward.

"He is her oldest friend, sir. They live only a mile apart, if one goes across the country rather than by the road. And if that were not enough for Sa . . . ah, Miss Marlowe, I believe she's reason to feel a particular obligation to him. Tom never told the whole, but once, when he returned to school sporting a quite rivetingly black eye, he did allow he'd gotten it from James Marlowe. James is Sarah's cousin, sir, and has a very unsavory reputation when it comes to ladies.''

A hard look in his eyes, Ravensby said slowly, "I see," then fell into a frowning abstraction before, at length, addressing Johnny again. He did not, as Johnny had feared, dismiss the tale he had heard as too fanciful to be believed. Indeed, going straight to the point, the earl asked, "Where would he take her, I wonder. Certainly not to his rooms at Whittingham's. There would be servants to come to her assistance if she cried loudly enough for help.''

"I've been considering the question, sir." Johnny cleared his throat, discomfited to be putting himself forward so, but when the earl accorded him his full attention, Johnny was emboldened. "Kendall frequents Maude O'Neil's gaming house in St. James Square. She would . . ."

Ravensby nodded. "Yes, I know Maude. She would do anything for a little silver." Suddenly he smiled, and though it was not a pleasant smile, Johnny found himself smiling back. "She'll unseal lips supposedly sealed, so long as one has the means to persuade her.''

Whether the earl meant he'd the silver with which to buy Maude O'Neil's cooperation, or some other means to persuade her, Johnny was never to learn. Ravensby did not explain, nor was Johnny present for the meeting between the two. Indeed, he was not even at the gaming house, for the earl thought it best that Johnny remain behind.

"As we are rarely seen in the other's company, there would be speculation as to the link between us. I doubt anyone would guess what it was, but I would rather avoid the possibility altogether.''

Johnny bowed to the impeccable logic, but he could not, quite, contain the chagrin he felt at missing what was certain to be a far more exciting final act than the one to be played out on the stage at Covent Garden that evening.

Seeing the young man's expression, Dominic clapped him on the shoulder. "You'll be the first to learn the outcome, Mr. Carstairs, I promise you that. Come to my house tomorrow at ten. I'll tell you the whole, and we'll discuss as well a position I have been considering offering to you. You've proved yourself clearheaded enough for it, that is certain." Even as Johnny, openmouthed, gathered his wits to nod his assent, Ravensby whirled to go, only to turn at the last moment and say over his shoulder, "Will you make my excuses to Lady Ruth, Mr. Carstairs? Best to do it quickly and say you're naught but a messenger, or she'll have the truth out of you before you know it."

With that, he wheeled away, striding toward the stairs with a look on his face that boded ill for Captain Charles Kendall.

It was the door had made that crack. Sarah comprehended it was not that her pistol had gone off after a second made agonizingly long by the fear that she might have killed a man. As the knowledge came to her, she saw Kendall's eyes flare with the same understanding; then a cool voice confirmed what they knew.

"Am I interrupting?"

Sarah did not have the time to sort out the identity of the voice. Kendall flung her from him so forcefully she went reeling. Half her mind on her pistol, she nearly lost her footing, but managed to clutch the one chair that had remained upright through her struggle with Kendall.

It was the captain found voice first, exclaiming in a hoarse, stunned croak, "Ravensby!"

The earl's eyes were upon Sarah. She could not utter a sound, could only stare, panting for breath, until he, apparently satisfied as to her condition, shifted his regard back again to the captain.

"How observant you are, Kendall." A cold smile lifted his lips. "But what an odd position it is in which I find you. I had not thought a lady would be obliged to resort to a pistol to persuade you to her purposes. Or could it be she was attempting to fend off your purposes, Captain?"

The hairs on the back of Sarah's neck lifted. Ravensby spoke pleasantly enough, as if he were only idly curious in the answer to his question, but no one was deceived.

Least of all Kendall, who colored. "I would not have you make more of this than there is, Ravensby!" he cautioned, while, his eyes never leaving the earl, he made haste to smooth his hair and right his coat. "I don't know what your interest is in Miss Marlowe, but I can assure you we are here at her request. She'd something she wished to win from me. I gave her a fair crack at the thing. When she lost, she did not take her loss well, and thus you saw us."

"That is a bald lie!" Sarah had regained her powers of speech and the ability to glare contemptuously at Kendall. "I did ask for this match," she admitted, turning to address Ravensby. "The captain does have something I wish restored to its rightful owner, and I did agree to meet him here alone. I was foolish beyond belief. I know it, for I trusted him as a gentleman, while he's not the honor of a slug."

"Why you little . . . !" Kendall made a move toward Sarah but recalled, in time, Ravensby.

"Yes, Captain?" she inquired with a pointed glance at his hands balled into quite impotent fists. "Have you thought better of continuing your assault upon me now we are not alone? But never mind, that little display quite proves my point, I think."

Pale, but with her chin high, Sarah again faced Ravensby. He had not moved from the door against which he casually reclined, arms crossed over his chest.

"I did lose the game, and the opportunity to recover the . . . the item I wanted. I cannot deny the loss was bitter. I would not have come if I had had no hope at all of winning. But as I had lost, I gave the captain the five hundred pounds I had said I would put up. It is now our story differs, for the captain would not accept the stakes about which he made no demur at all at Vauxhall. Five hundred pounds was too little for him, and he meant to take what he thought he deserved. By my honor, I'd never have come if I'd known I was wagering my . . . person against his valuable!"

"Where is the five hundred pounds?"

"There." Sarah pointed to the table, only to be reminded it

had been overturned. "And there and there and there," she went on, pointing at the notes scattered about the floor.

"And the necklace?"

"What?" Sarah looked at him in astonishment. "How did you come to know of it?"

But Dominic was looking pointedly at Kendall. A flush mounted on the captain's cheeks. "I, ah, could not bring it. I . . . thought it too valuable."

"Well, you may send for it while we play." Ravensby matched his brisk tone with sudden, decisive action. Pushing off from the door, he gathered the hundred-pound notes from the floor.

"What do you mean?" Kendall demanded, face paling. "I've no intention of playing you, Ravensby!"

"Limit yourself to boys and young ladies, do you?" The earl rose to give Kendall a thin smile. "Not very sporting, Captain. And you will play"—the smile faded entirely—"or I shall have you cashiered from the army. You may take your choice."

A murderous glitter lit Kendall's eyes, and Sarah looked anxiously from one man to the other. Ravensby was larger, taller, possessed of broader shoulders. But Kendall, if slighter, was wiry, and he'd been trained for combat.

Still, Sarah was glad it was Ravensby stood as her ally. While Kendall's anger made him seem wild and even frantic, the earl appeared hard as ice.

For safety's sake, however, Sarah tightened her hold on her little pistol. She would not hesitate to use it a second time. She knew Kendall better now.

But it did not come to that. His jaw clenched tightly, he ground out, "I shall have to go and speak to my man."

It was then Sarah and Kendall were both made aware the earl's arrival in their room was by no means a hastily contrived thing.

"Maude's man is at the door. He'll take your note down to the fellow." Kendall's dark eyes went black at the implication that he could not be trusted to return from a conference with his servant, but Ravensby only added helpfully, "He's pen and paper for you."

Anyone who might have been in the hall would have thought it odd indeed to see Captain Charles Kendall wrench open the door to one of the private rooms and for all purposes tear writing materials from Maude O'Neil's most trusted minion. The older man swayed, so violently was he relieved of his burden, but he remained patiently by the door to take the note that was in a very few seconds smacked hard into his hand.

Sarah looked to Ravensby while Kendall was occupied with his note. She could not understand how he had known to come once more to her rescue, but she was exceedingly grateful, and even if he were furiously angry with her, as she thought likely, she allowed every ounce of her gratitude to show in her eyes.

Before she could give voice to her feelings, he asked, voice low and controlled, "Were you harmed in any way, Miss Marlowe?"

She shook her head. "No, my lord. Only my pride is bruised."

No flicker of amusement lit his golden-brown eyes, no faint smile lightened his expression. Indeed Sarah could not be certain he had heard her, for he looked more fierce than ever as he stood regarding her during the moment it took Kendall to complete his business by the door.

23

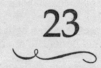

"You may wish to sit down, Miss Marlowe. This may take the captain and me a little time."

Ravensby did not wait to see if Sarah followed his suggestion. While she nudged a chair to his side of the table, he righted the one she had formerly occupied, and Kendall flung himself into the last.

"Champagne, Ravensby?" he asked nastily, as if he did not think the earl would accept the invitation.

But Ravensby surprised him. "Yes. Miss Marlowe?" When

Sarah did not answer at once, he added, "You look as if you could use it."

"There are not three glasses," Kendall noted churlishly. "I wasn't expecting company."

The earl shrugged. "She may have mine, then."

Preoccupied with pouring the champagne, Kendall did not see his opponent lay a pack of cards wrapped luxuriously in gold tissue paper upon the table until after he served Sarah. "What's this?" he demanded then, gesturing with the bottle.

"A new deck. Surely you recognize Maude's signature wrapping paper?"

Kendall's eyes narrowed. "Miss Marlowe and I did well enough with my deck."

"No, Kendall," Ravensby replied softly. "You did well with your deck. Miss Marlowe, as I recall the story, lost with it."

A crafty gleam lit Kendall's dark eyes. "How do I know this deck is not marked?"

"Do you accuse Maude or me?" Ravensby queried, seemingly uninterested in the answer. There was only one indication that lives hung on the captain's response, and that was the sudden cessation of all sound. Sarah did not breathe.

But once more Kendall swallowed his bile. "Neither of you, of course," he snapped.

"Good. Then shall we draw for deal? Oh, and by the by, I don't think I can stomach your company for more than one rubber. This will be it, winner take all."

Sarah shot an uncertain glance at Ravensby. Was he deliberately trying to goad Kendall?

If so, he succeeded to the extent that a muscle in the captain's jaw jerked uncontrollably. "I think the one should do it."

"And just to be certain we all understand, the stakes are the same as those to which you agreed at Vauxhall: Miss Marlowe's five hundred pounds against the Woodward necklace."

Pallor, Sarah observed, did not become Captain Charles Kendall. It gave his skin a dreadful greenish cast. Had he possessed even one highly placed friend in the military, he'd have refused the terms of the wager. But he did not. It was Ravensby had the connections in high places.

Sarah felt little pity for Kendall. He'd had none for her. She did feel wary, however, and kept a watch on the captain lest he should attempt to redress the situation by producing a pistol of his own.

Against Ravensby, Kendall did not play with the assurance he'd displayed in his game with Sarah. He hesitated interminably over his discards, hand hovering over one card, then moving to another, then back; all the while, he flicked his eyes to the earl's cards as if he would divine what Ravensby held.

Odd, that, Sarah thought, unless he was in the habit of reading subtle marks. Ravensby had been, she realized, quite right to produce a fresh deck.

Sarah was convinced beyond doubt Kendall was a cheat when he cried out in frustration at the sight of some card he'd chosen from the table. He had never been so unpleasantly surprised when he played her.

In the tense silence, the loudest sound, but for Kendall's curses, was that of the cards being played upon the table. No one spoke. Sarah did not think Kendall could have made conversation if he wanted. Beads of sweat marked his brow as he crouched over the table watching the play.

She could not tell how the game affected Ravensby. In contrast to Kendall, he lounged back in his chair, glancing without expression from his hand to Kendall, then to the cards lying facedown upon the table. Never once did he look at Sarah, nor did she try to engage his attention.

She wished to distract neither man. Ravensby for obvious reasons, and Kendall because she did not want to give him any reason to cry unfair if he lost. Still and silent, her hands clasped tightly over the pistol in her lap, she watched the flow of the play so intently, she did not hear the discreet rap at the door.

Ravensby did, however. "Will you go and receive the package I believe will be handed you by the man at the door, Miss Marlowe?"

Ravensby did not seem to desire a reply. He had not glanced up from his cards when he put the request to her. Only Kendall's head had slewed around jerkily.

She was aware the captain's eyes remained upon her as she opened the door and received from the elderly servant who'd been her guide, a wide rectangular box. Closing the door behind her, Sarah returned to the table.

"Verify its contents, if you will," Ravensby directed as he exchanged three cards from his hand for three on the table.

The captain missed the action entirely. His eyes were riveted to the box Sarah held, a hungry expression in his eyes as the splendid green stones came into view.

"It is Sir Adrian's necklace," Sarah said, looking to Ravensby.

"Not yet, it's not!" A hectic flush on his face, Kendall shot Sarah a furious look before jerking his attention back to his cards. Taking in that the earl had left him five cards from which to choose, he took four, and after examining them, cried, "Ha! Ha!" at which Sarah's heart sank.

With a mocking flourish, he laid down his hand, the last of the rubber. "Five clubs, four in a row, and three sevens, Ravensby. Eleven cards played! It's mine!"

"Tsh, tsh. You are hasty, Kendall," Ravensby admonished softly before one by one displaying his cards. Each was a face card, in sequence and in suit. When he was done, he held no card in his hand.

Kendall was ghostly pale as he stared in seeming incomprehension at the magnificent display. "But . . . but that is impossible! You'd need the luck of the devil to do that!"

"Careful, Kendall." There was that in the earl's eyes made the captain swallow whatever else he had meant to say about the amazing hand with which Ravensby had won their single rubber.

"Now, you will leave the Woodward necklace where it is, and after whatever night's sleep you can manage, will return to your regiment, wherever it is stationed. I do not believe it should be necessary for me to add that I would not care to hear even a whisper about what has occurred in this room tonight. However, should you be tempted to exact revenge by bandying Miss Marlowe's name about, you ought to know the consequences. Not only will I have you cashiered from the army in that case, Kendall, but I will produce the cards with which you played tonight. After I have done that, it will be my pleasure to call you out. Do you understand, sir?"

"Yes! Damn you!" His face contorted in a snarl worthy of a mastiff, the captain leapt to his feet. "I understand you would ruin me!"

Ravensby's movements, by contrast with Kendall's, were almost lazy. Only his eyes gave him away as he rose to his feet and leaned forward across the table to bring his face within an inch of the captain's.

"You are a cur, sir," he intoned, his voice as dangerous as the look in his narrowed eyes. "You cheat young men at cards, and tonight, had you not been stopped, you'd have raped an innocent young woman. My best advice to you is that you tuck your mangy tail between your legs and hie from this room before I chide myself for being too lenient with you."

When Kendall flung away from the table, Sarah did not fault him overmuch for cowardice. She thought there were few would have cared to face Ravensby down just then. They all understood that, had Kendall pressed him even once more, he'd have exploded upon the captain, mauling him with pleasure.

Only when he gained the door did Kendall find the courage to hesitate in his flight. Stopping, hand on the handle, he looked back at Ravensby, a strange smirk curving his lips. "I almost forgot! There is a flaw with your plan, Ravensby. I cannot decamp now. It would not be the honorable thing at all, when Charlotte Manwairing is carrying my brat."

Sarah gasped, but neither man seemed to hear her. They were fixed on each other. "Such confidence, Kendall," Ravensby chided, unmoved. "Despite what were, I don't doubt, your best efforts, you cannot know whether Miss Manwairing is breeding. The Whittinghams' ball was not quite four weeks ago."

Despite everything—the tension thick in the room, the not even yet fully realized joy of holding Tom Woodward's prize in her lap, the unsettling uncertainty of what Ravensby's mood would be when Kendall departed—despite all that, Sarah nearly giggled aloud at the look that came over the captain's face. His jaw dropped comically, and he stared at Ravensby as if he saw a sorcerer before him.

Nor did Ravensby explain how he could know when Kendall had found the opportunity to lure Miss Manwairing to a bed. He only went on to say, "Get you gone, Captain. Manwairing will find you, if he wants you."

* * *

The click of the door behind Kendall ought to have meant a sudden lightening of the atmosphere. It did not, however. To Sarah it seemed the tension actually increased. But that may have been because she, not Kendall, was now the focus of Ravensby's regard.

Her hands tensed, gripping more tightly to the box she held, but in the end, because she meant it so very much, she did not find it difficult to say simply, "Thank you, my lord. I—"

He waved off the rest of her thanks. "We must get you out of here, Miss Marlowe, and safely home. If we are quick about it, we shall just get you there before the Ponsbys' return. This is your cloak?"

Sarah nodded rather blankly as he brought it to her. Whatever she had expected, and she knew not precisely what that was, Sarah certainly had not anticipated this suddenly remote, entirely businesslike attitude.

"I am so grateful!" she tried again after he had placed the cloak upon her shoulders and once more stood before her.

His mouth quirked. Sarah could see very plainly the way it lifted at one corner, for he was leaning down close to her to lift her hood over her head.

She had not done it herself because, wanting most of all to talk to him, to hear him tell her why it was, and how, too, he had come to save her yet again, she had not thought to put down either the velvet box she held or her little pistol and do the honors for herself.

So impatient, it seemed, was Ravensby to go that he did not even wait for her to see the need to tie her own ribbons when her hood was raised, but set about performing that task as well himself. Their eyes met then. With a start she saw his were lightened by some emotion. She supposed it was humor when he finally replied to her exclamation of gratitude, saying, "You ought to be grateful."

"I do know it! Really, you cannot—"

Again he cut her off. This time by laying his finger across her lips. It was a very effective gesture. Sarah caught back her breath as well as her words. "We've not time now."

With almost annoying briskness he relieved her of the pistol, and if, ever so briefly, he did shake his head as he weighed it in his hand, he demonstrated no other emotion as he gathered up the pack of cards that had been Kendall's, then escorted Sarah to the door.

When he had assured himself there was no one in the corridor, Ravensby led Sarah back the way she had come, choosing all the correct doors with an ease of familiarity she could not but mark. Outside the gate in the back wall of the garden they found his carriage waiting.

Once inside, he did not call out an address, but rapped on the roof, and they rolled away. "Now, how did you plan to reenter your uncle's house, Miss Marlowe? Did you persuade a maid to leave a door unlocked?"

Had the lanterns in the carriage been lit, Dominic would have seen a flush rise on Sarah's cheeks; as it was, he only heard a slight intake of breath in the place where some reply ought to have been.

"Do not say you did not make arrangements to reenter the house! How did you get out?"

Sarah's voice was rather small when it emerged. "I, ah, I came out the front door."

Ravensby's most unexpected response was to throw back his head and laugh, if the short, sharp bark could be called a laugh. "I do not believe, Miss Marlowe, that secret missions are your forte, which is, I suppose in all, something of a relief."

She was on the point of saying she expected the front door would still be open as she had left it, but he spoke first. "I suppose the front door will still be open. Billings can go to the back, and saying he is a Bow Street Runner, ask if they've heard anything odd in the mews. That should set the servants buzzing away from the front of the house. Yes"—he nodded slowly to himself—"it should do."

Sarah could not fault the plan. It seemed not only sound but also admirably inventive. She wanted to say as much, wanted to voice any one of a dozen thoughts, but just as she turned to him, the carriage swerved to miss a drunkard staggering in the street, and she was thrown into him.

His arm went around her, holding her to him, not, she noted, pushing her away. "Can it be the captain, do you think?" he queried when the drunkard reeled out of their path shouting garbled threats.

Sarah said nothing, all questions and replies forgotten as she lay with her cheek upon his chest, listening to the strong, steady beat of his heart. His body was warm and powerful beneath the silken layer of his clothes. Slowly she turned her face up to him, bringing her mouth only a very few inches from his.

He seemed to catch his breath, looking down at her, his arm cradling her. His eyes lowered to her mouth, and then they both realized the carriage was rolling to a stop.

"I'm afraid we've made good time."

He smiled, she saw his teeth white in the dark, then he was entirely brisk again, putting her away from him and jumping out to confer with a squarish man who bounded down from his seat beside the coachman. No sooner had the fellow sped off than Ravensby reached into the carriage for Sarah.

"Come along, Miss Marlowe. I want you off the street as quickly as possible."

That was all well and good. Of course, Sarah shared his concern for her reputation. She also wanted to touch him again, even if only by the hand. Therefore, she put her hand in his, but recalling all her questions, she'd also the sense that she was being rushed along at the expense of her peace of mind.

"But, my lord," she protested, her toes only touching the pavement as he hurried her along. "Please! I must know how you discovered what I was about. And how you knew where to find me. And how you learned of the Woodward necklace. I thought no one in London knew Kendall had it."

"This is it, isn't it?"

Sarah looked up almost in surprise. "Oh, yes. It is my uncle's house. But—"

"Tomorrow. I'll come back then, or if you cannot wait, you may ask your cousin when she returns from the theater. You owe her a great deal, Miss Marlowe, and young Mr. Carstairs."

A quick scan of the neighborhood affirmed little but that no one was leaning out a window watching them. As that was all the assurance he was going to get, Dominic whisked Sarah up the steps of the town house and tried the door handle.

Only just stifling a cry of satisfaction, Sarah watched the

handle descend and the door open smoothly. "Off with you now, Miss Marlowe." Ravensby gave her a little push through the door when she seemed to hesitate. Nor did he give her the opportunity to turn and bid him farewell. Just as she was registering that her luck was still in, that there was no one in the entryway, she heard the door close softly behind her.

A little groan of frustration escaped her, but she recognized it would be the worst sort of thanks, after all Ravensby had done for her, if she were to make a public scene by rushing back into the night to call out to him, or, as she admitted she'd have liked to do far more, to hurl herself into his arms.

She'd not have long to wait for Kitty, she told herself, flying up the stairs to her room. And he would come on the morrow.

24

"I am pleased you would come for a drive with me, Sophy, though it is not the fashionable hour. The fine day is a more pleasant setting for a farewell than a drawing room. I shall be leaving town soon."

Lady Sophia shifted her parasol to look up at Dominic. "You are leaving town at the height of the Season?"

He gave her a light smile. "An estate knows only the seasons of nature, not of society."

There was a pause; then she said, "What of Lady Cowper's ball and Papa's gathering next week?"

"I shall be sorry to miss your father's gathering," he replied with every evidence of sincerity. "But as to Lady Cowper's ball, I've a notion Percy will make you a better escort than I. He seems quite in his element at such affairs."

Lady Sophia made no comment on Sir Percival's undeniable enthusiasm for the social round, nor did she remark that Dominic had not seemed particularly at sea at glittering galas. "Will you be away long?"

He shrugged vaguely. "I cannot say. It depends on several factors. But I doubt I shall return before the fall."

"The fall?" She turned to stare up at him. "Haven't you an agent to manage your estates, Dominic?"

"I've three, actually." He smiled a little. "But I'm of the opinion nothing can cause an estate to decline more rapidly than an owner's neglect. Too," he added more gravely, "I've Langston's affairs to look after. His condition is worsening."

There was a long silence as Lady Sophia digested his news. Dominic kept his eyes ahead upon the traffic and his pair of blooded chestnuts, their coats gleaming richly in the sun. At the park, he turned in, glad it was not the fashionable hour with its congested traffic. Near a small lake he drew up and threw his reins to his tiger.

"Why ever are we stopping?" Lady Sophia looked about in surprise.

Dominic had the grace to grin as he invited tardily, "Come, take a walk with me."

"A walk?" she queried, regarding him with all the astonishment she might have accorded someone asking her to trek across Asia.

Dominic smiled. "Only a short one."

He lifted her down. Over her head he noted the passage of a carriage he did not recognize but marked because he had the impression of sunlight reflecting off a sleek golden head. A rueful smile tilted his mouth as he gave Lady Sophia his arm and started off across the grass. He was seeing Sarah Marlowe everywhere.

"But the ground is not even, Dominic!" Lady Sophy protested, eyeing the grass with distaste.

"The path, then." He changed direction without protest, savoring with his eye the smooth roll of the lawns, the grace of the large willow by the stream, the scattering of bright daffodils along the walk. "I like this very much, you know."

Lady Sophia looked about, brow lifting. "What, pray?"

"The lawns, the willow, the flowers, even those motley ducks waddling over to demand a dole."

"What a pastoral enthusiast you are, sir." Lady Sophia gave him a long, considering look. "I didn't know."

He laughed. "Nor did I, at least not the extent of my enthusiasm. Not until I came to stay in town."

There was silence between them as they climbed an arched stone bridge. At the top they stopped to look out over the stream flowing beneath them. "You have changed, Dominic," Lady Sophy remarked at last, slowly, almost reluctantly. "I thought when you came to town, you intended to become a figure in political circles, to take your seat in the House of Lords, to entertain." She shrugged an elegantly draped shoulder. "Join the social round, in short."

"I did come to see if I were still interested in that life," Dominic acknowledged. "And I am, in aspects of it. I shall speak out in Parliament, when I've a notion, and I have every desire to discuss the issues of the day over a glass of claret with my friends. But I've little interest in becoming a fixture of the social round. I would have only a few guests for dinner, not hundreds for a ball, except on the rarest occasions. And I would be content to see my friends when it suits us, not night after night at one do upon another. Truly, Sophy, the social round is my idea of hell."

She gave a sharp, abrupt laugh. They both knew the social round was the breath of life for her.

Quietly he said, "You'd not be happy with me, Sophy."

She pulled in a deep breath, looking away. It had come, and with all the gentleness there was beneath that harder, unyielding side he showed to most. She ought to have been prepared. She had suspected for some time he would not make her his countess. Since that brief visit to Kent he'd seemed different. Remote, distracted, he had played her escort only occasionally. And even then his eyes had strayed frequently from her.

She'd had her chance at him years ago. She knew it. He'd have married her then, she did believe, if she had gone to him when he had nothing. He'd not have accepted a penny of her father's wealth, though, and knowing that, she'd not gone. No matter how compelling he was, and Dominic Moreland had been almost as riveting as a young man as he was now, she had not been able to contemplate life as a near-pauper.

"But now you've found someone who would live that life with you, haven't you, Dominic?"

Dominic's brow lifted. He'd not followed her thoughts at all, had in fact been saying how she would miss her parties, her *on-dits,* and come to resent him. She saw his surprise, but shook her head. "Never mind. It's best left. Well!" She lifted her chin, very much again the elegant, fashionable lady who is up to everything. And if her eyes were misty, she managed a small smile. "It's been a lovely novelty, this walk, my dear, but I think it's time I went home. I'm off to the Farquahars' tonight. . . ."

By the time a maid peeked around Sarah's door to announce that the Earl of Ravensby and Mrs. Ponsby awaited her below in the drawing room, Sarah had learned from Kitty the chain of events that had brought the earl to Maude O'Neil's gaming house. She even had an answer to the question that had, since a ride in the park earlier in the day, become the most important to her. When she had wished to know why Kitty and Johnny had chosen to apply to Ravensby for assistance, Kitty had giggled but gotten out at last that they had deemed him a better match for Kendall than Johnny. But why go to Ravensby in particular? Sarah had insisted, to which Kitty had returned with impeccable logic, "Who else could have wrapped the matter up so neatly?"

Sarah had wanted very much to hear something else. All through a restless night she had been thinking how he had come for her yet again; how he had not pushed her away in the carriage, but actually seemed on the point of kissing her; even how changed he had seemed at Vauxhall—and on those thoughts she had been building high, high hopes.

Those hopes seemed the merest sand castles the next morning, when escorting Becky off to play with the Ramseys' youngest child, Sarah agreed to a detour through the park and chanced to see the earl lifting Lady Sophia from his gig that they might enjoy a walk at an hour when there would be few people about to disturb them.

She knew she owed him her thanks now he'd gotten around to coming to Albemarle Street, but her feet dragged as she went down the stairs. She needed time to compose her features. She did not want him to know how wretchedly disappointed she was, and would have been mortified should he guess why.

It took only the sound of her aunt's voice to make Sarah's spirits plunge further. Poor Aunt Vinnie! Her hopes would have risen unmercifully at the earl's visit. And when nothing came of it, she would suffer her second blow of the Season on Sarah's account.

Sarah could not have been more correct about her aunt's mood. Mrs. Ponsby was positively giddy with raised hopes. But Sarah, dawdling in the hall while she summoned the will to appear breezy and unaffected, could not know Mrs. Ponsby's spirits had been lifted long before Ravensby's arrival upon her doorstep.

While Sarah had been proceeding through the park, Mrs. Ponsby had summoned Kitty to her room, intending to read the girl a severe scold on her behavior at the theater the night before, but her daughter had forestalled even the first harsh word.

"Mama! I know why you wish to speak with me, and you may cut up at me as deeply as you wish, only first I've something to tell you. It is about Sarah, and I think it wise you are prepared."

"Oh, my dear! What can it be now!" Mrs. Ponsby had wailed.

But Kitty, giggling excitedly, had bounced down on the bed beside her and said, "It is good news, Mama! I vow you will be beside yourself when you know."

"Well, what is it?" Mrs. Ponsby had demanded, intrigued, and beginning, despite herself, to smile.

"The Earl of Ravensby is, I truly believe, head over heels for Sarah."

"What!" Mrs. Ponsby clasped her hands together in the attitude of a saint experiencing ecstasy.

"And of course Sarah is head over heels for him," Kitty continued, eyes sparkling. "If I am not mistaken, the earl intends to come to Albemarle Street today, and if you will not take it amiss, Mama, I suggest that it would not be too terribly awful if you should find some pressing reason to quit the drawing room entirely."

"Dear girl!" Mrs. Ponsby chided, entirely in her element. "Do you not know that I am prescient? Of course, I can be certain poor Charles will . . . take a dreadful fall shortly after the earl arrives."

At which, of course, they both giggled until the tears came to their eyes. Eventually, when they both sobered, Mrs. Ponsby wished to know what had led Kitty to subscribe to such happy, happy theories, and Kitty, prepared, explained that the earl had shown great concern over Sarah's absence from the theater the night before. "It was on Sarah's account Johnny was late returning me to our box, you see." Kitty went on quickly, before her mother could press for an exact chronology of events or a detailed recounting of conversations, "And there is more, Mama! The earl has offered Johnny a position. No, more than that! Oh, I can scarce believe it, but I did have a note from Johnny, and in it he said Ravensby believes he owes, er, that is, the earl wishes to settle a farm upon us, if Sarah accepts him!"

Mrs. Ponsby's hand went to her throat, and seeming beyond coherent speech, she could only babble, "Oh, oh, oh, my! Settle a farm upon you! Oh! Kitty! Oh! My dear girl!"

"It is not a grand estate, you understand," Kitty cautioned, though almost as overcome as her mother. "It is only a small stud farm near Newmarket. It comes to the earl through an old friend, Lord Langston, and who can say if he really meant what he said to Johnny? It is such a grand gesture, he may think better of it, but, oh, Mama, I do have hope!"

As a result of Kitty's confidences, Mrs. Ponsby greeted Ravensby with such awe and gratitude, he had to exert all his charm merely to calm her sufficiently that she could remember to send for Sarah.

Sarah, ignorant of the reason for her aunt's elation, felt a worse villain than ever when she entered the drawing room. Mrs. Ponsby almost literally skipped forward to clasp her hand, squeeze it tightly, meaningfully, and lead her forward. "My dear, the earl has come to ask after your health. He was most concerned to find you absent from the theater last evening, but if you feel better, as I am certain you do, he wishes to take you for a drive in the park!"

''No!'' Sarah felt her cheeks go hot as Mrs. Ponsby looked at her with a start. ''That is, I, ah, do still feel weak.''

Mrs. Ponsby was all concern. ''Sarah, dear! I did not know. How very awful. I am not accustomed to you being peaked. I don't doubt it was that trip with Becky. She said she had persuaded you to lengthen your little journey that she might admire the park. Come and sit down at once!''

All the while her aunt was chattering, Sarah was achingly aware of Ravensby. He had risen from his seat when she entered, and stood watching her. She glanced up from under her lashes and saw he was . . . amused!

''Good afternoon, Miss Marlowe,'' he greeted her as her aunt brought her to him. ''I am sorry you do not feel quite the thing.''

She dipped a curtsy, mumbling good afternoon and thanking him for his concern, but did not dare meet his eyes again until she could determine why he should look so knowing.

It was almost as if he knew why she feigned illness again. But of course, he could not. He had been too intent upon Lady Sophia to see Sarah. The thought made her feel ill, and turning a complete coward, she decided to say she was so weak she could only thank the earl for his concern and retire immediately to her room. But before she could do more than open her mouth, one of the housemaids knocked and entered.

''Beggin' yer pardon, ma'am.'' The girl bobbed a curtsy and said, just as Mrs. Ponsby had instructed her, ''Katie wishes you to come to the nursery at once. Master Charles has taken a fall.''

Mrs. Ponsby rose instantly, saying to the earl, ''I know you will excuse me, sir! An emergency! Sarah, I leave you to see to Lord Ravensby's comfort until I return.'' And she bustled from the room before either party could do more than stare after her.

Dominic recovered first, and nearly smiled, for thinking on it, he realized Mrs. Ponsby's step had been exceedingly light as she rushed to her wounded son. Then his eyes came to rest upon Sarah, who was staring at the carpet as if it were J.M.W. Turner's latest work.

''Last night I very much feared you might come dashing back into the street to force an accounting from me, but now, when you may ask whatever you like, you will not even look at me. Sarah?''

His voice was low and deliciously lazy, and when he said her name, it was only with the greatest effort that she could resist looking at him. But, if even the thought of looking at him hurt, what, she reasoned, would actually glancing up and meeting those eyes that only laughed at her bring? Safest to keep her gaze averted.

Safest, perhaps, but impossible. He cupped his hand around her chin and lifted gently. Lord! but her eyes could go so wide, Dominic thought, and appear the deepest blue.

"Kitty told me everything."

It was a whisper, all Sarah could manage, looking into Ravensby's eyes. There was laughter in them. They sparkled with more gold than brown, but there was tenderness too, and something that had the effect of making her heart skip in its beating.

"Everything?" The lightest pressure of his hand lifted Sarah to her feet. She was so close to him, it seemed there was not enough air between them to breathe. "Did she tell you why I flew from the theater, not even taking time to make my excuses to my sister or my niece, but leaving the task to John Carstairs, Sarah?''

Her eyes never leaving his, Sarah shook her head slowly.

"Or did Miss Ponsby explain why I'd have taken pleasure pistol-whipping Captain Kendall to within an inch of his life last night, and only did not because of the inevitable gossip that would result when he appeared mauled and bloodied in the hallway of Maude's gaming house?"

"No."

It was the merest sigh, for Dominic was tracing the fine bones of her cheek and jaw with his fingers before trailing those sensitive fingers down to rest lightly on the back of her neck. "Then, perhaps," he continued, his voice as soft as his touch, "she was able to explain why it was I accompanied Lady Sophia Carrington to the park earlier today. . . ."

Sarah stiffened abruptly, and in response the hand lying just beneath her hairline began to move in slow, lazy, sensuous circles on her neck. To her dismay, a ripple of pleasure raced down her spine. "Ah, Sarah, Sarah." His voice was so husky, it caused a pool of warmth to form in the middle of her body to match the one growing at that place upon her neck he caressed so sensuously.

Sarah wanted nothing but to touch him, the problem of Lady Sophia Carrington rendered unimportant by his caress, his look, his voice. She laid her hands upon his coat and as slowly let them glide up the length of his chest.

Instantly the languid, amused look disappeared from Dominic's eyes. Intent, suddenly, they engaged her so deeply, she was aware of naught but him. His muscles, taut beneath her fingers, his dark hair thick and shining, the lean length of his body, the male smell of him, everything affected her, and she felt herself melting into him.

"Why did you come today?" she whispered.

"To say I love you, my love. And have for the very longest of times."

"Oh!" She could not quite believe it. Though he looked as if he meant it, and held her as if he did, Lady Sophia came back again.

"You," Dominic repeated, reading her doubts in her clear eyes. "No one but you. I was saying my farewells to Sophy. I owe her that. When you saw us, you jumped to the wrong conclusion."

"Oh!" she cried, for it was not she who had erred the most grievously in that realm. But Sarah's cry was less than fierce. Dominic had brought her up so that she lay against him, her breasts soft upon his chest and her delicate ear within easy reach of his mouth.

"I know, I know," he admitted, his whisper such a warm pleasure as it caressed her ear, she tilted her head for more. "Forgive me all I've said and done that was so beastly? I was mad with jealousy, but couldn't admit it. I had sworn I'd no intention of falling in love, and I can be so very determined. I refused to acknowledge the real reason I was raging around like a fool. It did not help, either, that I found it difficult to recognize an emotion I've never felt before."

She said, "Oh!" again, or something like it. It did not much matter what she said, for her heart was in her eyes. And then her eyes were on his mouth. "Kiss me again, my lord, will you? I have wanted you to for so very long."

It was the merest thread of sound, shaky and soft. Oh, but he heard. So long they'd thought of that one kiss they'd shared. So long they had both fought wanting it again that now they came together almost violently.

Sarah's heart beat so hard, it rang in her ears, and she grew feverish from the heat of his mouth.

He pulled back the merest fraction, after a moment. She looked to see there was no humor lightening his countenance. Grim, almost, intense certainly, he stared down at her. "You have not said you would marry me, and I want it clear between us that I will have you for my wife, Sarah. I've done with pretending to myself I don't want you so much I cannot keep my eyes off you, and entirely done pretending I do not care in the least as whole armies of men pay their addresses to you. I want you for my countess. You'll be equally at home in the country employing your easel, in a fashionable salon trading quips, or in the corridors of Carlton House receiving accolades from all the bucks, but most at home, I do truly believe, in my bed. Marry me!

"Don't drag out the answer, will you? Don't go on about my family or my rank or anything like that. You'll win over everyone at Ravensgate, from my mother to the lowliest tenant's child, as you have won over every hostess and hostess's son in London. I'll persuade your father. You needn't worry there. I'll have you, by the devil! Why are you smiling?"

She laughed, her face flushed, her eyes shining. "You, my lord, are as imperious as ever. It is customary to phrase a marriage proposal as a question, you know."

"Have you had so many?" He growled, but could not resist kissing first her nose, then her eyes, then her cheeks, then her mouth. Before he could succumb to the sweetness of her, however, he lifted his head. "Well?"

She giggled, giddy as Mrs. Ponsby could be at her most elated. "One or two, my lord."

"Dominic."

She let out a shaky breath, all the giddiness evaporating at the look in his eyes. "Dominic."

"Will you marry me, Sarah?"

"Oh, yes."

They kissed again, becoming so lost in the passion that could swirl between them that Dominic found his fingers on the tiny buttons of her dress before he recalled where he was. Expelling a long breath, he put her from him. It did nothing to strengthen his resolve to see her eyes were dark with longing and that her silky golden hair was coming loose from its pins.

"We must marry very, very soon, my love," he said raggedly, no humor at all in his tone.

There was, however, a suspicion of humor in the voice that answered him. "I am relieved you do intend to marry my niece, sir. I'd have regretted like the devil to have to call you out."

"Uncle William!"

Sarah turned very pink when she whirled about to find her uncle smiling genially upon them from the doorway, and she thought to put at least a step for propriety's sake between her and Dominic.

He did not seem to share her need for decorum, or perhaps he could not help himself. At any rate, Dominic encircled her waist with his arm as he addressed her uncle. "I do indeed, sir, intend to marry your niece," he began, fighting what he suspected was a foolish grin. "That is, of course, I intend to ask for her. Oh, Lord! I feel green as a boy!" A grin won over his best efforts when he heard Sarah's not-very-smothered giggle. "What I mean to say, of course, is that I intend to ask for the honor of Miss Marlowe's hand. I take it you will bless my suit?"

Mr. Ponsby chuckled. "My lord, any man who looks as head over heels as you deserves the girl, particularly if she looks as adoring as Sarah. I am delighted for you both, as I know Ivor will be. And I will add, as I've just had conference with Mrs. Ponsby, that I know Sarah is getting in you a most exceedingly noble man. You've my respect, sir, as well as my deepest gratitude."

"But what is this?" Sarah asked, turning to Dominic.

He told her then of the various properties he knew would come to him from Lord Langston, and of his plans for one, the stud farm near Newmarket. "I think we owe it them, do you not, my love?"

She'd tears in her eyes. "You are exceeding generous. It is I who owe you all."

"You'd give me all the repayment I desire, my sweet, if you swear you will always come to me when you are in difficulties. You've my word I want to share them."

Just in time, Sarah recalled her uncle, and did not fling her arms around Dominic's neck, only took his hand in hers. "You've my word, my lord. I shall always halve my difficulties with you."